Another cloud passed across the face of the Moon-Dog, plunging the clearing into deeper darkness. It felt like a sign that the ceremony was over, and a last ragged howl of happiness went up from the gathered Pack. More dogs joined in, near and distant . . .

Lucky froze, his ears lifting along with the roots of his fur.

Those aren't the voices of our Pack!

SURVIVORS

Also by ERIN HUNTER

THE NEW PROPHECY

Warriors: *Code of the Clans*
Warriors: *Battles of the Clans*
Warriors: *Enter the Clans*
Warriors: *The Ultimate Guide*
Warriors: *The Untold Stories*
Warriors: *Tales from the Clans*

MANGA

The Lost Warrior
Warrior's Refuge
Warrior's Return
The Rise of Scourge
Tigerstar and Sasha #1: Into the Woods
Tigerstar and Sasha #2: Escape from the Forest
Tigerstar and Sasha #3: Return to the Clans
Ravenpaw's Path #1: Shattered Peace
Ravenpaw's Path #2: A Clan in Need
Ravenpaw's Path #3: The Heart of a Warrior
SkyClan and the Stranger #1: The Rescue
SkyClan and the Stranger #2: Beyond the Code
SkyClan and the Stranger #3: After the Flood

NOVELLAS

Hollyleaf's Story
Mistystar's Omen
Cloudstar's Journey
Tigerclaw's Fury
Leafpool's Wish
Dovewing's Silence

SEEKERS

SURVIVORS
THE BROKEN PATH

ERIN
HUNTER

HARPER
An Imprint of HarperCollinsPublishers

Special thanks to Gillian Philip

The Broken Path
Copyright © 2014 by Working Partners Limited
Series created by Working Partners Limited
Endpaper art © 2014 by Frank Riccio
For information address HarperCollins Children's Books,
a division of HarperCollins Publishers,
195 Broadway, New York, NY 10007.
www.harpercollinschildrens.com

Library of Congress Cataloging-in-Publication Data
Hunter, Erin.
    The broken path / Erin Hunter.
        pages   cm. — (Survivors ; #4)
    Summary: "Lucky and the rest of his Pack encounter
another group of dogs that has survived the Big Growl—and
these new dogs may be their most dangerous enemies yet"—
Provided by publisher.
    ISBN 978-0-06-210270-6 (pbk.)
    [1. Dogs—Fiction.   2. Wild dogs—Fiction.   3. Survival—
Fiction.   4. Adventure and adventurers—Fiction.   5. Fantasy.]
I. Title.
PZ7.H916625Dat   2013   2013038557
[Fic]—dc23   CIP
                                                    AC

Typography based on a design by Hilary Zarycky
18 19 20   BRR   10 9 8 7 6 5
❖
First paperback edition, 2015

For Rachel Mansfield and Lucy Philip

TERROR'S FOREST

LONGPAW TOWN

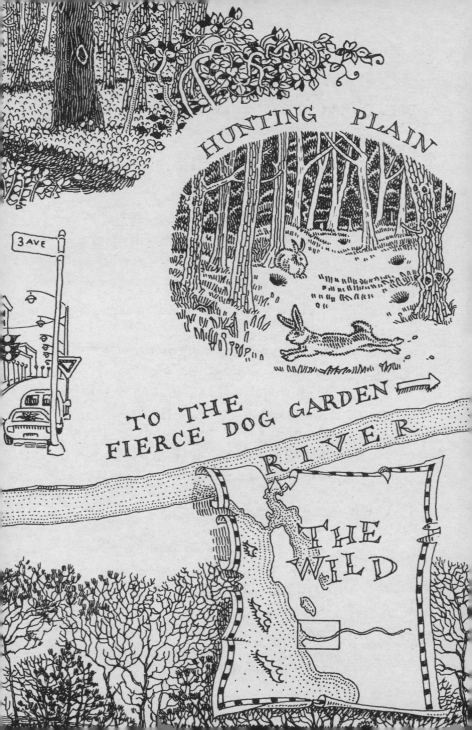

HUNTING PLAIN

3 AVE

TO THE
FIERCE DOG GARDEN

RIVER

THE
WILD

PACK LIST

WILD PACK (IN ORDER OF RANK)

ALPHA:

huge half wolf with gray-and-white fur and yellow eyes

BETA:

small swift-dog with short gray fur (also known as Sweet)

HUNTERS:

FIERY—massive brown male with long ears and shaggy fur

SNAP—small female with tan-and-white fur

SPRING—tan female hunt-dog with black patches

LUCKY—gold-and-white thick-furred male

BRUNO—large thick-furred brown male Fight Dog with a hard face

BELLA—gold-and-white thick-furred female

MICKEY—sleek black-and-white Farm Dog

PATROL DOGS:

MOON—black-and-white female Farm Dog

DART—lean brown-and-white female chase-dog

MARTHA—giant thick-furred black female with a broad head

DAISY—small white-furred female with a brown tail

WHINE—small, black, oddly shaped dog with tiny ears and a wrinkled face

OMEGA:

small female with long white fur (also known as Sunshine)

PUPS:

SQUIRM—black-and-white shaggy-furred male (pup of Fiery and Moon)

NOSE—black shaggy-furred female (pup of Fiery and Moon)

LICK—brown-and-tan female Fierce Dog

FIERCE DOGS (IN ORDER OF RANK)

ALPHA:

sleek black-and-brown female with a white fang-shaped mark below her ear (also known as Blade)

BETA:

huge black-and-tan male (also known as Mace)

DAGGER—brown-and-tan male with a stubby face

PISTOL—black-and-tan female

BRUTE—black-and-tan male

RIPPER—black-and-tan female

REVOLVER—black-and-tan male

AXE—large black-and-brown male

SCYTHE—large black-and-tan female

BLUDGEON—massive black-and-tan male

MUSKET—black-and-brown male

CANNON—brown-and-tan female

LANCE—black-and-tan male

ARROW—young black-and-tan male

OMEGA:

smaller black-and-brown male (also known as Bullet)

PUPS:

FANG—brown-and-tan male

LONE DOGS

OLD HUNTER—big and stocky male with a blunt muzzle

TWITCH—tan chase-dog with black patches and a lame foot

PROLOGUE

"Give up, Yap! I'm your Alpha!"

Squeak's bark was breathless as she tumbled over Yap, sending clouds of dust billowing around them both. The neatly clipped grass was dry from the long, hot days under the Sun-Dog, and both pups rolled together into the row of bright flowers the long-paws had planted. This small territory within the fence was so ordered and safe! A messy battle was exactly what it needed.

Kicking with his small legs, Yap wriggled out from beneath Squeak's weight and flung himself onto his litter-sister.

"No, you're not. I'm the Alpha!"

Sneezing out a noseful of grit, Squeak gave a high-pitched growl. "Just you wait, Yap."

As she sprang clumsily for his scruff, Yap rolled backward, letting her stumble over him, and grabbed her foreleg in his puppy teeth.

"Yow. Yow!" whined Squeak.

"Am I hurting you?" gasped Yap through a mouthful of leg.

"Ha!" Taking advantage of his guilty shock, Squeak twisted away and bolted. "Tricked you, Yap!" she barked back at him.

"Why, you—" Yap bounded to his feet and gave chase. "I'll get you yet, Omeg—"

He skidded to an awkward, startled halt. His nose twitched. *What is that smell?*

Squeak had vanished around the side of the longpaw house, her yelps fading, but suddenly Yap no longer cared. The strange odor tingled unpleasantly in his nostrils, making him cough. He pawed at his muzzle and shook his head, blinking.

Once again, Yap sneezed. Still out of breath, he had no choice but to take a big gulp of the tainted air. He whimpered in distress.

It was horrible. What could it be? And where was his Mother-Dog? Yap crouched miserably, shivering.

Wait a minute, he thought. *I'm a big pup now.*

Yap got to his paws and shook himself. The smell was very strong, and he was an excellent tracker—he was going to be the best ever! *I can investigate this by myself.* Yap sniffed the air and followed the odor, trying not to sneeze or cough again. The air burned his throat. . . .

There! A door to the longpaw house stood open, and Yap nudged it wider with his nose. The smell was especially strong in here, making his eyes water. *But I'm investigating. I can't turn back. . . .*

Tentatively he crept into the house, his claws clicking on the hard floor. There in front of him was that longpaw pup, the smallest one—the one with long, yellow hair twisted into a kind of tail. Yap liked her. She often barked at him, asking him to play, but she wasn't doing that now.

She was engrossed in a new game; she'd clambered up onto a sitting-box and was leaning over that shiny metal tower the longpaws used to singe their food. Yap wrinkled his nose and cocked his head to one side, perplexed.

The longpaw pup had something in her hands; Yap's ears caught a dry rattle as she shook it and pulled out a stick. *So it's just a game?* he thought. *She's playing with a new toy. Maybe I could join in!*

But something about the stick didn't smell right. Yap could catch its scent even at this distance. It had a red tip, as if it had been dipped in blood, and there was an acrid tang to it. And now he could hear a dreadful hissing, like a snake . . .

This isn't right. . . .

Suddenly Yap didn't care if he got in trouble with the longpaws. The smell and the noise and the strange stick were more than he could bear. *Stop that game, small longpaw, stop it!* Tilting back his head, he barked as hard as he could.

Startled, the yellow-haired longpaw dropped her toy. As it struck the ground it spilled more of the sticks in a scattered heap. Yap barked again, pawing the shiny ground, so scared of the little sharp-smelling sticks he couldn't bear to turn his back on them. And all the time, the hissing grew louder and louder.

The small longpaw's face creased in shock and upset, but that only made Yap's barks more frenzied. He didn't know what was happening, but he had to call his Mother-Dog.

It wasn't Mother-Dog who arrived, though. The room suddenly filled with bigger longpaws, shouting and gasping. One of them, the female one, gave a sharp scream and scooped up the yellow-haired one in her arms. She was making scolding noises and for a moment Yap stopped barking, wondering if he was in terrible trouble.

But the longpaws didn't take any notice of him. The male one raced to the clear-stone in the wall, flinging it open so that the horrible, choking smell could get out. Another male, smaller than the grown longpaws but taller than the little female, fell to his knees beside Yap, scooping him up in his arms.

Yap shivered, terrified, but the young longpaw didn't seem to be angry. He was making soothing noises, cuddling Yap against his chest and tickling his chin. "Good boy," was the sound he made over and over as he carried him outside. "Good boy!"

They were in the open air now, the smell fading, and the other longpaws were crowding around Yap, stroking his head and tickling his ears. That older female was cuddling the small one tightly in spite of the stern words she'd barked at it, and there was water in her eyes.

Yap gazed up at the longpaws, his tail tucked firmly beneath him, but none of them were scolding him for his outburst. "Good boy," they growled over and over again, and then, "Lucky. So lucky. Lucky . . ."

It was all too much. Panicking, Yap wriggled and squirmed until the young male longpaw set him on the ground. As soon as he was free he bounded for the shed.

Mother-Dog met him before he'd gone halfway, wagging her tail hard and watching him with bright, proud eyes. Yap skittered to a halt between her forepaws, and she licked his head fondly.

"Well done, Yap," she murmured. "You alerted the longpaws to something very important."

"Oh," he whined. "I thought they might be angry with me for barking, like before. But not this time?"

"No," Mother-Dog agreed, washing his ear with her tongue. "And I think they've found your name, too, for when you're a grown dog. Lucky."

Yap wrinkled his nose. He couldn't help the feeling of slight disappointment that crept in with the pride. "I thought I'd be able to choose my own name."

"Well, Wild Dogs do that." Mother-Dog looked a little disapproving. "And there are some Leashed Dogs who don't accept their longpaw names. But the name they've given you is a fine one—you should be proud of it."

"Lucky," Yap muttered, half to himself. He gave a last glance back toward the longpaws, but they were already retreating to their home and closing the door. "Lucky."

Mother-Dog nudged him gently. "It's a good name, Yap—Lightning was lucky when the Sky-Dogs saved him, and the Forest-Dog has always been said to be lucky." There was a hint of laughter in her voice. "It's a name that will keep you out of trouble, little one—and I have a feeling you might need that. Look on it as a gift from the Forest-Dog."

That made Yap's small rib cage swell with pride.

"Lucky." He licked his chops, tasting the name on his jaws. "Yes. If it's from the Forest-Dog, it must be a great name."

Mother-Dog whuffed with laughter as she nudged Yap back toward the shed where he slept with her and his littermates. The low sun glowed against its walls, and already Yap felt sleep stealing up on him. It had been a tiring day, and he longed for the soft sleeping-furs the longpaws had given them.

A home, and warmth—and now they had given Yap his dogname, too. The longpaws were good. They had always been kind to him. Yes, he knew he could trust them.

I am Lucky, thought Yap, nestling sleepily against Mother-Dog as she settled herself in the shady coolness of their shed. *I hope I always will be. . . .*

CHAPTER ONE

Lucky's paws crunched on the forest floor as he ran. Dappled bronze light, scattered by the branches above him, burnished the fallen leaves beneath him. Just ahead, he could see Fiery's powerful haunches as his huge Packmate bounded through the forest.

Lucky increased his pace, stretching his muscles to keep up. Somewhere behind him, young Lick ran too, and he had to trust her not to fall behind, because he didn't want to slow down. Heart pumping, tongue lolling to taste the cold Red Leaf air, Lucky felt stronger and faster than he had in many journeys of the Moon-Dog. He felt as if he could run forever.

It's good to be in the wild, he thought as bars of sunlight flickered across the rough track. *It's a long way from my old life, scavenging on the city streets, but this is a fine life. . . .*

There had been a time when he would have growled in disbelief at this change inside him. He had loved his time as a Lone

Dog, roaming the city streets and foraging for longpaw scraps. Once, he'd have been proud to sneak an old, half-eaten chicken from a Food House spoil-box.

And now here I am, far from the streets, under the eye of the Forest Dog— using all my senses to hunt down the fastest of prey.

Leaping over a fallen log, Lucky felt a surge of wild pride. Not so long ago he had been forced into the role of Omega as punishment for joining the Pack as a spy for his litter-sister Bella, and the Leashed Dogs she'd led out of the broken longpaw city. He'd hated being Omega, but he had to admit that demotion had taught him a lot about loyalty, and humility, and how it felt to be an underdog. He was a braver dog for the experience. And he valued his new rank so much more now. To be Omega was to be lowest of all the Pack, and it had been a shock to fall so far from his position as a valued hunter and patroller.

Every Pack needed an Omega, of course, to fetch and carry, to do the dirty and unpopular jobs. It was an important role; Lucky knew that.

It was just never going to be his role again.

Now that they were traveling, there was less need for Patrol Dogs, and more for hunters to feed the Pack. It had been hard work, fighting his way back up the ranks, but Lucky had been determined. He had done every low-down job that was asked of him, but he had kept alert for his chance, demanding the opportunity to prove himself in ritual fights against other dogs. Lucky still felt the sting of his first defeat—by the tan-and-white hunter Snap—but he had made it in the end. Now he too was a hunter, a dog of high status, valued and respected by his Packmates. He was seeking out prey again, providing for the Pack, who waited in their newest camp in the forest.

The narrow gorge wasn't the perfect home their old camp had been—that one was far back on the other side of the white ridge, between a low, protecting hill and a flower-dappled sweep of meadow. But for now the forest valley was a safe place to break their journey, and a comforting distance from the Fierce Dog Pack that threatened them.

This forest was unfamiliar, but Lucky was happy to trust his sharply honed instincts and his faith in the Forest-Dog. It stung his pride that Blade's attack had forced the Pack to move on yet again—but on the whole, Lucky was glad that they had. For the last few journeys of the Sun-Dog, life had been good. Lucky wanted that to last as long as possible.

"Lucky!" The huge, brown dog Fiery turned to bark over his

shoulder. "Remember—keep your nose alert for Blade and the others."

"Don't worry." Lucky wasn't about to forget the savage leader of the Fierce Dogs. He felt his hackles rise as he pictured her snarling, arrogant face. Lucky sniffed the frosty forest air for any trace of their enemy, but all he could detect were dying leaves, running water, and tiny creatures of the earth.

Blade won't get near the Pack while I can stop her. . . .

"Good. Just stay alert, and make sure the others do too." Fiery swung his great head to scan the forest. "Alpha's certain Blade will be back for revenge."

"I think Alpha's right." Lucky increased his pace until he was running closely at Fiery's flank. "And he's right not to let any dog go out alone."

Fiery's muscles bunched as he slowed his pace to a trot. "Let's move carefully now," he growled. "We're almost at the hunting ground."

The half-wolf Alpha had insisted that Fiery go out with Lucky on this first hunt of his new status. Lucky was fairly sure that was for strength in numbers, and not an indication of his leader's lingering distrust of him. It felt odd that Alpha should care about

Lucky's life after all that had happened between them, but Lucky and the half wolf seemed to have reached a kind of peace.

For now.

Lucky didn't think he would ever trust Alpha completely, but that wasn't a thought he could share with Fiery. He was the Pack's third-in-command after Sweet, Alpha's Beta, and had always been deeply, fiercely loyal to their leader.

"Lucky!" The excited yelp came from a clump of grass to his left, and Lick burst into view.

"You kept up," barked Lucky, amused. "Well done."

The young Fierce Dog visibly swelled, her head lifting. Lucky's surge of pride in her was mixed with a tingle of foreboding. Though she was young, Lick's Fierce Dog heritage already showed in her powerful muscles and her glossy hide, and in that strong jaw lined with ferocious teeth. Some of the other dogs were still nervous about accepting a Fierce Dog into their Pack.

Fools. Lick's about as vicious as a rabbit.

"Keep your eyes open, Lick," he growled softly at the young dog. "Remember, it's a white rabbit we're looking for, and Dart swears she saw one around this warren."

"Why does it have to be white?" Lick frowned. "I can smell so much prey here."

Lucky's heart sank, but he kept his voice cheerful. "Alpha insists on a snow-white rabbit for the Naming Ceremony."

Lick's head lowered, and all her energy seemed to seep out of her. "Oh. For Squirm and Nose. I bet it's going to be amazing." In a resentful growl she added, "Not that I'd know anything about Naming."

"Neither do I." Lucky shunted her cheerfully with his nose. "I never had a Naming Ceremony, Lick."

"Really?" She cocked her head, seeming a little more hopeful.

"Really. I don't even remember getting my name. Sometimes there's a vague memory, but . . . " Lucky shook his shoulders. "I remember a young longpaw, with yellow hair like a tail. She was in danger. I remember my Mother-Dog being pleased with me. I hear a voice saying, 'Lucky . . .' but the memory slips away just when I'm about to seize it, like a sneaky piece of prey."

Lick gave a rumbling laugh, a deep one that reminded Lucky just how fast the young dog was growing. "At least I'm not the only one, then."

"It's not something all dogs do," Lucky reminded her. "Think of the Leashed Dogs."

Lick sniffed wryly. "They don't know how to do anything right."

Poor Lick. She's putting on a brave face, but I know she's desperate to get her adult dog-name like the others. Covering his anger at Alpha, Lucky nudged her. "You'll get a Naming Ceremony, don't worry."

"I hope so." Lick scowled. "Why won't Alpha let me have one now?"

"Should I tell you how I found my name?" Fiery had fallen back to pad at Lucky's side again.

"Go on," said Lucky, relieved to have a story to distract Lick—even if it did involve naming.

Sure enough, the young dog looked eager to hear Fiery's tale. "What was your pup name?" she asked.

"Snail!" Fiery barked a laugh.

"Snail?" Lick shot him a disbelieving look.

"Really," Fiery assured her. "My Mother-Dog called me Snail because I was so fond of them. I spent all my time hunting them out, turning them over, and nosing about in their shells."

"Ugh," said Lick with a shiver.

"Hush, Lick!" scolded Lucky, though he thought it sounded disgusting too.

"I loved snails. Still enjoy one occasionally," added Fiery with another growl of amusement. "Of course, I couldn't be Snail forever. So not long after my back teeth grew in, I was asked by my Pack to choose my true name."

"How did you choose?" asked Lick, a tinge of envy in her voice.

"I knew that for such a big dog, I was fast. I knew it from when I first learned to run. I could run almost as fast as Lightning," laughed Fiery, "or so I thought when I was young and arrogant. I watched Lightning in the sky, and thought about how he looked like a streak of flame—and I just knew. I knew instantly that Fiery was my true name. Don't you think it suits me?"

Lucky growled his agreement, amused at Fiery's obvious pride in his fine name. "It does. So that's how the Naming Ceremony works? Dogs choose who and what they are?"

Fiery nodded. "Yes. A name sums up a dog's character. That's why it's so important. It's vital for a dog to get it right, because it will define him all his life."

"I like the sound of that," murmured Lucky.

"So do I," said Lick mournfully.

Lucky licked her ear in sympathy. "I was always a Lone Dog, and no Pack ever taught me to choose my name. But if dogs have to be in a Pack, then I think it's good for them to choose who they are in that Pack."

"Exactly," agreed Fiery. "A dog makes himself a true member of the Pack when he chooses his name. Or hers," he added, with a kind glance at Lick.

"It's more natural than longpaws giving us names," murmured Lucky, feeling a twang of regret deep in his gut.

"Much more natural," agreed Fiery. "It's—look! There!"

A shadow flashed through the undergrowth ahead. A dull, brown flash, not a white one, but it was definitely a . . .

"Rabbit!" barked Lick. The young Fierce Dog shot after the creature in pursuit, giving a volley of barks.

"Lick!" Pounding after her, Lucky gave her a sharp nip on the haunch. "Quiet!"

Lick skidded to a halt, sending up a fluttering shower of golden leaves. "Oh."

Fiery growled as he caught up. "There will be plenty more—as long as you don't scare them all off."

Lick lowered her head and tail, and whined apologetically. "Sorry, Lucky. Sorry, Fiery."

Lucky nibbled her ear by way of forgiveness. "Don't worry. Every dog makes mistakes." Still, his fur prickled with unease. Fierce Dogs were bred by the longpaws for attack, not for the stealthy hunt. Lick was a sweet-hearted dog but she didn't take naturally to caution and cunning, and that would not help her position in the Pack.

Hunching his shoulders, Lucky crept carefully forward through the tangle of branches and twigs. Fiery mimicked his movements, slinking off to his left so that he would approach the warren from a different direction. Their prey was clearly alarmed already; even though the dogs were careful to approach from downwind, some rabbits skittered away down holes. Others sat up on their hind legs, long ears erect, noses twitching suspiciously at the brisk Red Leaf air.

That wasn't unusual—it was hard for even the most careful dog to catch rabbits unawares, Lucky reminded himself as another three rabbits dived for their tunnels. Seeking out the dark shape of Fiery among the foliage beyond the warren, Lucky caught the big dog's eyes, and blinked in acknowledgment. Lucky knew what Fiery wanted, and Fiery trusted him to do it. *That's what Pack life's all about. . . .*

Turning his head, Lucky pricked one ear at Lick. Subdued now, she lowered her forequarters and crept close, her eyes eager and her tail quivering only a little.

"Lick, you can use that energy of yours now," murmured Lucky. "You're still smaller than we are, so you can be really helpful here."

He was pleased to see the young dog's face brighten. "That rabbit hole, there? Pretend to attack it. Go after them and start digging."

"Only pretend?" She tilted her sharp head.

"For now. Go on." Lucky nodded at the entrance to the warren. "And make as much noise as you like this time!"

Lick gave a bark of joy and tore toward the hole. The few remaining rabbits scattered, vanishing down the more distant holes with a flash of white tails, but Lick concentrated on the burrow Lucky had shown her. Barking ferociously, she forced her head in, hindquarters trembling and tail thrashing, and tore at the earth with her foreclaws.

It worked as if the Forest-Dog himself had planned it. From holes across the warren, rabbits burst into the open air, fleeing in panic. Brown streaks of fur flashed across the yellowing grass of the glade, and Lucky sprang, pouncing and snapping, killing as quickly and cleanly as he could. He smashed a paw onto another fleeing rabbit and bit into its spine; then, catching his breath, he glanced up in Fiery's direction.

Three rabbits had emerged almost under Fiery's nose, but he didn't lunge for them. Though his tensed muscles quivered with hunting instinct, the huge dog let them run; one tripped and tumbled over his muzzle in its panic, but he held on to his control, crouched low in stalking position.

"Now!" Lucky barked the signal as a flash of white shot from a burrow.

But Fiery was ahead of him. One swift leap, a crunch of his powerful teeth, the snap of fragile bone—and a limp and bloodied white rabbit dangled from his jaws. For an instant, Lucky felt the usual blood-tingling rush of delight that signaled a successful hunt.

Then an unexpected tremor of foreboding shivered through his body. The forest seemed to become still around him, the corpse of the white rabbit dazzling his vision so that he couldn't move. Fiery tilted his head, and stared at him quizzically.

What's wrong with me? We succeeded! "Well caught, Fiery!" Lucky shook himself and the paralyzing feeling faded. He raised his head and tail high as he trotted across the clearing.

Lick was still half-buried in the burrow, her muffled barks high-pitched with the thrill of the chase. Lucky paused, amused, and nudged her trembling rump. "All right, you can stop now, Lick."

Wriggling backward, she tugged her filthy head free. Her ears were pricked high and her jaws were stretched wide, tongue lolling as she licked clotted earth from her muzzle.

"That was fun!" she whined.

"I'm glad you enjoyed yourself," growled Fiery drily through his mouthful of white rabbit. "You did well."

Lucky wagged his tail slowly as he sniffed at the white-furred carcass. Again his spine prickled, but he turned to snatch up his own kills.

"Come on, Lick. You may not have killed this prey yourself, but you can help carry it back."

"Yes, Lucky!" Happy as a small pup again, Lick seized two rabbits together in her jaws.

As they left the clearing, Lucky glanced back once to the spot where Fiery had killed the white rabbit. Dark red blood was pooled on the pale rock. He clenched his jaws hard around his own prey.

It was a hunt. A normal, everyday hunt, that's all. There's nothing special about that rabbit. Nothing but the startling white color of its pelt.

CHAPTER TWO

The way back led them through a shallow valley lined with thorn-scrub and thistles, the shadows of even the smallest trees thrown far across the ground by the Red Leaf rays of the Sun-Dog. The camp was not far ahead, but Lucky had no intention of letting his guard down.

The air was still, with a hint of frost, so Lucky was immediately alert when something rustled close by. He paused to see a golden shape push through the leafless twigs of the bushes.

"Bella," he greeted his litter-sister warily.

Bella glanced awkwardly toward Fiery and Lick. She shook herself, but held her ground. "Hello, Lucky."

Lucky laid his rabbits on the ground and barked to Fiery. "I'll catch up with you."

Fiery looked back over his shoulder, nodded, then summoned Lick on.

Lucky shifted his attention to Bella, who was pacing back and forth, not meeting his eye. *My litter-sister,* he reminded himself; and yet she seemed more of a stranger than Fiery. Not so long ago she had been ready to sacrifice him for the good of her Leashed Pack.

Bella stopped pacing at last and scuffed the ground with a forepaw, her claws raking gashes like wounds in the dry earth.

"Lucky," she mumbled at last. "We haven't really spoken since—"

"Since when?" barked Lucky sharply as her voice trailed into silence. "Come on, Bella. Can't you say the words for what you did?"

She lifted her golden head and watched him steadily for the first time. Lucky saw her throat muscles contract.

"Since I abandoned you with Alpha's Pack," she growled in a low voice. "And since I led the attack with the foxes."

"I'm your litter-brother," barked Lucky bitterly. "But it seems I'm just here to be used like a sacrifice."

"Oh, Lucky." Bella's voice was full of misery. Wrapping her tail tightly around her rump, she crouched down on her fore-quarters. "Do you remember the Pup-Pack? Do you remember all those nights we curled up together, staying warm against our Mother-Dog?"

Lucky growled, deep in his throat. "Do you think reminding me of our Pup-Pack will make me forget what you did?"

"No! That's not what I'm trying to do, Lucky. Do you remember all the stories Mother-Dog told us?" Bella's soft brown eyes were pleading. "She taught us about wolves, didn't she? *Stay away from wolves,* she used to say. *They're bad. Keep your distance, pups!* I thought that trying to defeat Alpha was the right thing. I thought it was the most important thing."

"Huh. You let pup-tales scare you into betraying me. Is that what you mean?"

"He's only a half wolf," Bella went on desperately. "But he looks like a wolf, doesn't he? I thought he was a threat to all of us. To you as well!"

"Which is why you asked me to spy for you in his Pack?" snapped Lucky. "And lied to me at the same time? You've got very strange ideas about how to protect me, Bella."

"I was trying to do the right thing, truly. I thought you'd be in more danger if you knew what we were planning."

Lucky twisted his muzzle contemptuously. "And where does that leave you now, litter-sister? You're living with the half wolf! In his Pack! What happened to keeping your distance? That's not doing what the Mother-Dog told you, is it? You can't use her words as an excuse."

Bella lowered her body deeper into the dirt and shuffled forward, thumping the grass pleadingly with her tail. She pressed her jaw to the earth, and blinked up at him. "I know now it was wrong, Lucky. I never intended for you to get hurt. I meant well, but it was a mistake."

Her eyes glistened and her ears drooped miserably. *She's waiting for me to forgive her,* thought Lucky, tormented. *The trouble is, I can't. Not yet.*

"You think meaning well excuses what you did?"

Bella sprang to her paws suddenly, and Lucky flinched. Her eyes, so dark and unhappy before, now flashed with anger as she growled:

"Stop feeling sorry for yourself, Lucky!"

"What?" Lucky lifted his ears in shock, his body still.

"What about when Alpha threatened to kill me?" Her bark was furious. "Yes, I'm your litter-sister. And you did nothing to defend me!"

Shame twisted in Lucky's gut, undermining all his anger. *She's right. Bruno spoke up for Bella, but I didn't.*

Lucky sat down on his haunches, studying his litter-sister. Her expression was a tormented mixture of fury and remorse.

He remembered the day when he'd found Bella again, the day she and her makeshift Pack had fought off the foxes that had threatened him in the longpaw mall. He remembered his shock at seeing her after so long, and his happiness. He remembered the surge of joy when he'd decided to stay with her and her Pack for a while. And what dog would have thought it would turn out as it did?

I don't want it to be like this between us.

A scent tickled his nostrils. Glancing toward the scrubby thornbushes that protected the camp, Lucky caught sight of two dark eyes in a slender, pointed face. The young Fierce Dog had been watching them the whole time—and listening.

"Lick," he barked.

Hesitantly Lick squeezed through the thorns and padded across to Lucky and Bella, her tail tucked low. The late Red Leaf sunlight made her glossy hide a dark, shining bronze, reminding Lucky uneasily of Lick's former Pack-Alpha, Blade.

Still, the humble voice was nothing like Blade's. "I'm sorry, Lucky. I shouldn't have eavesdropped, but I was worried."

Lucky gave Bella a bemused glance, then turned back to Lick. "What in the name of the Earth-Dog were you worried about? You know Bella."

"That's just it. You and Bella." Sitting down on her haunches, Lick lowered her ears. "I wish I still had my littermates. You don't know how truly lucky you are."

Lucky felt a heavy weight of shame in his belly. Of course, Lick had lost her siblings, Wiggle and Grunt—one dead, and the other taken by the vicious Blade.

"I'm sorry, Lick," he growled quietly. "I hadn't forgotten your loss. But between Bella and me, it's just—things have happened. We need to . . ."

Lick raised her sad eyes. "You should be grateful to still have each other," she mumbled awkwardly. "That's what I think. That's all."

The young Fierce Dog rose and padded back toward the camp, tail drooping and shoulders slumped. Lucky's heart turned in his chest and his tail thumped the ground in pride. Lick had shown wisdom beyond her years.

I wish Alpha could have heard that pup just now, he thought. *That would have shown him what a kind-tempered dog she is.*

There was a soft whine from Bella, and he finally met her eyes. He recognized an aching there, one that felt familiar.

Lick's right. We're both upset right now, but—

He had barely opened his jaws to speak more kindly to his

litter-sister, when a deafening crack shattered the sky, and brilliant light burst from it. Both of them jerked their heads up, startled, their quarrel forgotten. Above them the clouds were dark and grim, looking heavy enough to crush the world.

"Lightning!" yelped Bella. "He's barking!"

"We need to take cover," whined Lucky.

He snapped his jaws to pick up his rabbits. Then they bounded together across ground that was already spattered with huge drops of rain. Again Lightning leaped, and his roaring bark shook the sky.

"Lucky!" howled Bella in terror.

"Quick! This way!" Lucky had spotted a sandy bank, already sodden but smoother and closer than the little gorge. He sprang up onto the shifting surface. Only at the last instant did he spot the dark mouth of a small cave, right beneath his paws. And where there were small caves like this, there could be—

A badger! It lunged from its burrow in fright and fury. Lucky's speed had already taken him beyond the badger-hole, but Bella was at his heels—and the creature turned on her, scrambling onto her back. Lucky caught sight of vicious, beady eyes and the broad, white stripe down its face just as it sank its teeth into Bella's neck and raked long claws into her shoulder. She yelped and staggered in pain.

Dropping his rabbits again, Lucky sprang down from the top of the bank, putting out his paws to knock the badger back—but its speed was astonishing. It whipped around and lashed its claws at his muzzle, digging them deep. Pain like fire shot through Lucky's face and he shook his head frantically, but the vicious creature clung on, its small teeth bared in a savage snarl.

White light flooded the bank as Lightning leaped again. The badger, startled, loosened its grip at last, and Lucky flung it off; it tumbled and rolled. Bella pounced, pinning its tail to the sandy ground. Lucky sank his teeth into the back of its silvery neck, holding it down as it wriggled and thrashed.

His chest ached, and pain still shot through his muzzle like hot spines, but Lucky focused on pressing all his weight down on the badger. *I can't let it bite!* He'd had encounters with these creatures before, and knew that they'd fight to the death if they had to.

Once again Lightning sprang, shaking the clouds. With his flash of light came a scent that singed Lucky's nostrils—something horribly familiar.

It's coming, he thought. *The bad rain—the rain that burned our hides in the last camp!*

He twisted in fear to look at the sky. The badger took its

chance, flinging him off and hurling itself aside to elude Bella as she lunged for it. Enraged, it lashed its long claws at Lucky's flank.

In the instant after its strike, Lucky felt nothing; but then the rain hit them, a torrent of water and wet ash. Black flakes clung to his sodden fur and trickled wetly into the wound. The rain burned worse than the badger's claws; it seemed to cut right through his flesh and eat at his bones.

Wild with pain and fury, Lucky turned savagely on the badger, snapping his jaws shut on its neck. He shook it violently and dropped it, a limp and sodden bundle.

"It's dead, Lucky!" panted Bella. She was crouched low to the ground, trembling.

"Bella. Are you all right?" Lucky panted hard and sniffed anxiously at her side.

"I'm fine." His litter-sister staggered to her feet, shaking off the clinging wetness. "But you're hurt!"

Already the burning rain had slackened to intermittent drops and a few black flakes whirling in the cold wind, but the wound in Lucky's side was still on fire. He nosed it and tried to lick it, but shuddered at the acrid taste and the touch of ash on his tongue.

"I'm fine," he told Bella. "It's only a scratch. But the rain stings."

Lucky lifted his head to watch the purplish-black cloud drift away, the drenching torrent now a smear of shadow across the far hills. The Pack hadn't escaped the bad rain, then—one more reason they needed to keep moving. They had to get far away from whatever was poisoning the land. Their new camp on this side of the white ridge was no safer than the others. Ever since the Big Growl had destroyed the city and their homes, the dogs had had to keep moving, form new packs with half wolves, fight off Fierce Dogs . . .

When will it all end? Lucky wondered.

He thought of Twitch, the lame dog who had left the Pack. Lucky had always thought of himself as a solitary dog, but it was Twitch who had struck out alone, feeling rejected by his own Pack. How was he surviving in these terrible times?

"You saved me," murmured Bella. "Thank you."

Lucky licked his chops, and shook himself again. He had to cling on to hope, in the face of all these changes. "Perhaps the Sky-Dogs are telling us that life's too fragile these days to hold a grudge."

Bella shuffled forward on her forepaws. He nuzzled her neck. Lick was right—they were fortunate to have each other. Whatever Bella's faults, however angry he was, he couldn't hold it against her.

"Come on," he said gruffly. "Let's get back to the camp. We should tell the others what just happened. And there's a ceremony to be held."

"We're already late," agreed Bella, trotting at his side as he set off back up the sandbank. "I hope Alpha understands about badgers."

"Whether he does or not, I need to speak to him," muttered Lucky, half to himself. "There are a lot of decisions to be made." He and Bella picked up his rabbits between them, and then set off.

The Sun-Dog beyond the hills lit their way with a last few darkly glowing rays as they picked a path through the gloomy twilight. At the very edge of the trees, Lucky halted and sniffed the air, startled.

"That's a pup's scent," he said, pricking his ears and scanning the glade. "Can you smell it, Bella?"

Her nostrils flared. "You're right. And it's fresh. So soon after that rainstorm?"

Lucky nodded. "Whoever it was, they've only just passed by."

"Is it Lick?" Bella sounded doubtful.

"No. I know her scent well, and this isn't it." Lucky creased his eyes in confusion. "I don't think it's a pup from our Pack at all."

"There she is, though." Bella pricked her ears at the young Fierce Dog, waiting anxiously for them at the edge of the camp.

"What are you doing out here?" Lucky asked as they padded over.

"I was worried." Lick bounded forward in greeting. "I had to come back and make sure you were okay."

"We were fine," Lucky told her. "It was just a visit from Lightning." But Lick was whimpering with anxiety.

"There wasn't anything else?" she asked, her gaze roaming the forest and the jutting rocks. "You didn't see any other creatures?"

"Only a huge badger!" Bella said, her bark full of pretend bravado. "But we defeated him. Didn't we, Lucky?"

Lucky didn't know which was more confusing—Bella's sudden show of confidence or Lick's behavior. How could the young dog have possibly known they might have encountered another animal, and why couldn't she tear her glance from the land behind them?

Lucky nuzzled her ear as the three of them walked on into the camp. "I caught a scent out there," he told Lick, watching carefully for her reaction. "A pup has passed by, very recently. A strange one, not from the Pack. Did you see it?"

"No. What would a strange pup be doing around here?" The

muscles of Lick's face twitched, and she licked her chops. Lucky frowned, but she avoided his gaze. "Oh, I think Spring wants me!" She shot off toward a small group of dogs relaxing under a bush.

Lucky hesitated, staring after her. He hadn't heard Spring call Lick—he couldn't even see her black-and-tan hide in the huddle of dogs into which Lick had vanished.

Remembering that strange pup-scent, his neck prickled. Lick had been in a mighty hurry to get away from his questions.

Something's going on, he thought. *And I intend to find out what it is.*

CHAPTER THREE

"What took so long?"

Lucky twisted to meet the piercing yellow eyes of Alpha, watching him with hostile curiosity. Drawing a deep breath, Lucky padded across to the half wolf, who sprawled on a small hillock where the last light lingered, away from the rest of the dogs, who were gathered in small groups around their dens. Already frost touched the air in the camp, and tendrils of mist crept through the grass where the shadows lengthened. Lucky shivered.

"Well?" Alpha's voice was a low growl. "Fiery returned long ago with the white rabbit. Where were you?"

"I'm sorry I was delayed, Alpha." Lucky kept his words calm and measured. "I stopped to speak to Bella. We had things to . . . discuss. And I should tell you I scented something—"

"Enough!" snarled Alpha, rising suddenly to all fours. "Didn't I make it clear enough to you, Street Dog? No dog should take risks beyond the camp. That includes lingering and gossiping beyond the perimeter while the Pack waits for you!"

Lucky bristled. "It was nothing like that—"

"Why do you isolate yourself when we both know Blade's Pack is out there? They are hunting us, Lucky, and unless we keep on our paw-tips and moving, they will track us down." Alpha's eyes widened suddenly as he caught sight of the wound in Lucky's side. "What happened? Were you attacked? If this is Blade's doing, I'll—" The huge dog-wolf stiffened and snarled.

"No!" Lucky barked hurriedly, then dipped his head in apology. "No, Alpha, it wasn't Blade. She was nowhere in sight. It was a badger, that's all."

Alpha's muzzle curled. "You were distracted by a badger? Pathetic. A stupid skirmish!"

"It wasn't like that," Lucky told him firmly. "And something much more worrying happened. The rain came again—the bad rain."

Alpha raised his ears. "You're sure? We didn't see any bad rain."

"It blew away, but I saw the black flakes, and I felt it burn this wound. We haven't outdistanced it."

For the first time, Alpha looked uncertain, and his hackles

flattened as his anger faded. "So we have to move on again," he growled, half to himself. Then his eyes flashed gold. "But not until after the Naming. Nothing will stop that."

As if they had heard their leader's words, Squirm and Nose came bounding over, skidding to a halt in a flurry of leaves. They seemed to have forgotten their awe of the ferocious dog-wolf, and their high barks brimmed with excitement. "Alpha, is it time yet? Is it?"

Behind them Lucky noticed Lick, trotting hesitantly in their wake. Her ears were pricked and her eyes hopeful; it hurt Lucky's heart to see how eager she looked.

No, he thought, *there'll be no Naming Ceremony for you tonight, Lick.* Not only was she younger than Fiery and Moon's two pups, Lick was also a Fierce Dog—and every dog knew that Alpha could barely stand to have one of them, however young and small, in his Pack. Not only would there be no Naming for Lick tonight, there might never be one at all. *Unless I can help.*

But he couldn't think how. And now Sweet, the swift-dog Beta, was calling the Pack together with her commanding barks. All around the camp dogs leaped to their feet, the Leashed Dogs as eager as their wild comrades. The gentle Farm Dog Mickey loped forward with Snap, and burly Bruno joined the black-and-tan hunt-dog Spring in the center of the glade, obviously keen to be at her side.

Though the former Leashed Pack still liked one another's company best—and no doubt sometimes reminisced together about their lost longpaws—Lucky was glad that they were so at ease with the Wild Pack. Dart, the black-and-tan hunt-dog, continued to keep herself a little aloof from them, but she was amiable enough. No dog, Leashed or Wild, really liked the snub-nosed Whine, but Sunshine was content to trot at his side, yapping friendly comments. Martha the water-dog chatted affectionately to the much wilder Moon, bonded by their shared maternal instincts; little Daisy bounded up to Fiery and yapped a greeting, not at all intimidated by his size. *My Leashed friends are truly fitting in with this Pack,* thought Lucky happily.

The Pack members trotted toward the prey-heap; no languid stretching or easy ambling this evening. Every dog was always eager for food-sharing time, but there was a special tingle in the air tonight. The Moon-Dog in her fullness hadn't quite risen over the horizon yet, but the Pack was eagerly anticipating the moment, their ears pricked and their eyes bright. Tails wagged, tongues lolled, and Lucky could smell the excitement.

And I feel the same, thought Lucky, *though I do feel sorry for Lick. I want to see what happens!*

Even the sharing of the prey felt different tonight—strict discipline was almost forgotten in the mood of excited celebration. Dogs talked and barked over one another, only occasionally quieted by a warning glance or a growl from Sweet. Alpha, oddly enough, seemed content to tolerate a little misbehavior, simply watching with narrowed yellow eyes.

"Spring, it's not your turn!"

"Sorry, Beta!" yelped the black-and-tan dog. "Whine, hey! That doesn't mean you can sneak in."

"Quite." There was a note of humor in Dart's growl. "You're not exactly Alpha yet, Whine."

"When will the Moon-Dog wake up?" That was Nose, almost beside herself with anticipation. Her tail lashed so frantically, she swiped Squirm's face.

"Not long now, Nose. Have patience!" But there was amusement in Sweet's stern bark.

"And don't touch the food before Beta has finished," growled Alpha, swiping a paw at the pup. But the blow was light, and barely ruffled Nose's fur.

The Naming must be a very big occasion, Lucky realized, *if even Alpha is relaxed about the rules tonight.*

One by one, the dogs ate their fill, though excitement seemed to have blunted all their appetites. Lucky himself ate less than usual, eager to begin the ceremony. He glanced up as a big shadow settled over him. It was Martha, the huge water-dog, and she looked as curious and perplexed as he felt. She stretched out one webbed paw and nibbled at her claws.

"I don't really understand all this," she murmured to Lucky. "Why is it such a big deal? I never had a Naming Ceremony. And neither did my littermates. But we still have names!"

"I was wondering that too," said Daisy wistfully. The little white terrier squeezed between Lucky and Martha, and Lucky noticed Sunshine creeping in on his left flank. Clearly the old Leashed Dogs were looking to him for some kind of explanation. *They lived such protected lives with their longpaws,* Lucky reminded himself. *I still forget sometimes how little they know, even now.*

"Fiery explained some of it to me," Lucky told them. "I know they have to choose their own names—it's not like when the longpaws gave yours to you. As soon as a dog grows teeth at the back of his jaws, he's allowed to choose the name he'll carry. And it has to be one that fits."

Sunshine cocked her head, her silky fur gleaming in the moonlight. She'd had to be even more patient than the others, Lucky knew—she was Omega now, and that meant she was always last to eat. He was glad the little dog didn't seem to mind too much, and tonight she'd been left half of a big and juicy rabbit at the end of the meal. Clearly every dog was to be encouraged to celebrate.

"I'm glad I didn't have to go through a Naming Ceremony," Sunshine yapped softly. "It all seems terribly serious. And I like the name my longpaws gave me. I think it suits me just fine, and better than anything I'd have chosen."

"Your name does suit you, Sunshine." Lucky was amused. Would Sunshine ever realize she didn't have "her" longpaws anymore—that she belonged with the Pack?

Still, she wasn't the spoiled little lapdog she had once been. And Sunshine would probably go on calling them "her" longpaws until the day she went to the Earth-Dog. It seemed to be a very hard habit for the little dog to break.

"Bring the white rabbit!" Alpha's bark cut across Lucky's thoughts, and every dog sat up straighter.

"That's my job!" Sunshine whirled around and dashed to join Whine, excited at her important role. In only moments the two little dogs—the former Omega and the new one—had emerged from the undergrowth, bearing the carcass of the white rabbit between them in their teeth. With great care they laid it on the flat rock in front of Alpha. As they both turned away, Sunshine holding her tail proudly high, Lucky couldn't miss the look Whine threw him. There was an expression of loathing on the snub-nosed dog's petulant face.

"What's up with him?" whispered Lick, creeping to Lucky's side.

"Quiet," Lucky warned her. "The ceremony is beginning." Besides, he didn't want to start explaining the former Omega's resentment. Even though the nasty little dog had risen in the ranks as he'd longed to, Whine was clearly still unhappy with Lucky.

But that's his problem, not mine.

Alpha must have noticed Whine's look, though, because the dog-wolf glared at him. "Whine! Sunshine! Your work is done. Get to the back of the Pack."

Sunshine obeyed at once, content to know her place. But Whine's muzzle curled over his teeth, and his left eye twitched. *There's a dog,* thought Lucky, *who wants to fight but is too scared.*

Whine wore a look of angry humiliation as he slunk through the ranks of watching dogs. This time, he avoided Lucky's eye.

Could he still be trouble? Lucky shook off the thought and concentrated on Alpha, and on Sweet. The swift-dog looked solemn and graceful beside her leader.

Alpha took a pace forward to stand before the pale corpse of the rabbit. "Snap. Spring. Come forward."

The two dogs clearly knew what was expected of them, each placing their forepaws on the rabbit: Spring on its front legs, Snap on its long hind legs. Alpha laid one of his huge paws on its head, crushing it down, then raised his other paw high above the corpse. His paw swooped down, and with precision, he dug a claw into the rabbit's throat. Slicing the rabbit open from throat to belly, he bared his fangs and sank them with a crunching noise into its neck.

There was a soft ripping sound as Alpha tore the pelt free in a single intact piece, and then slapped the white fur down on the rock. Sweet stepped forward, seized the carcass, and tossed it aside. Lucky swallowed. He had never seen a rabbit skinned with such precision; it seemed unnatural in contrast to the hungry rip-and-chew of feeding.

Lucky realized the whole Pack was holding its collective breath. On the gray slab, the bloodied white fur gleamed ghostly in the light of the risen Moon-Dog.

"Squirm. Nose." Alpha's growl was commanding as ever, but proud too. "Take your places on the Moon Pelt."

The two pups trod nervously forward; Lucky noticed that they were both trembling. First Nose and then Squirm hopped up onto the rock, turned, and sat down stiffly on the white fur. Nose sniffed at it anxiously.

"There's nothing to worry about, young ones," murmured Alpha. Lucky had never heard the half wolf sound so gentle. "The time has come for you to choose the names you will carry until you meet the Earth-Dog. So close your eyes, and turn your faces to the Moon-Dog. Now that she is at her brightest, she will show you who you are."

Alpha gazed around the watching, silent Pack. He met each pair of reverential eyes; then slowly he tipped his head back and released a ringing howl to the night sky.

One by one, the dogs joined in. Every voice added to the eerie, echoing sound, rebounding from the rocky cliffs and filling the woods and the gorge. When it was Lucky's turn, he gave a howl that seemed to come from his heart and guts and bones, yet he was filled too with the howls of the others. It was as if all the voices merged and swelled until they were a great single presence in the night.

Lucky's skin tightened and his fur prickled as the howl surged over him like a wave, drowning all thought. The Great Howl was the moment when he was always most certain of his place in the Pack, of the rightness of it; tonight the sense of belonging felt stronger than ever. He opened his eyes to take in the full silver glow of the Moon-Dog, but as he watched, a thin cloud drifted across her face, and a shiver ran through the Pack from one dog to the next. The whole Pack was in shadow now—all but the pups Nose and Squirm. The pale light still bathed them where they sat frozen in awe on the white rabbit fur.

Beside Lucky, Daisy shivered as a thrill ran through her. "It's as if the Moon-Dog knows," she whispered.

Lucky didn't shush her. He was thinking the same thing. Many times, when he'd wanted a peaceful night's sleep, he'd sent a prayer to the Moon-Dog to protect him, but it had felt like nothing more than wishful thinking: How could the Moon-Dog hear what he said? Tonight he truly believed she heard this Howl, and understood its special importance.

"I think you're right, Daisy," he murmured.

The Howl quieted, then faded altogether, dying to a charged silence. Alpha lowered his head to gaze at the pups again.

"What are your chosen names?" he growled softly but clearly.

Squirm's eyes were closed, but now he snapped them open; they glowed in the silver light. "I will be . . ." He paused. Something was moving on the side of the rock, a quick shadow that scuttled into a crack and vanished. Squirm's voice grew loud and certain. "I will be Beetle," he declared. "Fast, and hard to see! But my hide is tough and strong!"

There was a sound behind Lucky, a gruff noise from Dart that might have been amusement. But it turned quickly into a growl of approval that was taken up by the other dogs.

Hmm, thought Lucky. *Well, it's different.* Beetle, he decided, would have to grow into his name. . . .

Beside her brother, Nose's eyes were open too. There was something much calmer about her, and she didn't glance around in search of inspiration. Her whine was a little shaky, but determined.

"I've thought about this for a long time," she announced, glancing up shyly into Alpha's yellow eyes. "I will be Thorn. Sharp and deadly."

Alpha gave a low growl of approval, but Lucky pricked his ears forward in astonishment. *I never thought of Nose as being* deadly! he thought. But maybe a dog chose what she intended to be, not what she already was. . . .

And perhaps there was more to Nose than met the eye. What kind of dog, he wondered, would she become?

"That's a fine name she's chosen," he murmured to Bella.

"Yes." Bella sounded vague and distracted. "Aren't we all afraid of thorns?"

"But they're good protection for a Pack, too," Lucky pointed out.

"Mmm . . ." Bella nodded, clearly caught up in thoughts of her own.

"What is it?" whispered Lucky.

"I was just wondering what name I'd have chosen." Bella twitched her nose dreamily. "If I'd had the choice, that is. I never thought I'd regret any part of my Leashed life, but . . ."

"You said yourself, Bella means beautiful," Lucky reminded her with a nudge. "It's a good name. And it does suit you."

Bella gave him a rueful sideways glance. "Thank you, Lucky." But she still looked a little sad.

Lucky was about to say something else reassuring when he felt the gentle bump of a body squeezing up alongside him. It was Lick, desperate for a better look at the two newly named young dogs on the Moon Pelt. Her eyes were wide and awestruck.

"I'd love to have a new name one day, Lucky," she whispered.

Lucky's heart tightened in his chest. Lick had been so pleased with the pup name Mickey had found for her when he and Lucky had first rescued her and her littermates, but it was time to move on now. Little Lick was growing into a fine adult dog, and she deserved her true name. "You will," he told her softly. "What would you call yourself?"

Lick shook her head. "I can't tell you that," she said patiently. "I can't tell anyone—not until I've taken my place on the Moon Pelt. I won't know until the Moon-Dog helps me choose."

Lucky felt a surge of affection for Lick, so good-natured and gentle despite her Fierce Dog blood. *To think that some of them still have doubts that she should be in the Pack!* His fur prickled with resentment on her behalf. *Surely,* he thought, *on this night of all nights . . .*

"Alpha," he spoke up, shunting Lick forward a little until they were both standing in the clear space within the Pack circle. "When will Lick be able to have her Naming Ceremony?"

Alpha rounded on them. Lick stood her ground, brave but uncertain, tail between her legs. Lucky gave Alpha a challenging stare.

But Alpha didn't rise to Lucky's challenge. "Back in your place, pup!" he snapped at Lick. "The Naming is over and this is not the time."

Lucky opened his jaws to argue, but found himself speechless. As Lick scuttled back against his flank, he realized the moment had passed.

For now.

The new Thorn and Beetle were jumping down from the rock, mobbed by a mass of happy dogs licking their heads and congratulating them. Fiery and Moon were by their pups' sides, tails wagging hard with pride and happiness. Fiery in particular looked as if he might burst with delight, his dark eyes shining as he gazed at Beetle.

At the edge of the crowd, Lucky saw Sunshine take hold of the skinned, sacrificed rabbit and begin to bury it under a thick layer of earth. He blinked in surprise.

Spring caught sight of his expression and stepped close to him for a moment. "We don't eat the white rabbit," she said quietly. "We leave it as a gift for Moon-Dog and Earth-Dog, so that they'll approve of the pups' choice." Then she moved off to give Thorn a long, hard lick on the ear.

Lucky wished he could join in with the general rejoicing, but he felt too sorry for Lick. She pressed close to his side, small and dejected.

"One day, Lick," he consoled her with a sweep of his tongue.

At that moment, another cloud passed across the face of the Moon-Dog, plunging the clearing into deeper darkness. It felt like a sign that the ceremony was over, and a last ragged howl of happiness went up from the gathered Pack. More dogs joined in, near and distant . . .

Lucky froze, his ears lifting along with the roots of his fur. *Those aren't the voices of our Pack!* Lucky's blood ran cool as river-water as his eyes met Alpha's.

"Quiet!" roared the dog-wolf.

A horrible silence fell.

The guttural howling did not sound so distant now. It drifted eerily through the trees, a sound filled with menace.

"Fierce Dogs," whimpered Sunshine.

Alpha sprang up onto the flat rock, baring his fearsome teeth. "Listen to me," he snarled, meeting the eyes of each of his Pack in turn. "Those dogs aren't attacking. Not yet. For tonight we're safe, but they're close and it would be unwise to stay here. Go to your sleeping places, and do not leave this camp. Not for any reason." His muzzle curled in rage, but Lucky thought he heard defeat in his growl. "Tomorrow, we look for a new camp."

There were a few growls and whines of muted protest, but they were quickly silenced by a glare from Alpha. Every dog, including Lucky, knew their leader was right.

With a heavy heart, Lucky set off for his own sleeping place, only to see a small shadow slink across his path and pause. Coming to a surprised halt, Lucky recognized him at once: Whine. The little dog swiveled his head, exposing his teeth in a mocking sneer.

"Did you enjoy our little tradition, Street Dog?" He cocked his ugly head. "Of course it was new to you, wasn't it? You've never earned a proper name yourself. That's why you'll never be a proper Pack Dog."

His temper already on edge, Lucky was about to bite Whine's ear when Bella bounded between them. She growled threateningly at the former Omega. "You think not? That shows how much you know. Lucky did earn his name!"

For a moment she and Whine glared at each other; then he jerked his head contemptuously and waddled off.

"Thanks," murmured Lucky to his litter-sister. "I'm glad you said that, even if it's a lie."

"But it isn't." Bella pricked one ear forward, confused. "Don't you remember? That day at the longpaw house, when you got your name? They didn't give it to you—you took the word they spoke, and kept it for yourself!"

Lucky stood still, lost. The memory stirred again at Bella's words—a longpaw pup, a bitter scent—but as the recollection slipped away, he shook himself free of it in relief. Some instinct was telling him not to explore that memory, and he was happy to listen to it.

"Time to sleep," he yawned. "The others may want to celebrate longer, but all I want to do is get to my den. Come on, Lick." He nudged the younger dog. "You must be tired too."

A lot had happened that day, and there was too much to think about.

The two of them padded over to their dens and slumped down beneath the moonlight. Lick's flanks were snuggled warmly against Lucky's, and soon they rose and fell with the deep breathing of sleep. Her paws twitched as she chased something in her dreams, and she let out a small growl.

You don't need to run tonight, Lucky silently told her. *Stay safe, little one.*

CHAPTER FOUR

Lucky woke with a start, shivering in the darkness. The remnants of a dream slipped away like a molting coat—ice shards, stinging and cutting, whirling in a blizzard, while dogs tore at one another in a battle that never seemed to end.

The Storm of Dogs...

It was the same dream he'd been having since the Big Growl.

The cold he felt was real enough. Beyond the snug nest of leaves and moss where he lay, he could hear the wind whining in the trees, and a breath of it whispered across his flank. He shuddered and scrambled up.

The space at his side, where Lick had fallen asleep against him, was empty. The warmth of her body was gone. *Lick! Where is she?*

Lowering himself to his forequarters, Lucky crawled out beneath the branches and stood up on all four paws, stretching. Surely the reckless pup had not gone far. Not in the middle of the night, when the Fierce Dogs had howled so close that the Pack could hear them. Surely not?

Fear for Lick making his fur spring erect, Lucky slunk through the camp, giving Alpha's sleeping body a wide berth. The dog-wolf sprawled, sound asleep with a trickle of drool at his jaws, his huge, webbed paws twitching in a dream. Lucky's heart was pounding against his ribs, but if Lick was out here—and she wasn't anywhere to be seen in the sleeping huddles in the clearing—then Lucky had to find her, and soon. If Alpha woke and found her missing, he would throw her out of the Pack for good. No dog was permitted such disobedience, let alone the already unwelcome Lick.

Why, Lick? Why wander off tonight of all nights? But even as he asked himself the question, Lucky knew why. Her hurt at her exclusion from the Naming Ceremony must have gone deep.

You silly pup—Alpha will come around! He'll soon realize you're worthy of your place in the Pack.

But Lucky had to find her first. After a moment's hesitation, he stepped over the border of the camp. Now he was really disobeying orders. Sniffing the air silently, he trod through the mat of dry leaves toward the edge of the forest, trying not to make them rustle. There was frost in the air, but through its crisp smokiness he could make out that other smell again, that strange-pup

53

scent he'd caught earlier. It hadn't faded much. Lucky frowned. Could it be Lick's after all? Surely he couldn't be mistaken?

He stood still at the brink of the sandbank. This was where Lick had waited for him and Bella earlier, and it seemed a good place to try first.

Sure enough, as Lucky slithered quietly down the sandbank and into the clearing beyond, he made out a moving silhouette. The Moon-Dog was lower in the sky now, and did not glow as brightly as she had at the ceremony, but still Lick was outlined in frosty light. Lucky breathed a sigh of relief.

Lick was tugging at something, her forepaws down and her haunches high, and Lucky was about to whine to her when he saw a small, dark shape tumble out of the bushes. Another pup! And Lick was playing with him, mock-fighting over a stick. Their low, friendly growls and whines were clearly audible on the cold air.

Lucky started forward, then halted in astonishment.

Grunt!

It was Lick's litter-brother, the one who had left willingly with Blade when she came to Alpha to demand the return of the pups. Something had changed about Grunt, though—Lucky could detect the difference in his scent: a sharp hardness. The pup reeked of aggressive confidence. There was so much in him that Lucky didn't recognize.

Lucky's heart tightened with anger. Grunt had been the only one of the Fierce Dog pups who was eager to be taken by Blade—and he'd stayed willingly with her even after she killed his other littermate, Wiggle. Grunt truly was a Fierce Dog in his bones!

And what about Lick? Lucky had risked his own life and reputation to keep her in Alpha's Pack—yet here she was, secretly meeting her Fierce Dog kin. Tensing his muscles, Lucky sprang down the slope and flew across the hollow. He was on the pups before they knew what was happening.

Lick gave a yelp of alarm, but too late. Lucky rolled them both over and slammed a paw onto each pup's belly, pinning them to the ground. They lay on their backs and stared at him, panting, frozen with shock.

They had both grown a lot since they were helpless pups. Grunt, recovering from his fright, wriggled and growled, and Lick's muscles bunched as she resisted, but in moments the pups had quieted.

Resentment and aggression were burning in Grunt's eyes. Lucky vividly remembered him endangering his Packmates by trying to pick a fight with a giantfur. Together the Fierce Dog pups could no doubt fight Lucky off, but there was more to this than sheer strength, and they knew it as well as Lucky did. *I'm Lick's Pack superior,* thought Lucky, *and a higher-status dog than Grunt, and his instinct is still to submit.* He found himself grateful for the strictness of the hierarchy. This was how dogs survived.

The silence stretched until Lucky knew they had accepted his authority; at last he stepped back, releasing them and sitting back on his haunches.

"What is going on?" he growled.

Lick rolled onto her forepaws and crept forward, Grunt just behind her. But the male pup's muzzle was curled and his shoulders hunched with aggression.

"That pup-scent yesterday," Lucky snapped at Lick. "It was Grunt, wasn't it?"

She nodded miserably. "Yes. I'm sorry, Lucky. I couldn't help but come. I had a dream—"

Lucky made a gruff sound of disbelief. "A dream?"

"Yes." She met his eyes more confidently. "Don't ask me how, Lucky, but I knew if I came here I'd find Grunt. The dream told me so."

Lucky blinked at her, unsure how to react. Was the pup lying? Making up stories to get out of trouble? *But I've also had strange dreams.* He remembered the ice shards in the air and the terror he'd felt as he'd watched the Storm of Dogs raging, soaking the frozen ground with blood. . . .

But this is different. Lick is saying the dream told her what to do!

"She's telling the truth," muttered Grunt angrily. "I had the same dream. And I sneaked away from my Pack, so why shouldn't she?"

Lucky bristled at the pup's defiance, and a memory tugged painfully inside him: little Wiggle, so shy and timid and vulnerable, so desperate to stay with Lucky in Alpha's Pack. Lucky had let him down; they all had. And now he was . . .

"Wiggle is dead." He turned savagely on Lick. "Have you forgotten how he died? Grunt was involved in that. There are dogs it's better not to know, Lick—even if they are your own blood and flesh."

Grunt took a pace forward and bared his teeth, his tail quivering. "I did not kill my brother!"

"You were there when he died," Lucky pointed out sharply.

"Yes, but it wasn't my fangs that drew his blood. I wasn't responsible!"

"Did you do anything to save him?" Lucky snarled low in his throat. "Did you even try to stop Blade?"

Grunt fell silent, lowering his head. From his throat came a faint whimper of shame.

"Nothing," said Lucky. "You did nothing to help him, did you, Grunt?"

Grunt's head came up sharply. There was a stronger gleam of aggression in his eyes now, and his growl was cold. "That's not my name anymore. I'm Fang."

Lucky saw Lick's head droop at the news. *Another pup with his true dog-name,* he thought dismally. *Poor Lick.*

In the silence that fell, Lucky stared at Grunt. He saw that the young dog's ears were oddly misshapen, torn and stunted so that they stood erect, their edges ragged. How . . . ?

Lucky's eyes widened as he realized: Grunt's ears were a crude copy of the older Fierce Dogs'. Those brutes had had their ears neatly trimmed erect by their longpaws. Now Grunt's had been torn to the same shape—by the teeth of Blade, or one of the others. *They're mimicking what the longpaws did,* Lucky realized, as a cold tremor ran the length of his spine. How it must have hurt. Lucky wondered if they'd had to pin the pup down to keep him still. . . .

How could that Pack be so cruel? Lucky couldn't help shuddering. *Is there anything Blade won't do?*

As pity for Grunt—no, Fang—swelled inside him, Lucky felt

his anger draining away. "What happened to your ears, Grunt?" he asked gently.

Fang looked away. "That's private," he said sullenly. "It's my Pack's business."

"Maiming a fellow Pack member? That's every dog's business, I think." Lucky took a pace toward the pup, but Fang shook his injured ears and gave a low growl.

"I told you," he snapped. "It's for the Pack. It's tradition."

Lucky sighed and shook his head. "Lick," he said softly. "Why have you risked everything to come here? Even your life! You know what Blade's capable of—and Alpha too. If Alpha finds out—" He took a breath, imagining the possible consequences. "Your brother has always taken foolish risks, but not you. Why, Lick?"

The young dog blinked up at him, but before she could speak a great shadow fell across the pups, and the air seemed to grow suddenly colder.

A sleek shape emerged from the trees. Lucky's heart almost stopped as he recognized the glittering eyes, the glossy, muscled body.

Blade!

Teeth glinted in the starlight as Blade prowled forward, her eyes locked on Lucky. "To me, Fang," she snarled.

Lucky half expected the pup to protest—he'd always resisted being ordered around—but Fang immediately bowed his head and slunk to Blade's side, his tail tucked between his legs. Blade lashed out with a paw. Blood sprayed from the pup's flank, and he yelped and stumbled sideways.

"Get out of my sight," she snarled, and Fang limped miserably away, heading for whatever temporary camp the Fierce Dogs had established. He didn't look back once at Lick.

There was silence in the glade, though Lucky was sure Blade must hear his heart thumping.

"Street Dog," she growled silkily. "You have something that belongs to me."

Lucky tilted his head and sighed, hoping he looked confident. He hoped Blade couldn't smell his fear.

"Lick doesn't belong to you, Blade. She's not your Leashed Pet."

Blade stiffened. Raising a hind leg, she scratched meaning-fully at her ear. "I don't think I heard you right. Perhaps you'd better say it again. Differently."

"A pup isn't a possession—yours or any dog's. Lick has made her own choice, and that's to live with our Pack." Lucky's mouth felt as dry as dusty rock. "You don't have a say in it, Blade. You're not even Lick's Mother-Dog."

"I am *more* than her Mother-Dog. I am her true Alpha!"

"But she's no milk-pup anymore!" Lucky's curiosity overcame his caution. He truly wanted to know. "Why, Blade? Why are you so determined to have them?"

Mistake! He realized it as he heard Blade's throaty snarl. All his bravery deserted him and he cringed low, rooted to the spot. She leaped for him, jaws wide, teeth glistening.

I can't fight her alone! Earth-Dog, am I coming to you now?

Lucky flinched, waiting for the agonizing rip of teeth and claws. Instead he saw a small, blurred shape hurl itself at Blade. There was a furious yelp of pain from the huge Fierce Dog as she tumbled sideways. Stunned, Lucky gaped at young Lick, who was gripping Blade's hind leg with her needle-sharp teeth, gnawing savagely. Blood trickled from the wound, and Blade's face was rigid with shock.

Startled, as if she'd just realized what she was doing, Lick released Blade.

"Run!" barked Lucky. They both spun and fled.

Behind them, Lucky heard Blade crashing through the under-growth. Terror drove him faster, Lick at his tail, but he could hear from the uneven lurch of Blade's paws that she was limping. The young Fierce Dog had wounded her enough to slow her. *We might make it!*

At the border of the camp Lucky gathered himself and leaped, rolling and tumbling into the camp, panting with relief as he glimpsed Lick race in behind him. Staggering up onto his paws and turning, he could hear no crashing branches. Blade had pulled up before she reached Alpha's territory, but Lucky made out the glint of her malevolent eyes through the shadowy trees.

Will she attack? Even though I could raise the Pack with a single bark?

"I'll be back!" Her maddened growl echoed in the silence. Then Blade turned and padded away into the trees without looking back. Beyond her, in the distance, Lucky heard the baying of Blade's Pack, echoing their leader's menacing fury. *How do they know?* he wondered, fear chilling his bones. *How do they always know?*

There was a muttering and whining as the Pack Dogs started to stir, their ears pricking up at the sound of the Fierce Dogs howling.

"What? What's going on?" came Fiery's deep growl.

"I smell Fierce Dogs—and blood!" Sunshine yelped.

All at once, the whole Pack seemed to be on their feet, blinking as they bounded up to Lucky with growls and whines.

Lick was lost among the other dogs, and he just caught sight of her, dodging their heedless paws as they milled around. She managed to wriggle back to Lucky's side, and he heard her mumbled apology at his ear.

"I'm so sorry, Lucky." Then she was drowned out by the concerned voices.

"Lucky, what is it?" barked Dart.

"What in the name of the Earth-Dog—" yelped Snap.

"Was that Blade?" Sunshine's whine was high-pitched with terror.

"Quiet! All of you!" Alpha's deep bark silenced them all. The half wolf came stalking through the commotion, his yellow eyes blazing.

As they all fell silent, Lucky just managed to whisper to Lick, "Stay quiet." Then Alpha was standing over him, his muzzle curled back to show his teeth.

"What happened?" he growled.

Lucky dipped his head. "I heard a sound, Alpha. I thought it was probably nothing, but I went to check the perimeter just in case, and I found Blade sneaking around near the camp."

Alpha said nothing for long, agonizing moments. Lucky was staring at the ground—he didn't dare catch Lick's eye in case he gave her away—but he could feel his leader's stare boring through his skull.

Then Alpha gave a gruff snarl. "It's almost dawn. Get ready, all of you. We will regroup and move on. Now go!"

Lucky found himself trembling as Alpha stalked back the way he'd come, Sweet falling in at the half wolf's side. The elegant swift-dog spared Lucky a single thoughtful glance before turning back to murmur to her leader.

Lucky's gut churned with dread. *I couldn't have told them anything about Lick, about her secret meeting with Grunt. Alpha would have thrown her out—or killed her.*

I just hope I made the right decision.

CHAPTER FIVE

The Sun-Dog was shrouded in gray clouds as the sky lightened, and tendrils of Red Leaf mist lay in the hollows. Occasional glimpses of sunlight sparkled on dewdrops, but they faded quickly, leaving only wet coldness on the grass. The Pack was subdued as they assembled under Sweet's watchful eyes.

Alpha came padding from his den, resolutely silent. He walked on, nodding briefly to Sweet, then turned at the edge of the camp to face them all.

"Dogs are to walk behind me and Beta in pairs. Fiery and Lucky first. Patrol Dogs, stay to the right and left of the group and keep an eye on the youngest dogs. Snap and Spring, stay at the back and look out for any dog following us. Leave no obvious traces, and bury your waste if you make any. Dart, make sure that order is followed. Omega, you stay toward the rear, just in front of the rest of the hunters. Whine, you stay with her, and do not move forward. Full Pack discipline—do I make myself clear?"

"Yes, Alpha." The growl rose from every one of the Pack, and Lucky found himself joining in without a thought. What a long way it was from his own leadership of the Leashed Pack when they'd escaped the city, stumbling along in chaos. Reluctant respect for Alpha stirred inside him. Alpha wasn't always calm under pressure, and maybe his behavior was too controlling, but control was what was best for the Pack right now.

The mood was tense, as if the air buzzed with invisible long-paw power. The Fierce Dogs were close—and now that violent, hostile Pack bore an even worse grudge. The story of Lucky's encounter with Blade had raced around Alpha's Pack like a fever-sickness, exaggerated with every telling. Some dogs even gave him resentful glances, as if he'd deliberately provoked Blade.

Lucky shuddered. *The sooner we're gone from here, the better I'll feel.*

As they made their way from the camp, paws light and nervous on the forest floor, Lucky kept in his allotted place. Every dog did, obeying their Alpha and bristling with alertness as they eyed the undergrowth for movement. But when the forest was a few rabbit-chases behind them, and they were making their way through a gully fringed with thick bushes, Lucky trotted up alongside Alpha.

"What's the plan?" he asked in a low voice. "Where are we going?"

"The river," said Alpha brusquely. "If we follow its flow, we should be heading toward . . ."

The half wolf hesitated, his eyes narrowing, and his tongue came out to lick his chops. Lucky waited for him to go on.

He doesn't have a plan, realized Lucky with a sickening jolt. *He sounds arrogant, but he doesn't know where he's taking us.*

But it was no time to point that out, and humiliate Alpha. Brightly Lucky yelped in agreement. "Of course! I know where we must go—the place where all running water leads."

"The place where the water never ends," growled Alpha, "and it moves all the time but goes nowhere."

"It's a good move, Alpha," said Lucky. "It will be far from the Fierce Dogs."

Lucky noticed his leader's head lift in pride, and suddenly the half wolf's shoulders were straighter. "Of course. I don't need you to tell me that. Or to approve my plans."

What plans? thought Lucky in irritation. *Has there ever been a more arrogant dog? He's Pack leader, of course—but is that what leadership is? Sneering at every opinion?*

He kept his thoughts to himself, and not only from fear of

Alpha's reaction. The Pack was nervous enough—they didn't need a quarrel between Lucky and their leader to unsettle them any more.

Martha was walking behind Lucky, and he noticed that Lick had sped up and was now trotting alongside the huge water-dog. The two had been close since Lick was tiny, when Martha had looked after the Fierce Dog pups, but they'd always made an odd pair, and it was no different now that Lick was older. Lucky watched with amusement as Martha explained her webbed toes to the young Fierce Dog.

"No, Lick, all my littermates were born like this," Martha was telling her patiently. "We're a very special breed. My longpaws always said—"

"You! Lick!" Alpha twisted around to snarl at her. "Get back in line where you belong."

Lick gave a hurt yelp. "But Alpha, I—"

"That's enough! For that disobedience, you can walk with Whine and Omega."

Dejected, Lick fell back, her tail tucked between her legs. With an annoyed glance at Alpha, Lucky turned and loped over to keep her company. He doubted Alpha would complain—but if he did, Lucky would let him know exactly what he thought.

The former Omega, Whine, gave Lick a nasty glance but said nothing to her; Sunshine was trotting behind them both, dutifully clutching a big wedge of moss in her jaws. *She's already thinking about our bedding for the next camp,* realized Lucky affectionately. He was glad now he'd fallen back in the line; Sunshine was preoccupied, and he didn't want to leave Lick to the company of the bitter and twisted Whine. As if reading his thoughts, Whine snorted and picked up speed.

"I'll leave you and Lucky to enjoy each other's company," he sneered at Lick, and hurried to catch up with Beetle.

I'm not sorry to see the rump-end of you, Whine, thought Lucky. Ignoring the snub-nosed dog, he licked his jaws and glanced at the Fierce Dog pup. There was so much he wanted to say, but he kept his muzzle shut. Lick must feel humiliated, and no doubt she'd confide in him when she felt like it.

Sure enough, she gave a long and heavy sigh, and shook her head. "Why does every dog hate me, Lucky?"

Lucky blinked in surprise. *Does she really feel that bad?* "No dog hates you, Lick!"

Even as he said it, though, the words felt awkward and untrue. *I'm lying to her,* he realized with a jolt. He snapped idly at a fly as he tried to think of some reassuring words. Up ahead, Fiery was urging on the slower dogs: nudging Daisy gently to go faster, encouraging Beetle to watch the undergrowth for danger. Sweet had fallen back a little to discuss something with Moon, and both dogs scanned the trees as they talked. All the Pack members seemed so at ease with one another, yet it struck Lucky that no dog but himself had shown any sympathy for Lick after Alpha's snarling.

"You see?" whined Lick sadly into the silence. "You know it's true. And Alpha can't stand the sight of me."

"Oh, Lick. He's not used to having a Fierce Dog in his Pack; it's true, but why are you thinking about this now?"

"It's Grunt," she muttered guiltily. "Seeing him again. Not Grunt, I mean—Fang. He seems so happy in his Pack. He's so . . . well, he's wanted. He has his true dog-name, and he's been initi-ated, and . . ." Her voice trailed off, and she took a deep breath. "Lucky? Fang invited me to go with him."

Lucky's heart thudded, and he felt his fur bristle. *I fought hard to keep you in this Pack, Lick!* he thought with a stab of anger. *Your pre-cious litter-brother can keep his invitations to himself!*

But he couldn't say that to Lick. "What do you think would be better about it? Being in Blade's Pack, I mean?"

"Well, Fang's happy. He knows where he stands. They all do."

"They know their places, you mean," snapped Lucky. "Below Blade. And what's this 'initiation' you talk about? All I can see is that his ears have been mutilated—painfully, and for no reason!"

A stubborn light sparked in Lick's eyes. "At least Blade's Pack isn't always on the run. And the pups get good training."

"They're trained to be killers," said Lucky, "and not just of prey."

Lick shook her head in bewilderment, sighing as she raised her gaze to the treetops. "I understand what you're saying, Lucky; I do! But can it all be so bad? Fang's happy—and Blade loves him! She fought so hard to get him back!"

Careful, Lucky told himself grimly. *She's so unhappy right now. Don't say anything that might push her away.*

He took a deep breath. "Lick, are you sure 'love' is the right word? It means so many things, and a dog can twist it. Especially a dog like Blade."

"Can it? Are you sure it isn't straightforward, Lucky?" Lick turned her dark eyes directly on his. "What do you think love is, then?"

Lucky hesitated, confused. A vague memory prowled at the back of his mind, a memory made up of smells and sounds . . . the sweet, comforting scent of Mother-Dog, the softness of her voice as she told her stories of the Spirit Dogs, the warm, squirming bodies of his littermates. Suddenly he thought of Bella—and as if she had been called up by the memories, his litter-sister came bounding over to him.

"Come on, Lucky—bring Lick! Some of the hunters went foraging, and they've brought back food!"

The very mention of food made Lucky's belly rumble—loudly. For an instant he was embarrassed, and then all three dogs were barking with laughter.

"Let's go," he yelped. "Even my stomach's telling us to eat!"

As they trotted to join the other dogs, he felt a wave of relief. He hadn't wanted to continue that conversation with Lick. Not one bit.

By the time they'd eaten and walked on again, the Sun-Dog was bounding down toward the edge of the sky. Lucky's paw pads were aching. Sunshine looked bedraggled and exhausted, and though she hadn't let go of her mouthful of moss, it trailed on the ground below her drooping head. The young dogs Beetle, Thorn, and Lick were almost asleep on their paws, and even the stoic Mickey was staggering with tiredness. Lucky noticed that Sweet, with her slender, long legs made for sprinting over short distances, was limping.

Yet Alpha plowed on, leading them uphill along a dry stream-bed. He seemed intent, as if he hadn't noticed the state of most of his Pack. *That's not leadership,* thought Lucky. *That's rock-headedness.* At least they'd had a meal—without it Lucky thought they might actually have lost dogs by now; Fiery was almost having to drag on Daisy's scruff to keep her going. Still, hunger was growing in Lucky again, and he was sure the younger dogs must be starving.

A chill wind blustered down the hollow of the streambed, and the sky above them had remained cold and dark gray through-out the whole journey of the Sun-Dog. In fact, glancing up, Lucky thought it had grown darker than ever—almost black . . .

A blinding flash made him almost leap out of his skin. Light-ning! The Spirit Dog's thunderous bark resounded across the valley. Heavy spots of cold rain splashed onto Lucky's fur.

"The rain," he yelped. "It could be bad rain again. Quick—we need to find shelter!"

No dog questioned him. They all sprang for cover, racing and bounding toward a shallow cave in the steep walls of the dry stream. It was little more than a rocky overhang and a water-dug hollow, but it would have to be enough. Snap and Spring were last in, and they had barely whipped their tails beneath the rock shelf when the rainstorm exploded in earnest, drumming hard on the earth outside.

The dogs huddled together, staring out at the torrent. The black flakes were clearly visible, whirling among the raindrops and hissing where they struck the ground. Frothing puddles were forming quickly, fringed with yellowish foam.

I was right, thought Lucky. *The poisoned rain can still reach us. Will it ever stop? Because it looks as if we'll never outrun it.*

He started at the sound of shrill and frantic squeaks, and scuttled backward to avoid two rats. They darted into the cave, heedless of the Pack of dogs crowding it. The creatures scurried dementedly around the rock, desperate to escape, and as one paused on its hind legs to glare at him, Lucky saw that its tiny eyes were red and raw, its fur greasy from the rain. *It's in pain,* he realized, shocked. *It's not afraid of us—the rain is worse!*

Daisy watched the rats listlessly, and even Sweet did no more than click her teeth together with an exhausted growl. Fiery's wary gaze lingered on the creatures, but he made no move toward them. Not one of the Pack lunged at the rats, despite their hunger. Every dog must have realized, as Lucky had, that these rats were not good prey. As he eyed them, nervous, he felt Alpha at his side.

Both dogs turned back to look out into the rain once more. "We're no safer," muttered the dog-wolf. "Whatever has poisoned the land, it's getting worse."

Lucky shook his head. "There seems to be no escaping it."

"Even Lightning doesn't protect us," growled Alpha. "He brings the bad rain. When this storm passes, we must press on. This whole land is a place no dog can live."

Some of the Pack had heard him, and now they were muttering among themselves, and whimpering in distress. Daisy pressed her small body low to the ground, trying to hide beneath Martha's furry coat.

"It reminds me of the day the Big Growl hit," she whined.

"Oh, Daisy, don't say that," whimpered Sunshine.

"But she's right," said Mickey mournfully. "It's just like the day my longpaws left. The ground shaking, and that terrible scent in the air."

"I was hunting near the loudcage path and a power snake broke above my head," barked Snap. "When it fell, the invisible power set the ground on fire. I could have been burned alive."

"I remember that," agreed Dart. "And Whine almost fell into the earth when it opened."

"I was nearly hit by a falling tree," offered Moon. "It almost killed me, and my pups—their eyes weren't even fully open."

"Lucky and I were caught in a Trap House when it struck, in locked wire cages," said Sweet, sounding almost proud to be telling the awful story. "There was nothing we could do but hope we'd survive. Plenty of other dogs didn't."

Lick sidled up to Lucky, her gaze darting left and right as she muttered from the side of her mouth, "What was the Big Growl, Lucky?" She sounded embarrassed not to know.

Lucky opened his jaws and closed them again, surprised. *How can any dog not know what the Big Growl was?*

Then he realized—of course, Lick was born after it! The thought struck him with force, but he found it to be a cheering notion. One day the Big Growl would be entirely in the past, and no dog on Earth would have actually lived through it. All the time, pups were being born, and surviving—Lick was proof of that. The Big Growl wasn't the end of the world. Not yet.

"It was the worst of days, Lick. A day when the world shook and the city fell and the longpaws ran far away. Even the Earth-Dog trembled that day. Many dogs died."

"Oh." Lick shivered. "I'm glad I didn't see it."

Lucky touched her muzzle with his own. "So am I, Lick."

Lucky gazed back out of the cave mouth toward the stream-bed. He could hear the river they were heading for, and the rush and roar of it in the valley ahead. It was flowing fast, sounding furious and urgent. It was as if it was determined to get some-where, somewhere the River-Dog had commanded.

And where that river led, the Pack would follow. Just as soon as this dangerous rain ended.

CHAPTER SIX

Half of the Pack was dozing on the sandy cave floor when Lucky lifted his head and pricked his ears. It wasn't noise that had alerted him, but the absence of it. The roar of torrential downpour had been replaced by a steady, ominous dripping.

Alpha and Sweet sat at the cave mouth, staring out, and Lucky padded over to join them. Sure enough, the rain had stopped, leaving a maze of rivulets and puddles; the dry bed had become a web of real streams, flowing between the stones down toward the river.

Alpha gave Lucky a glance, then turned back to look at the sodden valley. The dog-wolf looked nervous. "This rain will have washed away all scents," he muttered. "It could be a chance to throw off the Fierce Dogs—or a chance for them to catch us unawares. We'll have to be alert. Beta, tell the Patrol Dogs. Lucky, since you're here, get every dog moving."

Paw pads had been rested, breath caught, and despite their hunger, most of the Pack was eager to get going. The air seemed to reek of nervous expectation as they set off into the valley, following the path of the sparkling new stream. The dogs heard the river before they saw it, and when they crested a crumbling ridge, there it lay: angry and fast and frothing. Out in the middle, the water was churned white around cruel, jutting rocks. Yellow scum swirled in the idle water at its fringes.

Lucky felt his heart sink. *This is going to be quite a challenge.*

"Every dog be careful," growled Alpha. "If any of you fall in, I won't allow Martha to rescue you. Understood? I won't risk two dogs."

Lucky glanced at the huge water-dog.

"River-Dog, protect us," Martha said. She looked solemn and anxious, but she didn't argue with Alpha. Even she was intimidated by that swirling, deadly current.

One by one, the dogs trudged nose-to-tail downstream, keeping their distance as well as they could from the water. The force of the nearby torrent sent shivers down Lucky's spine to the tip of his tail. Any dog who fell in there would be beyond help.

Walking at the river's flank made Lucky's nerves tingle and prickle. More than once he heard Daisy whimper with fear. Beetle and Thorn shivered as they trudged on, tails curled tightly at their flanks. Every grown dog was on edge, flinching at the noise of splitting branches and tumbling pebbles.

When the river valley flattened out at last, the river widened and calmed, straggling into a broad stretch of sandy plain. The dogs instinctively spread out, away from the edge of the water, and Lucky could hear them panting with relief. But though the terrifying white torrent was behind them, this new landscape unnerved Lucky too. It was vast and very exposed. He halted, Daisy shivering at his side. Just ahead, Mickey sniffed the air uncertainly, and Fiery gave a low, indecisive growl.

No longer funneled by its narrow streambed, the river split into many silver rivulets; the largest divided around two small islands crowned with tattered and forlorn pines. Searching the broad plain to find their path, Lucky saw with a sinking heart that the valley divided too, in several directions. In the distance he could make out at least three narrow passes between the low hills.

Oh, River-Dog! What now? Do we follow your biggest stream, or take one of the other valleys ahead?

"Where do we go now?" Echoing Lucky's thoughts, Snap stepped hesitantly forward, and turned to Alpha.

Every dog faced their leader, their eyes hopeful. But Alpha

simply stood there, turning from one river-fork to the other. His hackles rose slightly, and his tail was low, the tip of it twitching nervously. He wouldn't look at any of them. Around him, dogs were glancing at one another, growling and muttering, their ears pinned back with anxiety.

"Alpha," Lucky gently repeated. "Where do you think we should go now?" There were so many routes they could take, but which would lead them to safety?

Alpha's tail twitched, but he kept his eyes fixed firmly on the horizon.

"Be quiet. I'm thinking," he said eventually, but any dog could have heard the uncertainty in his voice.

Alpha's struggling, Lucky realized. *He has no idea what to do.*

Suddenly Sweet loped confidently forward and turned to face them. Her ears were pricked, her tail high, and her voice was steady and firm.

"All of you, wait and keep calm. There's an important decision to be made. Be patient."

The elegant swift-dog was a natural at being Alpha's second-in-command, Lucky thought with a twinge of pride and regret. *Maybe Sweet and I once shared a connection, but not anymore.* Sweet had chosen to be Alpha's loyal Beta. She padded from dog to dog, looking each firmly in the eyes, daring them to defy her. Lucky barely recognized her from the old days. Sweet had spoken of the Trap House, but she was no longer the gentle dog he'd met there. She'd accused Lucky of betrayal; she'd taken the side of dogs who hated the Fierce Dog pups. She'd held Lucky down when Alpha wanted to scar him for life. . . .

But at least Sweet had the guts and the quick thinking to step in when Alpha was floundering, and Lucky was grateful for that. *She realizes, too. She knows Alpha's in trouble.*

Now Sweet was sniffing at the branching streams, paddling carefully in the mud and lifting her slender head to scent along the dividing valleys.

Sweet's nostrils flared. Abruptly she leaped forward, racing gracefully down the bank of the right-hand stream. Her long legs took her swiftly out of sight around the curve of a low hill.

She reappeared within moments, streaking smoothly back up the valley to the Pack. As she came closer she barked with delight.

"This way! There are fish in the river, and it's clear of yellow scum—if they have survived, then this must be a safe route for us."

"Right," barked Alpha, his confidence restored. "Follow me." He looked around at the others before trotting proudly ahead. The rest of the Pack fell in behind.

Lucky watched his Packmates in disbelief. Hadn't any of them noticed that moment of weakness from their leader? They were all padding along dutifully in his wake as if nothing had happened, as if Sweet hadn't just saved them all with her confidence and quick thinking.

Snap loped past Lucky, shooting him a look of amusement. He caught up with the little tan-and-white dog, and trotted at her side. "What's so funny, Snap?" he asked irritably.

"Nothing. I noticed you looking unhappy back there. But, see, everything is fine again! Alpha's a good leader, Lucky. Strong. We all trust in him, and we shouldn't stop believing. All of us. You understand?" Picking up her pace, she bounded ahead.

Lucky couldn't help but stop in his tracks. He liked Snap, and he knew there was a lot more to her than met the eye—but he had a feeling he'd just been told off. *How did she even know that I was doubting Alpha?* Sometimes the subtleties of Pack relationships still made Lucky's head spin.

With a sigh, he shook himself and followed Snap. *Maybe she's right. I'd better stop worrying so much.*

Snap was trotting after the rest of the Pack, who had disappeared around a shoulder of a low hill. As he picked up his pace to follow, Lucky heard a loud bark of warning. Forgetting his confusion, he raced around the hill and caught up. All the dogs had come to a halt, and Lucky drew in a shocked breath, feeling his hackles lift.

Longpaw houses!

Ahead lay a small cluster of buildings, neatly lining one of those rock-hard longpaw roads that hurt the paws if a dog walked on them too long. *There must be a town at the end of it,* Lucky realized, tucked comfortably into the valley at the edge of another pine forest that sloped up into the hills. Among the red and gray roofs and the low longpaw houses he could make out regularly spaced trees and more hardstone tracks, as well as the signs and lights the longpaws always put beside them. The lights didn't flash and change now; they all seemed dead. There were no high clear-stone buildings in this place, so the distant hills were visible. This was a far smaller longpaw settlement than Lucky's old city.

The houses didn't seem to have been too badly damaged by the Big Growl, Lucky thought with a shudder of unease as the dogs padded cautiously toward them. With their intact white walls, their neat roofs, and little fenced gardens, they looked as if they might still contain living, breathing longpaws. Which might not be good news for a Pack of Wild Dogs.

"I don't like this," he growled under his breath.

No sooner had he said it than a white ball of fur flashed past his paws. Sunshine was racing for a row of longpaw houses, her fluffy tail in the air, her long, white ears blowing back, barking in delight.

"Lucky!" Alpha barked angrily. "Bring that long-haired rat back here!"

Oh, Sunshine! Lucky sprinted after her, not wasting breath on barking. With her short legs she was easy enough to catch up to, for all her eagerness. "Stop, Sunshine!" he barked, nipping at her tail. "Stop!"

"But—" She glanced over her shoulder but ran on, ducking her tail away from his teeth. "Food! Real food! Soft sleeping nests! Come on, Lucky!"

Lucky growled and snapped at her sides this time, nipping her flesh beneath the silky fur. "I said *stop*!" He couldn't believe this! After all they'd been through, she still turned into a lapdog at the sight of a longpaw's front door. "STOP!"

Lucky seized the scruff of her neck in his jaws, dragging her to a halt and shaking her.

She wriggled and squirmed in his grip, her barks high and desperate: "Let me go! Let me go, you bully!"

Snarling, Lucky pinned her down with his jaws, just managing to stop himself from giving her a real, hard bite on the neck. She thrashed a little more, feebly, and Lucky grew aware that Alpha had come closer and was watching them with interest.

Lucky panted into Sunshine's fur and gave her another small shake. "Come back to the Pack right now," he growled quietly. "Unless you want Alpha to throw you in the river with the fish. And Martha won't be dragging you out."

Beneath him, Sunshine went still, and he felt her begin to tremble.

"If there are longpaws here, they're *not yours*. They'll see you as a wild animal. You know it's true. Come back," he murmured again. "And get ready to apologize."

At last Sunshine went limp, defeated. Lucky nudged her to her paws and led her to Alpha. She was shaking by the time she stood before her leader, looking very small in front of his huge forelegs.

She flopped onto her side before the half wolf, showing her belly in submission. She looked petrified. *Acting sensibly at last,* thought Lucky with relief. Her nose in the dirt, she thumped her tail once, miserably.

"I'm sorry," she whimpered. "I'm so sorry, Alpha. I didn't think. I couldn't think."

Alpha glared down at her. Lucky held his breath, afraid even to intervene on her behalf. But young Lick crept close to Sunshine's flanks. Comfortingly she began to nuzzle Sunshine's silky coat.

Lucky was touched, but Alpha gave a sharp snarl of disgust. "How did my Pack ever come to this? Home to a foolish bunch of Leashed Dogs."

Lucky opened his mouth to protest, but he was interrupted by a low clatter from the nearest longpaw house.

"Something's in there," he exclaimed, forgetting Sunshine's troubles for the moment. *Sky-Dogs, protect us—this can't be good.*

"I see no longpaws." Alpha frowned. "We'll investigate this place. There may be food. But be extra vigilant."

With a jerk of his head, Alpha led the dogs into the shade of a stone wall by the side of the track, and they slunk along the hard sidewalk. Lucky glanced nervously at the house where he'd heard the clatter, but no longpaw appeared. Perhaps it had been a rat, or a sharpclaw? He knew there could still be longpaws hiding somewhere. *Like that one I found in the city, with his firebox . . . the angry one.*

The hardstone surface felt odd underpaw, after soft grass and leaves and muddy earth, but it was familiar to Lucky. Even the smell of it evoked memories, and as he lowered his muzzle to sniff at it he felt an unexpected rush of longing for his old city life.

The click of the Pack's claws seemed very loud, and Lucky was amused to hear the rising murmur of complaints among the Wild Dogs.

"What is this stuff?" Spring's voice echoed, and she glanced anxiously up.

"It's not stone; I'll tell you that," Fiery growled. "Keep your voice down."

Snap sniffed at the surface, hackles rising. "I don't like the smell."

"I do!" piped up Daisy's voice.

"Quiet, I said!" snapped Fiery.

"It hurts my paw pads," complained Thorn in a low voice.

Lucky rolled his eyes in exasperation. "You'll get used to it. Longpaws walk on it all the time."

"So do Leashed Dogs," added Bruno with pride. "There's nothing to be afraid of."

"Yes," said Daisy mischievously. "You have to learn to be as tough as Leashed Dogs."

Ahead, Sweet made a gruff sound that might have been irritation or amusement.

"And," Lucky added, "there's one thing you can be sure of. If there are longpaws around, there's always food. Food that you don't have to chase and kill! Believe me, food tastes a lot different when you don't have to catch it."

"Yes," agreed Sunshine with feeling. "And when you're not too tired to eat it."

That seemed to improve the Wild Dogs' mood. Snap and Spring looked brighter already, exchanging optimistic glances as they trotted along with their paws lifted higher. Even Moon pricked her ears in anticipation. But Alpha called Lucky forward with a surly bark.

"Who leads this Pack?" he asked coldly. "You or me, Street Dog?"

It was on the tip of Lucky's tongue to say Sweet, but—thank the wits of the Forest-Dog—he restrained himself just in time. "Sorry, Alpha," he said meekly.

"Just watch your step," growled the half wolf. "Ah!" Turning a corner, he came to a halt. The Pack fell silent, and Sunshine gave a high whimper.

Lucky swallowed hard. The center of the longpaw settlement lay before them, huge and wide open, a place where they'd be visible and vulnerable. Hesitantly they crept toward the end of their narrow street.

The Big Growl seemed to have done less damage here than

in the city: There was broken clear-stone everywhere, but no collapsed houses. Ahead of them lay a vast area of neat grass with well-tended trees and a pool of blue water in the center. Tucked among the reeds that edged it was a massive, messy nest.

"Swans," whispered Bella. "Take care, everyone."

Lucky too had always respected and avoided those huge white waterbirds, but this nest was empty. "It's all right; the nest's abandoned."

"He's right," murmured Bruno. "There are no birds there."

Mickey shivered uneasily. "No birds anywhere. Even in the trees."

He's right, Lucky realized with a creeping sense of dread. *The birds have left this longpaw-place. None roosting, none flying.*

And no wonder. As the dogs padded out into the open space and gazed around, Lucky felt his stomach lurch.

There were bodies here: two on the black hardstone, one on the grass, and one half-in and half-out of the water—abandoned, decaying corpses of . . .

Sunshine gave a wail of horror.

"Longpaws!"

CHAPTER SEVEN

The Leashed Dogs sent up a volley of grief-stricken, baying howls. Even Lucky felt a stab of awful misery.

The bodies looked as if they had been struck down without warning. Lucky spotted a few more—one was caught on a fence; another lay propped against the door of a house. Some had wide-open, glazed eyes; others had none. *Crows must have found them,* thought Lucky, *and now even the crows have fled.* And there was something strange about these longpaws' hides: They were gray, the texture of wet bark. There were streaks of yellow spit at their lips, and their paw-tips were blue, turning to black.

Lucky swallowed. Longpaws like these had passed him scraps under park benches, had absentmindedly stroked his head, or thrown him leftovers from Food Houses. Even the Trap House longpaws had fed him, brought him water, given him a fairly comfortable place to sleep. Some had kicked or shouted at him, too, but none of them deserved to end up like this. Lucky could tell the bodies had lain here for a while. Some had been attacked by foxes or birds; some were almost skeletons. Over the whole settlement lay the sickly, powerful scent of death.

They should have been given to the Earth-Dog, thought Lucky, feeling sick. *Why weren't they?*

"Are they our longpaws?" wailed Sunshine in distress. "Are they here?"

"They might be." Mickey lay down beside her, baying his misery. "We never did find them, did we?"

"No. Oh please, no." Martha crouched, whimpering.

"Shut up!" Alpha's angry barks could barely be heard over the Leashed Dogs' howling. "Be quiet, I order you!"

"Our longpaws," cried Daisy, as Bruno let out harsh, choking howls. "Our longpaws are dead!"

"BE QUIET!" Alpha barked. But no dog was listening to him.

They're hysterical, thought Lucky, *and I understand—but they can't go on like this.*

Seizing Mickey's scruff, Lucky shook him gently, raising his head out of the dust. "Listen," he yelped. "Listen, all of you. These aren't your longpaws. They can't be!"

"How do you know?" Mickey barked in furious grief.

"You knew your longpaws so well—if they were here, you'd smell them, wouldn't you? And your longpaws escaped! These ones lived here, and they were trapped. They must have been killed when the Big Growl hit. They aren't yours! We aren't anywhere near the city."

"Lucky, you don't understand—"

Through the chaos and misery, a bolt of inspiration struck Lucky. "This is a good sign, Mickey! All of you, listen—this is happy news!"

As one the Leashed Dogs stopped midhowl and turned to stare at Lucky. Mickey looked at him as if he'd caught the deadly water-madness, as if he expected Lucky to start frothing at the mouth.

"How can this be good?" wailed Sunshine.

"Because these longpaws were trapped," Lucky said patiently. "Look at how they're lying—they were trying to get away. They hadn't come to this place; they were trying to leave it!"

Mickey stared, trembling, at the bodies. "But they couldn't escape . . ."

"Don't you see?" barked Lucky. "This is what would have happened to your longpaws if they'd stayed for you. You wondered why they left—well, this is why! Do you understand, Daisy?"

Gently he nudged the little terrier with his nose. "Now you know your longpaws didn't want to leave—but if they hadn't, this is what would have become of them."

The Leashed Dogs began to sit up awkwardly; still distressed, thought Lucky, but at least they'd stopped that awful wailing. Even Alpha flashed him an exasperated but grateful look.

"I didn't think of it like that," said Daisy in a small voice.

"So," said Sunshine, snuffling into her paws. "That means my longpaws are probably safe?"

"Safe and alive," agreed Lucky. "Because they got away from the Big Growl and the poisoned land in time."

The Leashed Dogs were all getting back on their paws now, shaking off the dust and looking a little embarrassed. Martha concentrated very hard on nibbling at her webbed claws. Mickey scratched his ear.

"Well," Bruno grumbled. "Let's get moving."

Lucky shook his head. He couldn't help but hear the stunned murmurs of the Wild Dogs around him:

"What bizarre behavior," Moon whispered to Fiery.

"Outlandish," agreed her mate. "I thought they were Wild Dogs now?"

"They're supposed to be," sneered Whine. "And then they

see a few dead longpaws and they can't control themselves. Hmph."

"Mother-Dog," yelped Beetle softly, "I don't understand this."

"Hush, Beetle. None of us really do." Moon licked his ear. "I'll try and explain later. Don't hurt the Leashed Dogs' feelings, will you?"

But Beetle's right, thought Lucky dismally. *They're not supposed to be Leashed Dogs anymore.*

"Listen, all of you." Sweet gave an authoritative bark that settled every dog quickly. "I can feel the air thickening. The storm's returning. Let's find shelter, and quickly."

She was right, Lucky realized. The sky had grown dark and heavy, as if the Sky-Dogs were assembling above the clouds for a battle.

"Where will we hide?" asked Thorn.

"Look around you, youngster," said Sweet with amusement. "These longpaw houses seem stable, and the longpaws don't need them anymore." She gave a slightly apologetic glance in the direction of the Leashed Dogs.

"I think we should keep moving," Dart argued, giving the corpses an anxious glance. "I don't like this place."

"We can't be outside when the rain comes," snapped Moon,

with a protective glance at her growing pups. "Don't you know that by now, Dart?"

"Moon is right, and so is Beta," barked Alpha gruffly. "Find a longpaw house where we can take cover."

He has no problem making a decision, thought Lucky, *when another dog makes a good suggestion.*

"But there was a noise . . ." began Beetle timidly.

"Only a rat after all, I think," Lucky told him. "No longpaw has survived here; I'm sure of it."

Martha shuddered unhappily beside him. "I'm afraid Lucky's right."

Keeping closely together, the Pack set off down the hardstone track, treading delicately between the bodies that lay sprawled across it.

"How about that one?" suggested Snap, nodding at a long, low building.

"Not enough exits," said Alpha dismissively. Before Snap could even suggest another house behind it, he said, "And that one's too close to the other—it could give our enemies cover."

"This one?" Moon pointed her nose at a small building made of wood.

"Too flimsy. Keep looking."

Is he being picky? wondered Lucky. *Or just trying to show he's still in charge?*

Snap seemed to have given up making suggestions; she padded at Lucky's side along with Lick. "Honestly, Lucky, I had no idea a few dead longpaws would upset your friends so much."

"They're still getting used to being wild," snapped Lucky. When Snap gave him a surprised look, he dipped his head apologetically. *I shouldn't be so defensive. Snap has a point.* "It's just—well, it hasn't been that long since they lost their longpaws. And I think . . . the longpaws were like their Pack. Imagine losing your whole Pack and being left all alone."

Snap was silent for a few moments. "It's a shame." She sighed deeply, wagging her stumpy tail. "Those longpaws would make a great meat source."

"Snap!" he growled. "Be quiet. They'll hear."

"Honestly, though—"

"If you thought the Leashed Dogs were upset before, just see what they're like when you suggest they eat longpaws," Lucky told her sternly. "Anyway, these aren't for eating. Have you smelled them?"

Making a doubtful face, Snap paused by a longpaw corpse to give it a sniff. She yelped, and hurried back to Lucky's side. "You're right. They smell like the foul river."

Lucky nodded. "They've been lying out in the bad rain. And I think they've been here for a long time."

"Here!" Alpha's loud bark brought them all to a halt. He stood stiffly beside a broken clear-stone panel set in a solid wall. "We'll shelter in this place."

"Good idea," grumbled Spring under her breath. "It's starting to rain."

Lucky jumped in alarm as two big drops splashed onto his fur, and soon it was pattering steadily down. The dogs scrambled through the shattered clear-stone panel into a broad room filled with toppled tables and sitting-boxes. Scattered around the place were squares of white longpaw fur, clear-stone bottles of thick, red liquid and white, salty powder, and broken jars spilling flowers that hadn't died. Dart sniffed at one of the jars.

"No wonder they haven't wilted," she blurted in astonishment. "These flowers aren't real; they smell like the hardstone path."

"What is this place?" Beetle gazed up and around at the strange room as the others huddled and stared.

Lucky nosed at the tables and gave a yelp of delight. "It's a Food House!"

"A what?" Fiery lifted an ear, puzzled.

"A Food House. This is where longpaws come to eat together, like a Pack. They take turns, like we do, while their hunters bring them food. Then they put the salty grain and the red sauce on the prey."

Alpha gave a disbelieving whine.

"And there was always lots of food. Longpaws had good hunting," explained Lucky. "Sometimes they didn't eat all of it, and they'd give the rest to me."

"Give it to you?" asked Moon skeptically. "You mean, willingly? Food they didn't want?"

"Really. I know it sounds odd, but it happened quite often."

"I saw one of these places, in the city," put in Sweet. "Lucky's telling the truth. There was a kind longpaw there who gave him spare food."

"Spare food?" echoed Alpha with a snort. "A kind longpaw?"

"There might be something left," said Lucky, ignoring his leader's contemptuous tone. Nosing through a pair of loose-swinging doors, he found what he was looking for. "Here! The Food Room."

The center of the floor was paw-deep in water that spurted now and then from a broken pipe, but the water was clean. Lucky bent to lap a few mouthfuls. Nothing had tasted so good in a long time. Licking his chops, he examined the steel boxes against the walls, as the rest of the Pack crept cautiously in behind him. They flinched at the swinging doors, but then gave yelps of delight as they discovered the clean, fresh water.

Beside him, though, a low harsh whimper came from Sweet's throat. *Maybe she's remembering how scared she was in that other Food House, when we found just one dead longpaw.*

And now look at her, Lucky thought—*confidently leading a Pack whenever Alpha loses control, and not even worried by a whole street covered in longpaw corpses.* Part of him missed the old Sweet, but surely it was better to see her like this, tough and independent, than running scared.

The world's such a dangerous place now, maybe we could all use a bit of Sweet's new hardness.

Mickey pawed at one of the big steel boxes. "Watch this."

"They don't open," Lucky told him. "They're always locked."

"They do," Mickey told him mischievously. He hooked his claws around one steel door. With a flick and pull of a dexterous paw, he yanked the heavy door and it swung wide with a creak.

Lucky stared, open-jawed and impressed. *I wish I'd known that trick in the old days!*

"Well done, Mickey!" barked Bruno, and every dog fell on what was inside.

Some of the food was too old to eat, crusted in blue mold, or foul-smelling, but a fair amount was edible. Bruno tugged out a big, covered pan with his teeth, spilling soft, cooked grains onto the floor. There were packets of dry food too, and when Mickey opened another steel box a flood of freezing cold water drenched him, but they discovered a bag of meat discs that were still good.

It was no hunt, and the food was plentiful, so after their hard journey none of the dogs seemed inclined to follow Pack discipline. Sunshine held nervously back at first, and Dart widened her eyes in surprise when Whine snatched a mouthful of grain from under her nose, but Sweet and Alpha seemed content to let every dog eat their fill without regard for rank. With the rounds of frozen meat there was more than enough to go around, and the dogs were hungry enough to eat those as they were, crunching and chewing and gulping them down.

"You were right, Lucky," said Spring though a mouthful of half-frozen meat. "Food Houses are useful places."

Lucky couldn't help thinking, though, that the longpaw food didn't taste as good to him as it once had. Was that because it was old, or because he was so accustomed now to fresh prey and a warm kill? *I'm changing without even noticing it.*

Strange, he thought, that he felt the same about this meal as Alpha must. The dog-wolf barely bothered to touch the longpaw food, haughtily pushing it aside after only a few mouthfuls. Alpha watched them all eat with an expression of disdain, especially the Leashed Dogs, who ate with far more enthusiasm than the wild ones.

"I haven't tasted rice in such a long time," said Sunshine wistfully, licking up a few last grains.

"And you won't taste it again," snapped Alpha. "When the Sun-Dog rises tomorrow, the hunting dogs can go into the forest and find some real prey."

Sunshine sighed, but said nothing.

When the dogs had eaten their fill, they settled in their sleep-groups as rain battered down outside. Treading his ritual circle, Lucky cocked an ear to listen to the downpour, and was glad they were indoors and out of the way of the bad rain. In the corner farthest from the shattered clear-stone, Alpha and Sweet curled up together; the hunters and Patrol Dogs found their own separate sleeping dens beneath collapsed tables. Sunshine lay by herself, closest to the rain that blustered in through the broken clear-stone, whimpering sadly; perhaps her Omega duties were finally getting her down, Lucky thought sympathetically.

Deciding to keep an eye on the unhappy little dog, he shuffled to the edge of the hunters' makeshift den. As the cold breeze touched his fur, a shiver ran through his hide. *Sky-Dogs, it's freezing! Poor Sunshine. And will I ever get to sleep myself?*

Then he felt warmth at his side. Glancing around, he saw Lick carrying a white longpaw fur in her jaws. She tugged it over him and gave him an affectionate lick on the nose, then slunk back to her place on the edge of the patrol den.

Lucky watched her go, grateful and touched. *How can any dog think Lick's evil?* he wondered. *She has a sweeter nature than most of this Pack.*

Drowsily his snout sank to the floor, and he drifted into an exhausted sleep.

Blinking awake to the dim morning light, Lucky realized the noise of the rain had faded; it was now no more than a drizzle beyond the broken clear-stone. He could smell the acid tang of its aftermath, and when he risked peering outside, he saw hissing tendrils of steam rising from puddles. Lucky shook himself.

The other dogs were rising, stretching, and yawning; Sunshine, shivering, crept past on her way to receive her orders from Sweet.

"Did you sleep, Sunshine?" asked Lucky.

She gave him a grateful look. "A bit. Thank you."

Poor little Sunshine, he thought. *She's trying so hard.*

"Hunters and Patrol Dogs." Alpha summoned them from his corner. "A small group of you will scout the rest of the longpaw settlement. Beta will lead you. Martha and Daisy, go with her."

"Really, Alpha?" Daisy, her tail wagging wildly, was almost bursting with pride.

Alpha rolled his eyes. "You were a Leashed Dog. You'll have special knowledge. Use it to find anything we need to know. See if there's any reason we should stay here and keep this place as a base—or if there's any reason we should leave."

Daisy's tongue lolled and she whined her eager agreement. But Lucky found his hackles lifting. How could Alpha leave him out of the scouting party? He was a City Dog, as Alpha was usually so keen to remind him! *Is he doing this to spite me?*

Lucky turned to Daisy. "Do you want me to show you how to open a Food House door, Daisy? Would you like me to explain how you pick out edible food from a spoil-box?"

"That's a good point." Daisy hung her head, eyes darting to left and right. "I don't really know how to do those things, Lucky."

Alpha cocked his head and eyed Lucky. "If you have a problem with my choice of scouts, I suggest you say it out loud."

"Why not me, Alpha?" challenged Lucky. "I have skills you could use."

Alpha examined a dewclaw. "I think Daisy and Martha will do the job best."

Lucky took a breath to argue, but Fiery intervened before he could speak. "Alpha, why wouldn't you send Lucky? He knows about longpaw settlements, like the Leashed Dogs do. And he survived in a city alone—they didn't!"

"He's right, Alpha," whined Daisy, pinning her ears back. "Lucky knows so much."

"I think so too," said Snap.

"It seems obvious to me," said Bella quietly. Lucky met her eyes and panted happily, glad of her support.

"I agree," added Sweet calmly. "I think Lucky should go."

"Please, Alpha," said Martha.

For a brief moment Alpha's yellow eyes blazed with cold fire. Lucky tried to still his wildly wagging tail. Alpha couldn't refuse now. If he did, it would look as if he was putting his feelings before the good of the Pack.

Alpha's muzzle curled, and his expression grew sly. "I made you a hunter, didn't I? Go hunting. You and Fiery, Snap, Bruno, and Mickey: Get out into the forest and find food. Prey will be hard to track down after that rain, and we'll need all we can get. We won't be eating longpaw muck again; you all gorged on it last night."

"But we could find more—" began Fiery.

"I lead this Pack!" barked Alpha.

"You lead it when—" The words were out before Lucky could stop himself, but he snapped his mouth shut before he could go too far. What could he say, after all? That Alpha only led it when it was easy? When he could seize on one of Sweet's decisions and pretend it was his own?

The Pack watched him in tense silence. "You lead this Pack," Lucky finished in a mutter.

"Yes." Alpha showed his teeth. "The patrols are my decision, and that's final."

Lucky lowered his head and growled in assent. At least he'd been sent hunting; but Alpha's stubbornness infuriated him. And that move had verged on sneaky, rather than clever. Why shouldn't the Pack try to stay here, where it was safe? The priority now should be to find decent food and better shelter in the longpaw settlement, and that was where Lucky would have been really valuable. But Alpha had wasted Lucky's knowledge out of sheer spite.

Lucky was glad to get away from Alpha and the Food House; it was good to run in the wild again, his nose alert for scents of prey, the breeze cold and fresh on his skin and fur. As soon as the hunting party left the town, Fiery and Snap gave huffing sighs of relief.

"Thank the Sky-Dogs," said Fiery. "Grass under my paws again! My paw pads were aching on that hardstone."

"Mine too," agreed Snap. "And I'm sure it was blunting my claws."

Lucky glanced at them both, surprised. It was pleasant to feel cool earth beneath his paws—that was true—but could two such tough dogs really be affected so badly by hardstone?

He looked at Bruno and Mickey. The two Leashed Dogs weren't complaining about the soft tracks, but they weren't quite as nimble or sure-pawed out here as they were in the longpaw settlement. Earth was clumping between their claws, and mud bedraggling and matting their fur.

Each dog to his own, thought Lucky with an inward sigh. *And we all have to adapt now.*

Once they were within the shade and dimness of the woods, the hunters walked more carefully, picking their way under bushes and between mossy trunks. The light was gloomy, the rain a soft constant mist that pattered off the remaining leaves. It would be hard to track prey in this, but perhaps the prey would be less likely to scent them, too.

Halting in a small glade, Mickey and Fiery, the two best trackers, raised their muzzles to taste and sniff the damp air. The dogs all cocked their ears keenly. Distantly a bird gave a weak twitter, and Fiery narrowed his eyes.

"I can smell something," muttered the big dog. "I'm just not sure what it is."

"It's all we've got," pointed out Bruno. "We might as well follow it."

"All right," agreed Fiery. "But be alert, in case it's a badger or a coyote . . . or a giantfur."

Lucky shivered. The memory of the last giantfur they'd met was all too fresh in his mind—the small, angry eyes in a round-eared head, the massive, black-furred body, the raking claws, and the snarling jaws in an earth-brown snout. No dog could stay brave for long before one of those enormous creatures.

"I hope it isn't one of those," said Snap drily. "I'm not in the mood for a battle."

"I don't know," Bruno said heartily. "A giantfur would make a pretty fine meal to take back to Alpha."

"Hmph," laughed Fiery. "I hope you're joking."

"You'd better be, Bruno. If I see a giantfur, I plan to turn tail and run," said Lucky. "I'm warning you now."

"I'll be with you, Lucky," said Snap as they trotted on through the forest.

"Me too," agreed Mickey, looking nervous.

"Oh, don't worry. It's not likely to be a giantfur," scoffed Fiery. Then his ears pinned back and he drew a breath. "What in the Sky-Dogs' name—"

He came to a halt in front of them. Their banter was cut off abruptly.

"It's not a giantfur," he snarled, his hackles lifting as his legs stiffened. "It's dogs!"

A volley of aggressive barks ripped the air, echoing through the trees.

"They're straight ahead!" howled Lucky. *And they're heading in our direction.*

CHAPTER EIGHT

Fiery stood rooted to the spot, immobile, horrified at his mistake at leading them straight into danger. Lucky realized he had to take command from the big dog, if only for a moment.

"Every dog, get in a circle!" barked Lucky. "Tight battle formation!"

Lucky was grateful that the Pack had been drilling and training since their last disastrous battle with the Fierce Dogs, when they'd submitted out of fear; Mickey, Snap, and Bruno fell instantly into a defensive line, keeping close together and showing no signs of panic. Fiery, too, recovered from his remorse and shock. Shaking himself, he took a place at Lucky's side, his muscles tensed, ready to face whatever was approaching.

They could hear the crackle and rustle of branches and dry leaves, growing louder as the other dogs plunged through the undergrowth toward them. *How many?* wondered Lucky. *Nine?*

Ten? More? They certainly outnumbered Fiery's patrol. Lucky stiffened his muscles and bared his teeth. If it was the Fierce Dogs, he and his Packmates would not go down without a fight.

The first enemy burst from the bushes ahead. It was not a Fierce Dog, Lucky saw with a surge of relief—this strange dog was stocky, his long, matted brown hair patched with pale cream. His eyes widened to show the whites and he skidded to a halt in a tumble of leaves. Spinning frantically, he yelped a warning to his Pack.

So they didn't know we were here, either! Lucky thought, as the rest of them crashed into the clearing behind him. Lucky felt his hopes rise. This new Pack was a rabble! They were wheeling and barking and knocking into one another as they let out a chaotic volley of warning barks. The mangy brown dog slipped and slid in the leaves in his panic, provoking a frightened, "Watch out!" from a thin dog who almost fell over him. These dogs might be a threat, but at least they didn't pose the kind of danger Blade's Pack would.

Facing them down, Fiery's patrol raised their hackles, and snarled as one.

Nice to know there's a Pack even less disciplined than the Leashed Dogs, thought Lucky wryly. Lowering his hackles, he sniffed cautiously.

The newcomers seemed uncertain, still giving occasional barks

111

as they sniffed and eyed the hunting party. They didn't appear too hostile, despite all their angry barking as they'd arrived.

Snap gave a sudden yelp of surprise and joy. "Twitch!"

Startled, Lucky watched her bolt forward to the bushes. Another dog was limping into view—a black-and-tan hunt-dog, clearly lame. It was Twitch!

He survived after he left us, even with that broken leg! Lucky felt a surge of gladness. *And he's found a new Pack!*

But then a thrill of horror ran down Lucky's spine. Twitch's leg was no longer broken: It was gone altogether. It had been cut off—no, probably chewed off—and all that was left was a stubby lump. Skin had grown back over it, warped and hairless, and there was no open wound. Lucky exchanged a shocked glance with Bruno and Fiery.

Still, Twitch didn't seem to mind. He lurched forward on three legs, moving fast and easily, and returned Snap's eager licks.

"What are you doing here, Snap? And the rest of you!" His voice was glad, but urgent. "I thought you'd found a new camp, after that black cloud fell."

"We did, but—" began Snap.

Twitch shook himself. "No, never mind that. There's no time. Listen to me—you have to get out of the forest." The three-legged dog gave a nervous glance over his shoulder. "Right now!"

Lucky opened his jaws to ask why, but a great crunching and snapping of branches made every dog look up.

The dog that emerged last from the bushes was a gigantic creature, as big as Fiery. His short hair was dappled all over with ugly bald patches, red and inflamed-looking, and his square face was bloated and twisted. But it was his eyes that were most disturbing, thought Lucky. They were wide and dilated, and nearly the same vivid yellow as the furs of those sinister patrolling longpaws.

As soon as the huge creature appeared, Twitch and the rest of his Pack flopped to the ground, meek and cringing.

"Terror!" yelped the patchy brown dog.

The massive, ugly dog surveyed them all with a sneering growl.

Fiery, with a last quick glance at his patrolmates, stepped forward and dipped his head in respect for the dog who must be Alpha of this Pack. "Greetings. We're part of a Pack that is passing through your forest, looking for new territory. We will be moving on soon."

His baleful yellow eyes glowed, but the huge creature said nothing.

"Will you as Alpha permit us to hunt here for a few journeys of the Sun-Dog?" Fiery went on.

Lucky listened with his ears pricked, impressed. Surely this mean-looking Alpha dog couldn't object to such a polite request? Fiery was quick-thinking and reasonable as well as huge and strong—no dog could fail to listen to him.

In fact, it suddenly occurred to Lucky that Fiery would be an ideal Alpha. If anything were to happen to the half wolf . . . first Sweet and then Fiery were the obvious candidates to be the next Alpha of their Pack.

Expectantly Lucky and the other members of the patrol turned back to the big yellow-eyed dog. Still he didn't reply. Instead he began to tremble, his patchy fur rippling, and suddenly he gave a barking laugh. The tremors became great shudders that shook his whole massive body.

Lucky was stunned. Snap cocked an ear at Bruno; Mickey's jaw hung open in disbelief, and Fiery's eyes narrowed—just before the big Alpha dog struck out with a paw, slashing hard across Fiery's muzzle.

With barks of anger, Lucky and the others sprang forward to Fiery's defense, but the other Pack dogs were on their paws too, even Twitch, snarling viciously at them.

In the standoff, the big yellow-eyed dog lifted his head, drool slavering from one side of his jaw. "I am Terror," he growled. "I am the Forepaw of the Fear-Dog, King of all the Spirit-Dogs. Show me respect!"

Stunned into silence, Lucky glanced at Fiery, who was slowly shaking his huge head. "What are you muttering about?" he snarled. "There's no such thing as a Fear-Dog!"

"Yes, there is!" The strange Terror's bark was high-pitched with fury. "All must bow to him!" Spatters of drool flew from his mouth and his yellow eyes rolled. "Bow to him!"

Around him, his Pack quivered and pressed themselves low to the ground, every eye fixed in fear on his face.

Terror struck the ground with his claws, sending leaves flying, raking gashes in the earth. "Where have you slunk from? Strange dogs are not welcome here. The King of Dogs does not share his prey!" He swung around, lifted one great paw again, and Lucky tensed to leap out of the way—but this time Terror's claws slammed down hard on the forepaw of one of his own Packmates.

The little, short-haired brown dog yelped with pain and cowered, and the rest of Terror's Pack trembled with a frenzy of fear. Lucky's fur prickled. What Alpha would do that to one of his own dogs, for no reason? Fiery shook his head and stared, then gave a bark of fury.

"You're crazy. And you and your made-up Spirit-Dog can go to the real Earth-Dog! I told you—we are travelers. My Pack and I will hunt in this forest, as is our right by the laws of the Forest-Dog. And if you know what's good for you, you and your pathetic Pack will stay out of our way."

"You!" Terror barked into the face of the short-haired dog he had just hurt. "Attack the intruder!"

At such a feeble threat, Fiery exchanged an amused glance with Lucky, who shook his head. *Ridiculous,* he thought. *That little dog's no match for Fiery!*

But the dog obeyed her Alpha, her eyes wide with fear. She flung herself at Fiery's head, clawing and barking frantically.

Shocked, Fiery batted her away, knocking her into a pile of leaves, but she leaped up instantly and flew at him again, teeth snapping. Lucky stiffened, but he couldn't interfere. Fiery would be livid at any suggestion of help—the little dog's behavior was absurd!

Fiery whacked her aside, this time pouncing forward to slap a great paw onto her belly and hold her down. Yet again, she wriggled free and flew at him.

As he tried to dodge, Fiery shot Terror a look of disbelief. The huge, mad-eyed dog was making a growling, huffing sound, as if he was amused. Lucky shuddered, and he could see the disturbed expressions on Mickey and Bruno's faces too.

"Now!" barked Terror. "In the name of the Fear-Dog! Attack!"

Lucky and his friends backed hurriedly into their disciplined line, but it was no defense against Terror's Pack. *We're seriously outnumbered,* thought Lucky.

At the rear of his Pack, Terror was biting and scratching at his dogs' haunches, driving them on into battle. Lucky growled and bit at the first dog to lunge at him, who was snarling and clawing insanely. To his right he saw Snap forced to fight against Twitch, who was striking out even as she barked at him.

"Twitch! Stop this! We were Packmates!"

In return Twitch gave her a hard blow on the side with one paw. He did not look as mad as the others, but there was a light of desperation in his eyes, and he didn't hold back from obeying Terror's howled orders and snapping teeth. And Lucky could see why, even as he fought off his own opponent. Terror's "leadership" tactics might be crazy, but they were effective.

It's working for him, thought Lucky, *but how can he fight this way? It's against a dog's honor!*

Fiery had managed to pin down the crazed little dog with two paws, though she still struggled, jaws snapping, growling and yapping crazily, and now he had a thin and mangy black dog hanging on to one of his ears. The black dog's eyes were rolling in their sockets, so wide and dark that Lucky thought they might pop right out of his head.

"Retreat!" Fiery barked. "All hunting dogs, back! It's no use!"

With a last hard swipe to dislodge the snapping brown dog from his throat fur, Fiery spun around and bounded into the forest, Lucky and the others at his heels. It was the only thing to do, Lucky knew. Fiery was right. There was no fighting those dogs, driven to deadly combat by fear of their leader.

His breath rasping in his throat, Lucky ran with the others until his legs and his rib cage ached—but they were easily outpacing that ragtag Pack. Surely they'd give up as soon as they'd driven the hunters out of the forest?

As they burst from the trees into the meadow, Lucky risked a glance back over his shoulder. For a moment there was no sign of movement—then, to his horror, Terror's Pack burst from the trees, snarling and wheeling, tripping over their own feet, but still chasing them.

"Are they insane?" he barked breathlessly at Fiery.

Fiery's eyes were shocked. "I think they are—at least their Alpha is."

Lucky could tell from their clumsy, pounding paw steps that the pursuing Pack was exhausted, yet still they came, breaking through the undergrowth, plowing on with sheer determination.

"Back to the Food House!" barked Fiery, and raced onto the first stretch of black hardstone in the longpaw settlement.

Lucky doubted that a mere longpaw building would be enough to stop this maddened Pack, and he could hear their rasping breaths and slapping paws behind them, echoing off walls and houses.

"They're afraid of Terror," he barked breathlessly to the others. "They'll go wherever he wants them to go—and he's making them follow us! We're leading them back to our camp!"

Fiery slowed again, casting an anxious glance behind him. "We have no choice."

"Those dogs will fight to the death," panted Lucky as he ran. "They're out of their minds with fear of their Alpha! Our Pack might be able to defeat Terror, but we'll have to kill every one of his followers. Maybe even Twitch!"

"That's Terror's fault," barked Fiery. "If we have to, we'll kill them all."

"Do we really want to do that? Even to mad dogs? And we'll lose some of our own; you know that."

"So what are you suggesting, Lucky? Keep running forever? They're not stopping!"

Bounding faster, Bruno barged to the front and interrupted Lucky and Fiery with a sharp yelp. "I've got an idea. Follow me!"

Swerving around a corner, the burly Fight Dog led them down a narrow alley and along a broken garden fence. Halfway along he crouched on his belly and squirmed underneath.

"There's a sharpclaw I used to chase," he panted as Lucky wriggled under the fence after him, followed by Fiery, Mickey, and Snap. They got to their paws and stared at an abandoned longpaw house, set in the middle of the garden. "I chased that animal around and around my old longpaw house. I think the fat, old brute used to enjoy the game, really. That's where I learned this trick." And Bruno set off running around the abandoned longpaw house, scattering tiny chips of stone.

With a last perplexed glance at one another, the four hunters followed. Bruno led them around the house and around again several times, until Lucky thought the old Fight Dog had gone as crazy as Terror. Then he skittered to a panting halt on the gravel, next to a pile of logs and a wooden structure propped against the house wall.

"I can hear them coming!" There was panic in Snap's yelp.

"That's all right. We've done enough." Tongue lolling with tiredness, Bruno wriggled his haunches, eyeing the roof of the wooden structure. He sprang up onto the wobbling pile of logs, then made another leap for the top of the structure. Though he didn't quite make it, he kicked with his hind legs until he was safely on the rickety roof. "Come on!"

The others followed, too desperate to ask what Bruno was up to. As Lucky landed on the thin sheet of wood, panting with relief, Bruno was already turning again, gazing up at the roof of the actual longpaw house. It sloped, but not steeply, and there was a brick tower sticking up at one end.

"Oh no," groaned Fiery. "No higher, Bruno!"

"Up!" barked Bruno, ignoring him, and jumped.

They had no choice but to follow. First Snap, and then Mickey and Lucky made the leap; Fiery was next, but he couldn't drag his massive body onto the roof. He began to slide backward, whining in panic.

"Fiery!" yelped Mickey, lunging forward, nearly losing his own grip to seize Fiery's scruff in his jaws.

Lucky slithered down the sloping roof and crouched to add his strength to Mickey's. Between them they dragged the wildly scrabbling Fiery up over the edge. As soon as his hindpaws had a grip, they all stumbled to the shelter of the little stone tower.

They panted, wide-eyed, but Bruno said, "Now we wait. Keep still!"

Lucky had no intention of moving a muscle, since the least misstep was likely to send him sliding down the roof and plummeting to the earth below. He hardly dared look over, but he saw Terror hounding his Pack into the garden, biting their haunches to drive them under the broken fence.

"Get the intruders!" he yelped. "Kill them, in the name of the Fear-Dog!"

Noses snuffling at the ground, the strange Pack loped to the longpaw house and began to race around the walls, shoving and snapping at one another as they squabbled over the scents.

"This way!"

"No, they've gone back—that way!"

"Don't get in my way—*yow*!"

They ran around twice in a circle before half the Pack doubled back in confusion and began to retrace their pawsteps. That led to collisions and more fighting and nipping.

"They've gone!" yipped the little short-haired dog. "Vanished!"

"Don't be stupid," howled Terror. "Find them!"

A wiry-haired black dog went down on his belly and crawled

trembling to Terror. "It's true, Terror; they've disappeared."

"Perhaps the Sky-Dogs took them away," whimpered another.

"The Sky-Dogs would not dare!" howled Terror in a rage. "The Fear-Dog rules the Sky-Dogs! Find that Pack!"

Terror's eyes bulged, foam flew from his jaws—then with a sucking gasp he went rigid. His whole body began to shake as if in the grip of its own Big Growl. From their place on the roof, Lucky and the other hunters watched, silent and horrified. The Alpha's head lolled and spittle dribbled from the corners of his jaws.

Terror's Pack didn't seem shocked. A hush fell over their whining and chattering and they formed a circle around their leader, backs to him, standing guard protectively as the huge dog collapsed to the ground, his legs buckling beneath him. He lay on his side, rigid, twitching and trembling. Still none of his Pack glanced at him. They gazed out, alert, hackles high, ignoring their leader's violent spasms and the slaver pooling under his jaw.

"What's happening?" whispered Snap in Lucky's ear.

Lucky shook his head, dumbfounded. He'd never seen anything like this. Was Terror dying? *But why isn't his Pack trying to help?*

Gradually Terror's spasms weakened, until finally, with one last jerk, he lay still. His sides heaved and his tongue lolled. Licking the foam from his mouth, he rolled over and stumbled to his feet.

He looked pathetically weak, as if he had no idea where he was.

His Pack gathered around him, licking him reverently.

"Terror! You've come back to us."

"You always do. Thank you, Terror."

"What did the Fear-Dog say? What did he say?"

Terror's eyes hadn't changed; they were still wide and glazed and yellow. "Fear-Dog told me . . . we must return to our camp," he growled, his voice throaty with drool.

"Now?" whimpered the little brown dog.

"Now. Immediately." Terror swiped a trembling paw at her face, though this time he missed. "He says . . . we are to kill any strange dogs. Kill them all. Kill them on sight. Now go!"

They turned tail and fled, squirming frantically under the fence, Terror lumbering behind them. Lucky saw Twitch pause and glance back over his shoulder. Then he lurched after his new Pack on his three legs.

"Well," muttered Bruno at last. "That was odd."

Mickey shivered. "Good thing you had this idea, Bruno, or I think we'd be dead dogs."

"Agreed," rumbled Fiery, his tail thrashing. "Well done, Bruno."

"Even if you did get the idea from a sharpclaw," added Snap, nudging Bruno mischievously. "What do you think, Lucky?"

"It saved our hides," growled Lucky thoughtfully. But to him it felt like an uncomfortably narrow escape. First Fierce Dogs, now crazy dogs. And what happened to Terror? *Is there really a Fear-Dog who rules the other Spirits, and gives Terror his orders?*

The idea sent prickling sensations through his fur. "Let's get back to the camp," he suggested, though he dreaded returning without food. What would Alpha say? And what would he say about their encounter with the other dogs?

"I agree," nodded Fiery. "Alpha will have to hear about this insane Terror, and sooner rather than later." Hesitantly he poised himself at the edge of the roof, and jumped down onto the wooden structure.

"Do you think he's really insane?" asked Mickey, paws skittering as he followed Fiery.

"Crazy as a cage of angry sharpclaws," growled Fiery.

"What happened to him just then?" said Snap. "That thrashing and jerking. It wasn't natural! Do you think he really spoke to this 'Fear-Dog'?"

"There's no such thing," growled Lucky, wishing he could feel as certain as he sounded.

He gazed out across the meadow toward the forest. It was

good to know that more dogs had survived the Big Growl—but what kind of dogs were these? Had their madness come from the Growl, or was that whole Pack infected by the insanity of their leader?

Of one thing Lucky was certain: Terror definitely lived up to his name.

CHAPTER NINE

"What is the meaning of this?" Alpha rose to his paws and snarled menacingly. "Where is your prey?"

The patrol lowered their tails as they slunk back into the ruined Food House. Beetle and Thorn bounded forward to greet their father, Fiery, and Moon's tail tapped the ground as she pricked her ears, but the rest of the Pack lay still, glancing warily at Alpha, subdued by his anger. The feeble sun cast long shadows across the room. *Have we really been away so long?* thought Lucky.

Fiery padded forward, giving Thorn's ear a quick lick in passing. He stood respectfully before his leader. "I'm sorry, Alpha. Things happened that were beyond my control."

"Explain!" snapped Alpha.

Fiery dipped his head, but Lucky noticed with growing respect that he didn't lower himself to the floor as the other dogs might have. "We were confronted by a strange Pack. A hostile one."

"Not the Fierce Dogs?" Alarm flitted across Alpha's face.

"No. Another strange Pack."

The gathered Pack growled and whined in astonishment.

"A whole Pack?" Snap's eyes widened and her ears pricked.

"Yes," said Fiery quietly. He raised his head to look at his Packmates one by one. "With a mad dog for a leader."

Alpha's muzzle curled in disbelief, but he went on watching Fiery intently. "Mad? In what way?"

"Insane," Fiery told him. "Like a dog with the water-madness"—at this several Packmembers gasped and growled nervously—"but not that. His jaws foamed and he had fits, but he was in control. Very much in control. He rules his Pack with fear."

Lucky glanced at Alpha. The big dog-wolf was nodding slowly. Again Lucky wondered if he should back Fiery up, reinforce his story and his warning to the Pack. *No,* Lucky decided. *I'll leave this to Fiery. He has a much better relationship with our leader than I do.*

Alpha sneered. "Fear might rule this other Pack, but it did not have to control you! You let a mad dog drive you from the hunting grounds?"

Fiery inclined his huge head, licking his chops. He waited a long moment before answering his leader; to Lucky it seemed that the big dog was only just holding on to his temper. "For now,

Alpha. I couldn't risk our hunters. And this dog's own Pack is petrified of him—they'd do anything for Terror. They could have killed us."

"Terror?" asked Alpha, wrinkling his muzzle. "That's his name?"

"Yes," said Fiery.

Alpha gave a snort of derision. "I see. Terror the Mad Dog. I suppose you had no choice, but this was a poor day's work, Fiery. To come back here with nothing."

"I'm sorry, Alpha," said Fiery calmly.

"And rightly so," growled Alpha. "This situation cannot stand. We'll challenge this brute, but in the meantime"—his voice rose to a howl—"the Pack goes hungry. That's your fault."

A note of shame crept into Fiery's whine. "I know, Alpha." The big dog glanced again at his pups and at Moon. Obviously, thought Lucky, he felt he'd let his family down. *But that's not fair. It wasn't Fiery's doing—it was Terror's.*

Lucky might have spoken up then in Fiery's defense, but it was too late. Alpha stood up straighter, gazed around the Pack, and gave a sharp, angry bark.

"Not one of you dogs is pulling his weight. Not one!" The dog-wolf, Lucky realized with shock, was glaring at Sweet. "Beta failed too. No food to be found, she tells me. Well, it isn't good enough! Remember your responsibilities. A Pack is not run for the convenience of one dog, the safety of the few. Pack involves commitment. Pack involves sacrifice. And don't any of you forget it!"

Again Lucky felt his hackles rise, but he swallowed his annoyance and averted his eyes from Alpha's glare. No good could come of a fight right now. *But this is not leadership!* he thought angrily. *This is bullying.*

"Perhaps," said Moon softly, "we should move on from here. I don't think there's anything to be gained by staying."

"I think Moon's right," said Dart, nibbling a paw with her teeth.

"But at least it's warm," whined Daisy timidly. "And we're protected from that terrible rain."

"Shelter isn't any use if we can't find food," said Moon, though her voice was kind.

"We can't travel on empty stomachs," protested Bruno. Lucky could almost hear his friend's belly rumble.

"I don't see any immediate way of filling them," snapped Spring.

Alpha gave an impatient bark. "We're certainly not going

anywhere before the Sun-Dog rises tomorrow," he growled. "So get some rest, all of you. You should conserve your energy since we have no food."

He glared at his Pack, and no dog argued. Slowly, unhappily, each of them padded away to his own sleeping place. Yet Lucky could hear whispered exchanges, and soft, alarmed murmurs.

"More dogs are in the forest. More of us survived."

"Not more of us . . . strange dogs, hostile dogs."

"I don't know what it means." That was Moon's quiet whine to Fiery. "But it can't be anything good. . . ."

It was a long and restless night. In the darkest hours Lucky rose, stretched, and trod a circle, trying to shake the empty feeling inside him; the hollow ache would not let him rest. He licked his chops, longing for one more mouthful of those cold, moldy Food House grains.

He heard Sunshine give a low whimper nearby, and some other dog's paw scrape the hard floor; clearly every dog was disturbed by the nip of hunger in their bellies. On the metal roof of the Food House, a gust of rain rattled. *Daisy's right. It will be hard to leave a place where we have a roof over our heads. But with Terror in the woods, keeping us away from the prey, we might have to.*

Sighing, Lucky shut his eyes. The memory of Terror's spasms haunted him, and he couldn't suppress a shudder. What did the crazed dog see when he went into those convulsions?

Is there really a Fear-Dog who speaks to him?

Across the room Fiery's eyes glowed. Perhaps he too was thinking about Terror, and the choice that lay before them.

Lucky feared he would never sleep, but when he next blinked his eyes open, the Food House was flooded with the pale light of the rising Sun-Dog. Clambering to his paws, he yipped at Snap next to him, and nuzzled Lick's ear as she stirred.

"Are we moving on?" he asked Alpha. The dog-wolf was already awake and alert, standing at the Food House door and sniffing the air with twitching nostrils.

Alpha took long moments to answer. At last he turned to Lucky, his expression full of disdain.

"No," he growled softly. "We aren't. We're going to start by finding some food around here."

"But Sweet said—"

"*Sweet* isn't a City Dog, is she?" Alpha's muzzle curled. "You are, Lucky. Or so you keep telling us."

"I can't produce food if there isn't any to be found," objected Lucky.

"There was once a whole nest of longpaws here," snarled Alpha. "You know all about longpaws, don't you? You brag about it—how they used to just *give* you food. How you could survive on nothing but your wits. Well, Lucky, I want to see if you still have those famous wits."

Lucky glowered at his leader, baring his teeth. "The longpaws are gone. I live in the wild now. I'm a hunter like you!"

"You're no hunter if you can't help feed this Pack," growled Alpha. "Show me what you're made of. Find prey in this longpaw-place, or you'll find yourself demoted back to patrols."

Alpha turned with a flick of his tail, and gave a summoning bark. "Spring! I'm sending out hunters, and I'm putting you in charge. Choose a patrol and find some food before we leave here." Without another glance at Lucky, he paced away, claws clicking on the floor. The rest of the Pack was awake now, blinking in a sudden shaft of sunlight that poured through the broken clear-stone.

Spring trotted cheerfully over to Lucky, obviously unaware of his angry exchange with Alpha. "We'll take Beetle and Thorn," she announced. "The more hunting experience they get, the better."

The two pups pricked up their ears and bounded happily to join Lucky and Spring. Behind them, Lucky caught sight of

SURVIVORS: THE BROKEN PATH

Lick's disconsolate face. Her ears drooped and her eyes were huge and sad.

"What about Lick?" he murmured to Spring. "She's good."

"You're right." Spring barked. "Lick! You come too."

As Lick trotted eagerly forward to join them, Lucky couldn't help noticing Alpha's angry backward glance, and he heard the dog-wolf give a rumbling growl. But Alpha said nothing. *There's nothing he can say,* thought Lucky. *Lick's earned the right to go hunting, just as much as the other two. He'd be no kind of a leader if he denied a Pack member the chance to hone her skills.*

"You lead on, Lucky," Spring told him as the five dogs trotted out of the Food House into the warm and welcome sunlight. "You have experience with longpaw-places."

There was no contempt in the black-and-tan hunt-dog's voice as there had been in Alpha's, and Lucky shot her a grateful look as he led the patrol down the edge of the hardstone track. "I'll do that, Spring. Though I don't know what we'll find in this deserted place."

"I know," she agreed wryly, "but it's worth a look. And it gives the young ones a chance to stretch their muscles."

She was right, thought Lucky. It had been wise of Spring to choose the younger dogs for this patrol—and not just for the

134

experience, but because it was so obviously taking their minds off their achingly empty bellies. Beetle, Thorn, and Lick's ears were pricked and they raised their noses high to sniff the air, but they seemed happy and excited too. Thorn went down on her forepaws to tease Lick, and while she was distracted Beetle leaped playfully at her back. All three young dogs rolled over on the cracked hardstone, giving muffled yelps of delight. Lucky was pleased that Spring didn't scold them, but only glanced at them indulgently.

"I'm glad they all get on so well," he told her in a low voice. "Lick doesn't resent Beetle and Thorn for having their names, and they don't look down on Lick for not having hers."

"That's true," sighed Spring. "Growing up is so complicated for pups, even ones of the same litter. It's all about learning to cooperate like real Pack dogs. I remember when Twitch and I . . . " Her voice trailed off wistfully.

Lucky nudged her gently with his nose. "Twitch is all right," he told her. "He's found a new Pack to shelter him; that's the main thing."

Spring shook her floppy ears. "I can't help worrying. We didn't always get along, but he is my litter-brother, and I don't want him to come to any harm. Or catch this madness from the others."

"He seemed sane at first," Lucky reassured her. "I think Terror's the only truly mad dog in the Pack; it's just that the others are so afraid of him. In fact, Twitch tried to warn us that Terror was approaching. And I'm sure he wouldn't stay with him if he felt endangered. . . ."

His voice faded, and he turned awkwardly to watch the antics of the younger dogs. *I'm not sure of that at all. Twitch has nowhere else to go. What is his life like, having to keep on the good side of that mad-dog leader?*

The silence was broken only by the grunts and thuds and growls of the young dogs play fighting. At last Spring sighed. "How is his leg? Did it look bad?"

"Oh." Startled, Lucky realized he hadn't told her. With a shudder he remembered that ugly stump, and the hairless skin that had grown over it. "Twitch's leg, it's . . ."

"What?" She pricked her ears, alarmed. "Is it worse?"

"Not worse, he . . . " Lucky licked his chops awkwardly.

"What? Tell me!"

"His leg . . . he doesn't have it anymore, Spring. It's been chewed off."

"What?" Spring came to a halt, shocked. "But why? Is he all right?"

"He's fine. Really, he is." Lucky licked her ear. "Actually, I think he's better without it. That bad leg always did give him trouble."

"But how does he manage? How does he hunt?"

"He can run; I promise!" Lucky told her. "If anything, he gets around better than he did before. You should have seen him chase us with the others!"

"Really?" Spring tilted her head hopefully and lifted her ears. "Well, I'm glad if that's true. Though I'm not glad that Pack chased you," she added hurriedly. She raised her voice in a bark. "Beetle, Thorn, Lick! Stop fooling around now. We're supposed to be hunting!"

Clearly she didn't want to think about Twitch anymore, and Lucky was relieved. The priority for the Pack right now was to find food—they could go no farther without it. Shaking Twitch from his mind, Lucky narrowed his eyes and tried to think. *How did I find food in the longpaw-place? I have to remember all my old tricks.*

He had almost stopped noticing the longpaws strewn on the hardstone and in their own gardens; the scent of death was a constant background odor. *There are no longpaws left alive to give me scraps—it's true; but there must be food here—food that they stored away.*

A slight breeze rose, whispering between the buildings and

bringing a sound to his pricked ears. Rustling little paws, and maybe a hint of squeaking?

"Here. Behind this building." He lifted his muzzle and let the scents of the house drift into his nostrils. "I think I heard something."

"It's worth a try," agreed Spring, twitching an ear.

Lucky took a few cautious paces toward the house, sifting the scents of living things from the overwhelming stench of death. "Rats!" he muttered to Spring.

"Yes, you're right." Spring's eyes brightened. "Well scented, Lucky!"

He glanced back over his shoulder. The three young dogs slunk quietly forward, their fun forgotten at the prospect of prey.

"There's a hole at the bottom of the door; look," said Beetle, snuffling at it. "With a little flap!"

"That's too small even for you," Spring told him. "That's for the sharpclaws who used to live here. We need to find another way in."

"Wait a minute." Hesitantly Lick shunted her way forward between the others, then pressed one paw against the door as if testing its weight. "I think I might be able to break this."

Spring raised an eye muscle doubtfully. "Really, Lick? Doors are hard to break."

"Maybe you're right." Lick shrank back, embarrassed. "I don't want to do anything stupid, anyway."

"No, wait," murmured Lucky, feeling his heart turn over at such timidity in a powerful Fierce Dog pup. "Spring, let her try. We've got nothing to lose. We haven't found anything else."

"All right." Spring still sounded doubtful, but she took a pace back from the door. Beetle and Thorn exchanged glances, Beetle's muzzle curling slightly.

Lucky gave Lick an encouraging nudge. "Go ahead. But if it breaks, be careful of what comes out. Rats can be vicious. Be alert for them, and don't let them rush you."

The young dog licked her muzzle nervously and swallowed, but she tensed her powerful shoulders, gathering her strength. Crouching, she flung herself at the door.

She rebounded, staggering. The door trembled in its frame, but didn't yield. Lick growled softly.

"I don't think it's impossible," she said, narrowing her eyes. "The wood's strong, but it does give."

"Try again," Lucky urged.

Once more, Lick clenched her jaws and sprang, slamming the full weight of her body against the door. This time Lucky heard a clear, sharp crack as the peeling wood quivered.

"It's damaged," he told her excitedly. "One more try should do it, Lick!"

A low snarl of determination rumbled in Lick's throat and she crouched back on her haunches. As she hurtled at the door she ducked her head, crashing into it with her full weight and strength. With a screech of splintering timber, the door collapsed inward, and Lick fell after it, tumbling and rolling.

Beetle and Thorn gave joyful yips of triumph as Lucky and Spring stared at the broken door. "I knew she'd do it!" yelped Thorn. "See, Beetle?"

"Well done, Lick!" said Spring, her whine full of admiration. "Now, let's go!"

Lucky squirmed through the doorway, ignoring the splinters that caught in his fur. As the others shoved in behind him, he could hear more splinters snap from the broken door. Lick was already on her paws and racing after the rats, her jaws snapping and slavering. The creatures were everywhere—scurrying across tables, clawing their way up torn lengths of curtain, surging in a wriggling mass over abandoned rotten food. A moment's stillness fell as the rats turned, and Lucky found himself staring into a pair of glowing, beady eyes. A rat was only a paw's length in front of his muzzle, and his fur sprang on end.

The rat squealed, spun, and bolted. Then the rest were shriek-ing and fleeing in panic, swarming over one another in their eagerness to escape.

There were so many of them, it was hard to not catch prey—Lick had broken the spines of two of them before Lucky had even caught up with her. The escape holes were blocked by a mass of squabbling, furred bodies, so some rats had no choice but to turn on the dogs and fight—and Lucky knew how savage they could be in a corner.

Spring gave a high howl of panic, and Lucky saw a rat fasten on her throat fur with its long, yellow teeth. He turned to dash toward her, but could only yelp as small teeth bit into his own leg, sending a sharp, hot stab of pain through his flesh. He shook the rat off, snatching and snapping its neck before it could fly at him again. As he heard Lick give a yelp of pain, Beetle barked, "Get off her!" But Lucky saw it was Thorn he was rescuing, grabbing a rat from her shoulder and shaking it to death in his jaws.

Snarling, Lucky twisted to drag another rat from his own back. Lick was snapping at one that clung to her hind leg, but she jerked her head up at a terrible noise from the corner of the room. Spring was howling and yelping in distress. *There are so many rats,* realized Lucky with a shiver of horror. *Maybe this was a mistake!*

"Lick!" barked Lucky. "Quick, help Spring!"

A huge number of the fierce-eyed rats had piled onto Spring, clawing and biting. One clung to her muzzle, its eyes red with fury as it sank its teeth into her face. Lick reached her in a moment, but as fast as she flung the rats off her Packmate, more attacked.

Lucky shook himself free of three more rats and bounded across the room, his paws slipping on blood. "Beetle! Thorn!"

The two young dogs raised their heads from their own battles, eyes alight with wild excitement. As soon as they saw Spring's distress, they raced to her and joined Lick, tearing rats from Spring's back and haunches. Lucky sank his jaws into the rat that clung to her face, ripping it free and crunching it between his teeth. The stench of it caught in his throat, almost making him choke.

With the help of Lucky and the young dogs, Spring at last shook herself free of the squealing rats. Maddened by their bites, she plunged into the fleeing mass and attacked them, flinging small bodies aside. By the time the last rat had scuttled into a hole in the wall, dragging its bloodied tail, the five dogs hunched panting in a small pile of dead creatures.

Beetle shook himself and licked at a bite on his leg. "That was fun!" he barked.

Spring tossed her head violently, as if a rat still hung there. Her muzzle and ears were bleeding from deep bite marks. "I'm glad you enjoyed it," she shuddered.

Lucky's flanks heaved, but he felt a rush of satisfaction as he gazed around at the pile of prey. "This was a good hunt. Well done!" he barked at the three young dogs.

Lick looked quietly proud, her eyes shining. "Are you all right, Spring?"

"Thanks to you," said Spring gruffly. "And Lucky and Beetle and Thorn, of course. Rats are nasty things."

"Nasty but tasty," yelped Thorn brightly.

Spring gave a bark of laughter. "At least Alpha should be pleased with us now. Let's get these back to the Food House."

By the time Spring and Lucky had divided up the spoils into manageable burdens for each dog, and they wriggled back through the broken door, the sky had completely cleared and the Sun-Dog shone bright and strong. There was something odd about the beauty of the day and the delicious warmth, thought Lucky, when longpaws still lay lifeless all over the settlement, the death-smell growing stronger all the time. Still, the Sun-Dog was out and they would eat well today, and Lucky's mood lifted. Lick,

Thorn, and Beetle were almost bouncing with pride and pleasure as they trotted off down the hardstone track, their jaws filled with rats. Spring was limping slightly at his side, but her wounds didn't look too deep and her eyes were bright with the pleasure of a hunt well executed.

Lucky's jaw ached with the strain of holding his own mouthful, but he was happy. Lick had well and truly proved herself to Spring, and they were returning to the Pack with a prey-haul they could be proud of. Each of the five hunters had pulled their weight, even the young ones.

All the same, Lucky felt tired as he padded with Spring after the three young dogs, and the warmth of the Sun-Dog made him long to drop the rats and have a satisfying pant. *That was a good hunt, but how long will a nest of rats keep the whole Pack fed?* They hadn't solved the problem for good. And that meant the Pack would have to return to Terror's forest—or leave this place, too, and set off again on the search for safety. At the thought, fatigue settled over Lucky's bones.

He felt almost sick at the thought of moving on again, and most of the Pack must feel the same. Surely their journey would end soon? They had to find a territory to call their own—a place to hunt, and raise pups, and howl to the Moon-Dog in peace.

As they passed through the center of the settlement, the broad, shining pool was too much for Lucky to resist. *That will make me feel better!* With a glance at Spring, they both dropped their rats and paused to sniff at the water's edge.

"I think this water's all right, in spite of the rain," Spring muttered hoarsely. "There's so much. The rain can't have been enough to poison it. . . ."

"I think so too." Lucky splashed into the pond, cooling his hot forepaws. With no more hesitation he dipped his muzzle into the water and began to lap. Delicious!

Spring followed his example. "Oh, that's much better," she said, sighing with pleasure and licking her dripping chops. "Let's go on."

Lucky was about to reply when he frowned. A scent tickled his nostrils—something familiar. A Pack dog. But who was it? Nervous curiosity tightened his gut. "You go ahead and catch up with the others," he told Spring. "I won't be long. There's something I want to check."

"So long as you're quick," muttered Spring, with a glance in the direction of the Food House. She seized her rats and set off at a trot after the younger dogs.

Lucky pawed his rats into a heap. He knew it should be safe

enough to leave them for a little while, and he had to find out which dog had passed so recently. Had one of the Pack wandered off alone? The scent was so familiar. Was Snap trying to get back in touch with Twitch?

No, not Snap. The scent had the tang that still clung to the Leashed Dogs—that faint sweetness that spoke of comfort and longpaw furs and bland, plentiful food. None of them had quite shaken it off yet, even after so many Moon-Dog journeys spent in the wild. Lucky quivered with apprehension as he padded along the scent-trail, nose to the ground.

When his muzzle bumped against a wooden barrier, he blinked. Hesitantly he licked his chops. The fence was partly broken and long, yellow grass pushed through the boards. Beyond it, the stench of death was stronger and closer than ever, but there was a smell too of raw, fresh earth—and a Pack dog. Clawing a gap wider, Lucky wriggled through into a wildly overgrown longpaw garden.

He stood up tall, alert for trouble—and found himself staring straight into a pair of sad, brown eyes in a black-and-white face.

"Mickey!" he blurted. "What are you doing?"

Mickey lowered his head, but his eyes held Lucky's, mournful and determined. He nodded at a longpaw corpse in the straggly, wet grass. Lucky swallowed.

"It's so young," whined Mickey. "Like my longpaw pup. My own longpaw, back in the city."

"But Mickey . . ." Lucky reminded himself to keep patient and calm; he understood the Farm Dog's feelings, even if he couldn't share them. The longpaw looked so pathetic, abandoned there in the weeds. "Mickey, we can't help this longpaw. It's not yours, remember? This is a stranger."

"I know that." Mickey's expression was sad but stubborn. "I do understand, Lucky, but he's so like my longpaw. The size of him, his hair, everything. I scented him here and—I couldn't just leave him like this. It isn't right."

Between Mickey's white paws, filthy with dirt and grass, the Farm Dog had dug a deep scrape in the earth. It obviously wasn't easy work. Out of longpaw control, the grass and roots had grown wild and tangled.

"You wanted to give him to Earth-Dog." Lucky nodded.

"I hope some dog would do it for my longpaw, if I couldn't," said Mickey quietly.

"I understand." Lucky sighed. "But Mickey, if Alpha finds out this is where you've been—"

A sound made him turn on his hindpaws, his lips drawing back. He relaxed when he saw three familiar dogs squirm beneath the fence.

"Lick, Beetle, Thorn." He eyed the young dogs warily. "What are you doing here?"

Beetle glanced at Thorn, and Lick took a pace forward. "Spring caught up with us. She said you'd scented some dog, and that you'd gone to check it out."

"We wanted to make sure you were all right," added Beetle.

Lucky felt a rush of affection for the three young dogs. "But your prey—"

"We've left the rats where we can pick them up later," Thorn told him. Mischievously she added, "Like you did, Lucky."

"We thought it was more important to come after you," said Beetle defensively. "Spring said it was all right."

"Well, I'm all right too," said Lucky, tilting his head in amusement. "But thanks for being concerned. That's good Pack responsibility."

Beetle and Thorn's chests swelled visibly. "We heard what you and Mickey were talking about," Beetle whined, with a glance at Mickey. "And we think Mickey's right."

"If he wants to give the longpaw to the Earth-Dog, he should," said Thorn. "And the Earth-Dog would want it, too."

She gave Beetle a nudge with her shoulder. The two of them and Lick trotted over to Mickey; then showers of earth and clods of mud flew as they began to swiftly turn Mickey's shallow scrape into a deeper hole.

Surprised and touched, Lucky watched the three young dogs dig with their powerful paws. Mickey looked a little taken aback but grateful as he joined in once again.

It probably isn't the best way to spend their time, thought Lucky, *but I'm proud of them. This is Pack behavior, too, isn't it? Knowing how Mickey feels, and helping him—even if they don't understand him.*

And I'm one of this Pack too. Biting back his misgivings, Lucky joined them to help claw out the loose earth.

With the extra pairs of forepaws, the work went far faster than when Mickey had struggled alone. In a short time his shallow scrape of a hole had been dug deep and long enough to hold the small body of the longpaw. Beetle kicked out a last flurry of earth, then scrambled up from the trench.

"Now," said Thorn, "let's bury Mickey's longpaw, and we can all go back to camp together."

"He isn't my longpaw," said Mickey, with a look at Lucky. "But he easily could be. That's why—"

Lick gave his ear a fond swipe with her tongue. "We understand, Mickey."

Once more Lucky felt his heart swell with affection for the young Fierce Dog; but he was glad this time that Alpha wasn't here to see her. The dog-wolf, he was sure, would disapprove of what they were doing.

Mickey trod carefully around the longpaw's body, then took hold of its fur covering at the shoulder. Following his lead, Beetle took the other shoulder and they gently dragged the longpaw until it slumped into the hole. Panting, the two dogs stepped back; Thorn, Lick, and Lucky scraped earth back into the trench with their hindpaws, covering the small body. Soon the longpaw was entirely buried; all that was left to show where he had been was a mound of fresh earth in the wilderness that had been a garden.

For a long, awkward moment, the dogs stood in silence and gazed at the grave. The death-smell was fading, smothered by the fresh, rich scent of the soil.

Thorn cocked her head and flared her nostrils. "Earth-Dog has taken him already. Do you smell her?"

"Yes," agreed Beetle. "That must mean she's happy with us. The longpaw will be fine there, Mickey."

"Earth-Dog will put him back into the world." Lick nudged Mickey gently.

Lucky felt a strange lump in his throat at the matter-of-fact sense of the young dogs. Blinking, Mickey crouched on his fore-quarters and touched his nose to the mound of soil.

"Take care of this small longpaw, Earth-Dog," he whined. Sitting back on his haunches, he let out a single low, sad howl.

Respectfully the young dogs waited until Mickey had got back to his paws and was walking away from the longpaw's grave, then fell in behind him. With a final glance at the buried longpaw, Lucky followed.

He knew Beetle, Thorn, and Lick had come through for Mickey when he'd needed them. But was it right to waste time like that? What they'd done was right for the longpaw, but was it right for the Pack? Lucky sighed. *Nothing about this new life is straightforward.*

Relief flooded through him when they found the pond and Lucky's rats undisturbed. "Nothing took them. I hope your prey is as safe," he remarked to the others.

"I'm sure it will be." Lick pawed at the sparkle of the Sun-Dog on the water, then dipped her head to drink, followed by Beetle and Thorn. She licked her dripping muzzle. "There's nothing in this place to steal our food, Lucky."

That's probably true, thought Lucky, *but will that last? Terror's Pack is just outside the town, and we haven't seen the last of the Fierce Dogs either.* Lucky picked up his rats and led the way back toward the Food House. The Sun-Dog had bounded up the sky almost to his highest point, and the puddles left by the previous night's rain had nearly all dried, leaving cracked fringes of yellow scum. If anything, the powdery remains smelled worse than the dead longpaws, and Lucky avoided the patches as best he could. It was hard to believe such deadly destruction had happened here, where the houses were still in one piece and there was barely a split in the hardstone tracks. Lucky paused to stare at a dead loudcage, its rainbow-colored blood leaking onto the ground. Where the liquid touched one of the dried-up puddles, it hissed and foamed, and a sharp odor scorched Lucky's nostrils.

Dropping his prey, he shook his head to clear it. Mickey, Thorn, and Beetle were padding ahead, but Lick had fallen behind, so he waited for her.

"Lick," he whined, "can I talk to you for a moment?"

She set down her rats, then sat back on her haunches. "What is it, Lucky? Have I done something wrong?"

"No, I—well . . . " Lucky flattened his ears in confusion and let his tailtip smack the ground. "Mickey's gone ahead, so I just wanted to say . . . What you did, it was kind. But I don't think you should encourage Mickey too much."

Lick cocked her head, puzzled. "Encourage him?"

"About the longpaws. I know he felt strongly about that young one, but he shouldn't be feeling that way—not after all this time. It's as if he can't let go—as if he has to keep the longpaws alive in his mind."

"It's only in his mind, though." Lick wriggled down until her forequarters were on the ground too, but she gazed up at Lucky. "He doesn't really try to get back to them, you know. He hasn't left the Pack since the time you found me and Fang and Wiggle. So where's the harm in it?"

Lucky felt exasperated, but whether with Lick or with Mickey he wasn't sure. When Mickey had left his longpaw's leather glove in the city, Lucky had thought he had finally broken the connection. Now he wasn't so sure. "His loyalties are torn, don't you see? He can't commit to the wild life—not completely. And that's bad for the whole Pack."

"I think he's brave," said Lick quietly.

"What?" Lucky was bewildered.

"Mickey does what he thinks is right. He can stay loyal to the longpaws as well as to the Pack—don't you see, Lucky? That's just who he is. He wouldn't be Mickey if he forgot the longpaws."

Lucky tapped the ground slowly with his tail, unable to think of an answer.

"It doesn't mean he's going to abandon us." Lick laid her head on her forepaws, her eyes downcast. "It doesn't mean he'll leave the Pack. He just wants to remember where he came from. That's all."

"I . . ." Lucky stared at her, but now she wouldn't meet his eyes. The truth hit him like a longpaw-kick in the ribs. "Are you really talking about Mickey, Lick?"

Lick's muscles stiffened and she looked away. Then her ears flopped down beside her head. "I was going to tell you, Lucky, I . . . I had another dream last night."

Lucky licked his muzzle. "About Fang?"

"Yes. Except it wasn't like a normal dream. It was so real, just like it was before I met Fang outside the last camp. We were standing at the place where the river divided, and Fang was there. He said he was dreaming too. He wanted me to meet him there and come back to the Fierce Dog Pack with him. And I just *know* that if I went, he would be there waiting."

Oh no, Lucky thought. *Lick, you can't abandon us now. . . .* "But I told him no," Lick whined. "I said I wanted to stay with my Pack."

Lucky's heart swelled with pride. "You chose right, Lick."

"I think so." Lick's tail gave a hopeful wag. "Fang was really angry. He said I'd abandoned my Pack, and if I wouldn't come by myself then Blade was on her way and she'd make me see my mistake."

Lucky suppressed a shiver. He thought of the massed bodies of the dogs that he saw in his dreams, battling while freezing shards of ice whirled all around them. *The Storm of Dogs isn't real,* he told himself, *and neither is this dream of Lick's. I just wish I were a bit more certain. . . .*

"*You're* my Pack, and I'm not leaving. But he's still my family. I can't just be one thing or the other," she barked.

"It's not something we can work out with a few words; I see that now," Lucky said. *Not Mickey's confusion—and not yours either, Lick.* "Let's get back to the camp."

As Spring had predicted, Alpha was in a far better mood by the time Lucky and Lick returned to the Food House. He sat up and barked a gruff welcome as the last two members of the hunting party carried their rats into the room and laid them on the prey pile. Stepping back to view the rats stacked there in the center of the room, Lucky's mood lifted as he realized just how well they had done.

"A successful hunt," barked Alpha. "Though it was unwise to split up at the end. Stay together from now on."

He can't resist a criticism, thought Lucky, but for once Alpha's complaints didn't seem important.

With so much prey to go around, the sharing of food was calm and disciplined. Dogs chatted amiably as each waited for their turn, and Lucky noticed Martha murmuring to Mickey. The conversation seemed to cheer the Farm Dog up, and his eyes lost their faraway expression as his tail tapped the floor.

When it was Lucky's turn to select a rat, he suppressed a shiver. He could ignore the greasiness of its fur and the clinging smell of rotten longpaw-spoils; after all, he was ravenous. Closing his eyes, he chewed into its flesh. Not quite as bad as he'd expected . . .

"You must be hungry, Omega," Moon told Sunshine, her voice kind. "But there will be plenty left; don't worry."

"I know," yapped Sunshine, sitting pertly with her furry ears pricked. "I don't mind waiting."

"Just as well," grunted Whine, but without his usual sneery hostility.

"Where did you go this afternoon, Mickey?" asked Bella.

Beetle put in, "For a walk. To stretch his muscles. Didn't you, Mickey? He met us on the way back from the hunt."

"That's true." Mickey gave him a grateful look, then stepped forward to take his share of the rats.

"Hmph," growled Alpha. "Dogs wandering off alone, splitting up on a hunt—discipline is slack in this longpaw-place. Don't imagine that will be tolerated forever."

"Alpha's right," said Sweet. "You all need to take more care. The Fierce Dog Pack is still out there, and now there's the threat of Terror as well. We can't let our guard down and start acting like Leashed Dogs." Martha and Daisy were in her eye line, and she shot them a meaningful glance.

"Of course not, Beta," said Martha meekly.

"Is Omega finished eating? Good." Sweet stood up. "We should howl now. And then get a good night's rest."

Alpha stretched, raking scratches in the hard floor with his claws. "Outside. There can be no proper Great Howl in this . . . longpaw cage." He glanced at their surroundings, his muzzle curling with disdain.

It's shelter, not a cage, thought Lucky, *and we should thank the Sky-Dogs for it.* But he rose and padded out into the street with the rest of the Pack.

The sky was still cloudless and clear, frosted with stars, and the Moon-Dog cast distinct shadows from the walls of the longpaw settlement. Alpha padded out to where the silver light shone full on the hardstone, then waited for his Pack to gather around him. Lightning and the Sky-Dogs were barking, but their voices were muted and distant, and Lucky knew the danger of the rain was a long way away for now.

A single howl rose from Alpha's throat, quietly at first. Then, as the other dogs joined in, he tipped his head back and gave a full-throated cry to the Moon-Dog. Lucky waited for his cue from Snap next to him, then joined his voice to the others, his mind drifting as the sound throbbed and rose and fell around him. As the Great Howl spun its magic, he felt his body grow lighter. The silver Moon-Dog light brightened, until he felt as if the stars themselves were floating loose and spinning around the Pack.

I belong here. . . . We all belong. . . . The Moon-Dog and the Sky-Dogs and us, we're all part of the same life. . . .

He closed his eyes, yet still he could see the stars. This time, when he saw the shapes of dogs form, leaping through the black emptiness between them, he was not surprised. Lucky had grown used to the feelings the Great Howl roused inside him, and he could let his own mind bound free, rising with the sound of the Pack. It felt wonderful to let the worries and the hunger of the daytime slip from his hide, to let the harmony of the Howl thrill into his bones.

A huge dog formed in the sky in his mind. Massive and noble, she was a great black shape that seemed to absorb the stars so that they glittered within her body. She was racing across the night, huge paws pounding the air as she ran toward something . . . something else that shone and glinted like the stars. It was a great expanse of black water that sparkled silver: a vast lake that went on forever. Excitement thrilled through Lucky, and he raised his howl in joy. Around him he heard the rest of the Pack raise their howls to blend with his.

Martha! For a moment confusion touched Lucky's mind. The ghostly black dog leaped and dived, plunging into the black water in a shower of silver starlight.

Not Martha—the River-Dog. Or is it both of them?

The stars blurred into a haze of white light as Lucky squeezed his eyes tight. The howl was ending, fading, when he wanted it to go on and on forever, like that starlit lake. . . .

He blinked. The night was no longer whirling. One by one, the dogs around him fell silent, until only Alpha's voice was left. Then, as the dog-wolf too lowered his head, there was only the quietness and the ordinary glow of the Moon-Dog.

Does this happen to every dog? But if it happened to us all at once, how could we ever stop howling?

Alpha's growling voice broke into his thoughts. "I have an announcement to make to the whole Pack."

Every dog sat up straighter, attentive. Martha shivered, and shook herself. *Did she see what I saw?* wondered Lucky. She looked as if she found it hard to stop howling, too.

"There is no food here worth having," said Alpha gruffly. "We ate well tonight, but you all know that one nest of rats cannot support this Pack for long. We have to take our hunt to the forest—whether this Terror likes it or not."

There was a low, general rumble of agreement from the circle of dogs.

"I've met Terror," said Fiery, "just as some of you have." He glanced one by one at Bruno, Lucky, Snap, and Mickey. "He's a dangerous dog, but we can't allow that to frighten us."

"I agree," said Sweet quietly. "He will fight us, but he must not be allowed to keep us from hunting in the forest. That is the Forest-Dog's law."

Again there were murmurs of agreement. Snap stretched and scratched her ear with a hindclaw. "Let's take the fight to him, then. I didn't like being chased away from my prey!"

"It's decided." Alpha rose to all fours, his muzzle curling in a determined snarl. "The whole Pack will go to the forest tomorrow.

Let Terror decide if he wants to fight us all. A show of strength should teach the mad dog to respect the true Spirit Dogs."

As the Pack rose and stretched, growling to one another, Lucky stayed silent. He glanced around at his friends, wondering if any of them felt the same foreboding he did. His sense of dread kept him still, rooted to the spot.

It makes sense when Alpha says it here, among the Pack. But I'm not so sure that it will work the way he hopes.

CHAPTER TEN

Snow crunched under his paws, but he didn't sink into it. He flew across the glittering white ground, and though pine trees stretched in every direction, they gave way before him, opening up to clear an endless, snowy road. He moved too fast for his paw pads even to feel the cold.

Lucky halted, sniffing the frosty air. Where was the prey? What prey? He couldn't even remember what he'd been chasing. A rabbit? A rat? He didn't know. Why couldn't he remember?

Because I'm dreaming . . .

Of course he was dreaming. Even now that he stood still, his paws didn't feel the cold. *This isn't real.*

The forest closed in again around him, hiding the snowy track. Now the branches were dense and he had to shove and shoulder his way through, but the trees didn't scratch him; thorns didn't snag in his fur. It was as if everything was made of snow.

Distantly he could hear furious, frenzied barking.

I have to go to those dogs. I don't know why . . . but I must.

He ran again, the branches giving way like mist. Far sooner than he expected, the foliage vanished and he was in a clearing, a shallow bowl of snow. There in the center, two dogs were fighting to the death, wrestling, biting, snarling. And he knew them—Blade the Fierce Dog, and Terror.

This is the Storm of Dogs . . . and all the dogs but these two are gone!

The mad dog's body shook with every blow and every bite, yet he didn't fall; he kept on struggling, fighting viciously to survive. But Lucky knew that Terror didn't stand a chance against Blade. As a shadow passed overhead, Lucky glanced up; the sky was a deep, dark gray, snow clouds whirling into a tight, ominous spiral. And the snow began to fall: flakes of gray and white that spun down thickly. When they reached the ground, Lucky knew they would smother them all. But the fighting dogs took no notice. He could see that the fight was turning, and he couldn't look away; now Terror was driving Blade back. He was going to win—Terror was going to kill the Fierce Dog Alpha!

A snowflake landed on Lucky's flank. Instead of a soft, cold tickle, there was a sharp stab of pain. Lucky yowled, though no sound came out.

This is a dream. I shouldn't feel pain in a dream!

But he could, and now the snow was falling fast on his hide, stinging bitterly wherever it touched him. *Something's wrong!* Lucky twisted and yelped, feeling the snow burn into him—and then he realized. It wasn't snow; it was shattered clear-stone! And the snow at his feet—that too was a deep layer of tiny clear-stone shards. It fell all around him, wicked, glinting pieces that pierced his skin.

Panicking, Lucky broke into a run, but he didn't know where to go. Back and forth at the edge of the clearing he dashed, the shards stabbing deep into his paw pads. The clear-stone blizzard was cutting his hide off in strips, ripping away his fur, and blood spattered the fallen snow-that-wasn't-snow. Yet still Blade and Terror fought on, ignoring the storm of clear-stone. Lucky's rib cage tightened until he couldn't breathe. There was nowhere to run, no dog to help him. Clear-stone showered him and his blood flowed. He was going to die.

How can I die in a dream?

But he was. Lucky was going to die. . . .

Lucky jerked awake, his head snapping up as he growled and whined with terror. No snow. No clear-stone. Around him the frozen pines and icy branches faded, becoming nothing but the peeling walls of the Food House.

I didn't die. Sky-Dogs, thank you; I didn't die!

There was warmth at his flank. Lick slept peacefully, her sides rising and falling with her gentle snores. Yet even though he blinked again and again, Lucky could still see falling splinters, could still hear the echoing growls and snarls of the battling dogs; he could still smell the smoky frost, tingling in his nostrils. And worst of all, he could still feel the stabbing pain of the clear-stone that had buried itself in his fur. He shook himself, then licked hard at his flanks. There were no real wounds and no blood—only the healing scars from his fight with the badger—but that didn't stop the stinging. Lucky whined, licking and nibbling at his hind-quarters.

Lick blinked awake and pricked her ears. "Lucky! What's wrong?"

"Nothing. I just—" Lucky shuddered again and whimpered, nosing his flank.

"Did some dog hurt you?" Lick sprang to her paws and spun around, baring her teeth at the shadows. "Where are they? I'll show them!"

Lucky's head still spun with the dream, the images clinging to his mind and making him feel dizzy and sick. "It wasn't that, Lick—I don't know—"

"They can't do this to you!" Lick snarled, hackles high. "Show me where they went!"

"No!" Lucky forced himself to stop fussing at his fur. "No, Lick, wait—you don't understand. No dog hurt me. It was just a dream."

"You're sure?" Her lips were still drawn back over those fierce fangs.

"Yes, really." He was touched by her loyalty, but something made him uneasy. Lick wanted to defend him, and did not think twice about coming to his rescue—but she was so quick to attack.

Maybe that's the trouble, he thought. *Maybe she* ought *to think twice.* At least no other dog had been awake to see her lightning-fast reaction, her instinctive aggression. The whole Pack was stirring now, though: yawning and stretching in the early Sun-Dog light. Lucky wished she'd get those hackles down.

"Honestly, Lick," he muttered, "I'm all right. It really was just a dream."

"Well. If you're sure." Lick tilted her head and gave him a

questioning whimper. "You looked so—so scared, Lucky."

I was scared. But that's stupid of me. It was only a dream.

"We'll be moving on soon." Alpha's growl disturbed his thoughts, and for once Lucky was grateful. "But first, we'll hunt. I'm sure every dog here is hungry."

"Oh, yes," whined Bruno. Daisy gave his ear an affectionate lick as Dart woofed in amusement.

"I'll lead a patrol," suggested Fiery, yawning and scratching at his ear with a hindpaw. "Bruno, you come, since you're so keen for food. And Snap, Lucky, and Mickey. Is that all right, Alpha?"

Alpha grunted in agreement. "Try not to get into pointless fights with the mad dog."

"We won't. I've got a good feeling in my fur today," Fiery reassured them all. "We'll find plenty of prey."

"And there's no way Terror will catch us off guard this time," added Snap. "We'll be ready for him and his crazy Pack."

Lick was on all four paws, gazing yearningly at the hunting patrol as they gathered at the Food House door. Her tail twitched at the tip, as if she was just managing to stop it from wagging. Lucky glanced at Alpha, then yipped to Fiery.

"Should Lick come again? She's a useful hunter."

Fiery opened his jaws, but didn't get a chance to reply. Alpha paced forward, claws clicking, and he narrowed his yellow eyes as he sniffed at Lick.

"Keen to go, is she? What makes you think she deserves to be a hunter?" His muzzle curled as he glared at the young Fierce Dog. "You, pup. You haven't even had a Naming Ceremony. The lowest dogs in this Pack don't get the honor of hunting."

Oh, no. Lucky saw the hackles rise on Lick's spine. *She's only just calmed down.*

The other Pack members went quiet as Alpha padded a circle around the young Fierce Dog. Sunshine whimpered fearfully and sidled closer to Martha. Spring gave a low woof of unease.

Alpha licked his teeth, sneering, as he prowled around Lick. His tail brushed her nose as he circled her again. She watched him warily, turning to try to keep her eyes on his. On his next circle, he bumped his shoulder hard into her flank.

Off-balance already, Lick went sprawling onto the ground, her legs flailing. She recovered fast, though. She sprang up and lunged at Alpha with her teeth bared.

No! thought Lucky in panic.

The young dog's jaws were about to close on Alpha's throat when Fiery leapt forward, knocking her aside. Her teeth snapped on the air and she snarled, then spun and attacked again. But Fiery was between her and Alpha now, his paws splayed firmly on the ground, his eyes blazing. Lick skidded to a halt, glaring, her muzzle curled.

"You want to challenge Alpha?" growled Fiery. "Then you'll have to do it properly. Declare your challenge before the Pack, and accept the consequences."

Lick breathed heavily, but there was a look of uncertainty on her face now.

"If you won't go that far," Fiery went on, his voice low and steady, "then you need to calm down. Right now."

Lick blinked and licked her chops. Her gaze shifted to Alpha, then back to Fiery. Turning her head slightly, she met Lucky's eyes.

He found himself holding his breath. *Don't be foolish, Lick.*

At last her head dropped and she slunk a pace backward.

"I don't want to challenge Alpha," she muttered.

Lucky could almost feel the sigh of relief that went around the whole Pack, and Sunshine gave another tiny whimper as the tension was released. Lick crouched low and backed off farther from Fiery and their leader, then crept across to Lucky and lowered her head to the ground.

"I'm sorry," she whispered.

Lucky licked his jaws, staring at her. The fear in his belly was hardening into rage now, and he found he couldn't speak. Alpha had a right to punish her now, and Lucky wasn't even sure he wanted to defend her. His fur prickled as Alpha stepped forward, but he said nothing. He couldn't intervene.

"You." Alpha's snarl was savage as he stalked up to Lick, so close his bared teeth almost touched her quivering nose. "You show me nothing but insolence and insubordination. You need a lesson—"

"Wait."

Every dog looked up at Fiery's low bark. The huge dog had turned to face his leader. His head was high, his paws square on the hard floor. A tremor of nerves went through Lucky.

"Alpha." Fiery's voice was clear and steady. "In sight and hearing and smell of the Pack, I challenge you for their leadership."

Every dog heard Alpha's indrawn breath of shock, but no dog could move. In the ominous silence, the dog-wolf drew himself up, his muscles bunching and his stiff legs quivering. He oozed so much rage and disbelief, Lucky could almost smell it.

Dart's jaw was open as she stared at Fiery. Whine wore an expression that was half surprise, half vicious curiosity. Beetle and Thorn pressed instinctively close to Moon's sides; she herself watched her mate with a steady, trusting gaze. Bruno and Mickey exchanged stunned glances, but even Sunshine made no sound; she pressed herself quivering against the floor, silky ears flopped over her eyes.

Lucky's breath was caught in his throat. *Why is Fiery doing this?*

Fiery turned slowly, watching each member of the Pack. "I respect Alpha," he said. "He has led us well and kept us together, in good times and bad. But I believe the Big Growl changed things. Our world has turned upside down, and I don't think Alpha can cope anymore. He has been hesitant; he has failed to make decisions. And"—Fiery shot a look at Mickey and Bruno—"his attitude to the Leashed Dogs is not helping. He scorns them instead of valuing the skills they do have, and he makes no attempt to hide his dislike for Lick. His attitude is beginning to cause conflict in the Pack." Fiery met Moon's eyes. "While I know and respect what he has done as our Alpha, I believe I would be the better leader now—the stronger leader. That's why I challenge him."

Alpha's fur bristled all over his body. Low in his throat he gave a menacing growl.

Still no dog spoke. Lucky felt as if the air itself was trembling. Beside Moon, Beetle crouched, looking as fearful as if he were a half-weaned pup again; Thorn, on the other paw, wore a bright, hopeful look. Martha gave Sunshine a quick, reassuring lick, then nuzzled the frightened Daisy.

At last Sweet stepped gracefully forward. She licked her slender muzzle hesitantly, but when she spoke her voice was clear and steady.

"Hear me, Packmates. Fiery the hunter challenges Alpha for the leadership of this Pack." She glanced at Moon, looking suddenly hesitant, and Lucky wondered if she had ever had to make this declaration before. She seemed to stumble over the unfamiliar words. "Such a challenge may not be refused, and . . . and it may not be withdrawn. Fiery and Alpha will meet in combat . . . so that Alpha may defend his position by strength."

"And keep it by strength," snarled Alpha.

Sweet did not respond to that. She tilted her elegant head. "Moon, come forward."

Beetle and Thorn shot anxious glances at their Mother-Dog, but Moon rose immediately and padded forward to stand at Fiery's side.

To Lucky's surprise, Sweet sounded gentle and calm—like the dog he'd first met in the Trap House, not the savage Beta he had come to know recently. "Moon," she declared. "As Fiery's mate, you have the right now to challenge me for the position of Beta. Do you wish to do so?"

Moon turned her head to give Fiery an affectionate lick on his muscular shoulder. As the mates' eyes met, Lucky looked from one to the other, shocked.

Moon knew! he realized. *She knew Fiery was going to challenge Alpha— they must have discussed it.*

A sense of dread rippled through his fur. *I don't want either of them to be hurt.*

To his surprise and relief, Moon dipped her head. "No, Sweet," she said quietly. "Should Fiery win the challenge, I will accept you as his Beta."

"It will not be something you have to accept," growled Alpha. "Fiery will not win."

Moon ignored him, her gaze fixed on Sweet. "I have no wish to take your place in the Pack."

Sweet gave a solemn nod. Both she and Moon looked perfectly calm, though Lucky's head whirled. His heart leaped in his chest at the thought of Fiery replacing the half wolf. How different Pack life would be with the brave and noble Fiery in command. Lucky blinked as a thought occurred to him. If Fiery won this fight, then Alpha would revert to his real dog-name.

Lucky realized he didn't even know what that was.

But what if Fiery fails? What if . . .

"Hear me again, Packmates." Sweet's commanding voice rang clearly into the silence. "Moon declines to challenge me, and I will remain your Beta. Fiery and Alpha will contest the leadership; according to the law of the Sky-Dogs, the battle may end only in full submission, or death."

Lucky's heart thudded against his rib cage. It was just as he'd feared.

But Sweet hadn't finished. "The fight will take place tonight, under the gaze of the Moon-Dog. Until then, Alpha remains our leader and his will is to be obeyed." She looked around the Pack, daring any of them to challenge her.

"Of course," agreed Fiery, taking a pace back and dipping his head to Sweet. The other Wild Dogs growled and whined their agreement, but the Leashed Dogs looked to Lucky in bewilderment.

"I don't understand," whined Daisy.

"Lucky," whispered Bella, "what do we do now?"

He wasn't sure. He opened his jaws to answer her, but Alpha's growl was right at his ear. He turned, shocked, to look straight into the half wolf's eyes.

"What do you do?" Alpha snarled. "You, Lucky, will take your Fierce Dog friend to the forest. You will hunt with her. And you will both pray to the Spirit Dogs that you catch plenty of prey, because you will answer to me on your return—as you will be doing for a very long time, because I will remain Alpha of this Pack."

CHAPTER ELEVEN

"Hunters, come with me," *Fiery's voice* rang out, strong and confident. "As Alpha commands, that now includes Lick." He gave the young Fierce Dog a swift glance, but Lucky could not read his expression. He could only follow Fiery outside, feeling Lick close at his hindquarters. Out on the hardstone track, the dogs broke into a steady run.

Lucky raced with them, his mind swirling. He couldn't believe that Fiery had challenged Alpha's leadership, but the prospect of seeing Alpha ground beneath Fiery's claws gave him a small thrill of pleasure—which immediately made him cringe with shame. *I know Alpha's been a bully—is a bully—but if I enjoy his defeat, what does that make me?*

"I'm sorry, Lucky." He could feel Lick's panting breath on his flank. "I'm so sorry."

"Don't worry," he growled. "Just keep up."

"It's my fault."

"No, it isn't." *At least, not completely,* thought Lucky. "Fiery's challenge has been a long time coming, I think."

"But if I hadn't lost my temper," she panted, "if I hadn't provoked Alpha, Fiery wouldn't have challenged him. Not right now. And it's not a good ti—"

"I said, don't worry!" He couldn't help snapping at Lick. It was true that her behavior had brought everything to a head. And in a way that was good. *But she had no business attacking Alpha. She confirmed every dog's fears about her!*

There was still no sign of life in the deserted longpaw houses, and Lucky had almost stopped noticing the corpses in the streets, though Bruno and Mickey still flinched at the sight of them. As the dogs left the settlement behind and the forest drew closer, Fiery slowed to a confident walk, the others behind him. *He has so much sense,* thought Lucky. *He's properly cautious, but he isn't afraid of Terror. Every dog is alert and focused—under his leadership, they are calm. . . .*

And he was, too, he realized, his fury at Lick beginning to fade. "What in the name of the Earth-Dog made you do it?" he sighed at last, falling back until he was walking at Lick's side. "Couldn't you see that Alpha was trying to goad you? You did exactly what he wanted."

Lick bowed her head in shame. "I know that now, Lucky. I really am sorry. I don't know what happened. I should have controlled myself, but . . . I just couldn't."

"Lick, you've got to learn," he sighed. "You're responsible for your own actions—not your blood, nor your family! Please don't prove Alpha right."

"I'll try," she whined.

"You've chosen to stay with this Pack," he went on. "That means you've left your Fierce Dog family behind. With us you'll be fed, you'll be looked after, but you're—well, you're the Alpha of your own life. You have to be master of yourself, of your instincts."

"I thought we should follow our instincts," she said as she trudged.

"But you can't let them control you," he told her. "It isn't easy, but you have to learn. You have to stay calm when you're challenged."

"Yes, Lucky." She looked away toward the meadow where the rest of the Pack was already heading into the trees.

"Come on. We're falling behind." Lucky nudged her, and they broke into a run through long grass that tickled their snouts.

She seems to be listening to me, but how can I really tell? Lucky had a sudden image in his head of Lick playing secretly with her brother Fang. She'd looked so happy, so mischievous. And the way she'd talked about Mickey, and his conflicted loyalties . . . Had she really left her blood family behind? Maybe not entirely.

All the dogs pricked their ears as they passed the first trees and padded farther into the dimness of the forest. Birds fluttered in the branches and they could hear the rustle of insects and tiny creatures in the leaves beneath their paws, but every dog was listening for something more than prey: a threatening growl, or the thunder of paws. So far there was nothing, but Lucky knew they couldn't let their guard down for even an instant.

Snap was at Fiery's side as the big dog led them on. "I want you to know you've got my support tonight," she growled. "I'd like to see you as Alpha."

Mickey joined in with a low bark. "Me too."

Fiery only grunted thoughtfully, but Bruno gave a warning woof. "I agree, but we're still a Pack. Whoever wins the challenge should have every dog's support."

"You're right, Bruno," said Fiery, nodding. "That was well said. But thank you, anyway, all of you."

He fell silent again, and Lucky wondered what was going through his head. Was he planning for tonight's challenge, or focusing entirely on the hunt and on the threat of Terror? *Surely he must be at least a little anxious. And that must affect his concentration.*

"Perhaps we should spread out," suggested Mickey.

"Yes," said Fiery, pricking his ears. "Spread out in a line—flank-to-flank, not nose-to-tail. Stay a few paces away, but don't lose sight of one another. And keep your noses sharp."

Lucky was glad Fiery was concentrating on the job at paw, but his command to be alert for scents was easier said than done. In among the trees the earth was still damp from the previous day's rain. Many scents were mingled, and some must have been washed away, but at least the Sun-Dog, much higher in the sky now, was pushing light through the leaves and warming the ground. That made the scents clearer with each passing moment.

Nose to the ground, Lucky didn't see Lick until she blundered across his path. He bumped hard into her and she jumped.

"There's something up there!" she whispered. She stared up into the branches. "Listen . . ."

Lucky strained his ears and tilted his head, but all he could hear was birdsong and the flutter of wings. He gave a low, exasperated whine.

"See!" she exclaimed, pointing with her muzzle. "There!"

Above them perched a huge, black bird, its head cocked to stare down at them before preening its glossy feathers. It knew as well as he did, Lucky thought, that it was perfectly safe up there.

"You won't catch that unless it flies to the ground, Lick!"

"But it's alone. Right there in front of us!"

"Oh, for the Forest-Dog's sake, move on," Lucky growled. "Unless you're planning to climb that tree. Or fly!"

"I've heard sharpclaws can do it," grumbled Lick.

"Yes, I've seen sharpclaws hunt in trees, in the city, but we can't. They're different from us. Come on!"

He trotted off, and heard Lick reluctantly follow him, her pawsteps hesitant. "So there were sharpclaws in the city. You've never told me anything about it before," she said. "What was it like? Was it like the place we've made camp?"

"A little, I suppose. Lots of hardstone paths and longpaw houses. But it was much bigger. So much bigger, it's hard to describe. And it had some houses made all of clear-stone, from top to bottom."

"Clear-stone houses?" Lick gaped. "But couldn't hunters see inside, then?"

"Well, yes. But that was how they were meant to be. Longpaws hunted in the clear-stone buildings, and the things they hunted were right there for them to see."

"Weird," muttered Lick.

"It's hard to explain. And there were lots of Food Houses.

And so many longpaws." Lucky licked his lips. "Kind longpaws, who would share their prey."

"I like the sound of that," said Lick wistfully.

"Well, they weren't all kind," added Lucky, picking his way through the dry leaves. "Some wouldn't share, and would rather kick a dog. And there were foxes—nasty things—and plenty of sharpclaws who'd scratch your nose if you even looked at them. But it was a good place to live."

"You miss it." Lick nuzzled him.

"I suppose I do, a bit." Lucky shook himself. "But that was a different time in my life. I'm a Wild Dog now."

Lick snapped idly at a fly that buzzed at her ear. "Would you go back? If you got the chance?"

Lucky was silent for a moment. "No," he said at last. "Something tells me—something inside—that I'll never be a City Dog again."

Lick gulped the fly and licked her chops. "Oh. Well, if you feel like that, I'm sure it's true."

"It's not just a feeling." Lucky sighed, feeling a small jolt of regret. "The fact is, my city doesn't exist anymore. I couldn't go back even if I wanted to."

"But you don't want to," Lick whined happily. "And I'm glad. I like having you in the Pack."

But then, you've never known things any other way, thought Lucky.

A little to their right, Fiery gave a growl, and Lucky paused, back on alert. He slunk low through the grass toward Fiery, Lick behind him, and the others creeping carefully from the other direction. A breeze whispered through the trees, stirring a few dead leaves underpaw, and every dog fell silent.

"What is it?" Lucky murmured to Fiery.

"I'm not sure," growled the big dog.

Lucky listened hard and tried to smell the air. There were definitely sounds echoing between the trees; it was as if there were creatures moving around just ahead of them—but he couldn't smell any unfamiliar dogs.

"Smells like . . . loudcages," he whined, his fur prickling. "But it's very faint."

Fiery pricked an ear and turned his head. "Maybe there are longpaws in the forest?"

Lucky trembled. *Longpaws? Here? I hope not!* The longpaws they had encountered since the Big Growl had been anything but kind and friendly.

"Stay down," muttered Snap. "We'd better not move until we're sure."

"And no running to the longpaws," growled Fiery to Mickey and Bruno.

"Of course not," whispered Bruno, sounding a little insulted.

"Just making sure. Now, hush!"

Lucky shivered as he lay low, thistles pricking at his belly and weeds tickling his nostrils. Beside him he could just hear Lick's nervous breathing, but she was keeping still. *Prove to me how calm you can be, Lick.*

A crash of undergrowth, a shower of leaves, and there they were—longpaws, directly ahead! It was those yellow-furred ones again, Lucky realized with a stab of fear. Glossy, yellow hides, black faces without eyes or mouths—and they were carrying those frightening metal sticks, the ones they used to poke and prod at Earth-Dog. *What are they doing here? Did they follow us?*

Lucky heard a high, terrified whimper close to him. Lick! Of course, she had never seen a longpaw at all—never mind these strange yellow monsters. Lucky risked wriggling closer to her, and nuzzled her fur reassuringly.

"They're not friendly," she whispered to him. "Can't you smell the aggression? They're not kind, the way you said. They're like—like Fierce Dogs, looking for a fight!"

"Hush, Lick," he murmured urgently. "You're right; we can't trust these longpaws. They're different from the ones I knew. But try not to move. We just have to wait for them to pass by."

He could see glimpses of the other dogs concealed in the grass. Mickey's black-and-white fur was the most conspicuous, but he lay obediently still, shadows dancing across him from the overhead branches. Surely the longpaws would walk on by. *They didn't follow us,* thought Lucky as panic rose in his belly. *So they're not interested in us. Right?*

Lucky was horrified to see the longpaws stop only a few rabbit-chases in front of the Pack's noses. *What are they doing?* He could hear them talking to one another, but he could understand even less of their language than usual; they spoke in crackling hisses as they jabbed their metal sticks into the soil. One pointed at a hollow among the trees; another shook its head and turned to stare—

Right in the dogs' direction!

Lucky cringed closer to the ground, wishing he could press himself right through the surface and into the protective paws of Earth-Dog. The longpaw's black face was turned toward him and Lick, but with its eyes invisible Lucky had no idea if it had noticed them or not. He had never felt so helpless, so incapable of a decision.

Please, Forest-Dog. Please don't let the longpaws see us!

A volley of sharp, hissing barks made Lucky snap his head up, terrified. It was the yellow-furred longpaw, barking furiously in that crackling voice. And the longpaw was pointing as he shouted—pointing straight at the crouching dogs.

"Run!" Lucky barked, scrambling to all fours.

The other dogs leaped up with him, and together they took to their paws and fled. Lucky ran blindly, dodging tree trunks, crashing through bushes and thorny undergrowth, hearing the panicked panting of the others as they raced close by. Bruno grunted as he leaped a fallen trunk, and Lucky heard Mickey yelp as if he'd stepped on thorns—but they were all still with him, flying as fast as their paws would go.

Fiery was pounding at his side, tongue lolling, but the big dog managed to bark out a furious order. "I'll run behind. You take the lead, Lucky!"

"Why?" panted Lucky. "What are you going to do?"

"I don't know. But if the longpaws want to hurt a dog under my command, they'll have to go through me to do it!"

There was no more time to question Fiery. Lucky took the lead, but plowed almost immediately into a patch of mud, his paws slithering and slipping. One forepaw sank deep in the stickiness, and he stumbled, but recovered. Behind him he heard yelps, and knew that the others too were having trouble with the mud, but he couldn't look back. Fighting his way free, paws still slipping, he struggled up a bank, then turned to bark encouragement.

"You're nearly there, Snap. Come on, Bruno!" His chest heaved.

"Why run? We should fight!" The savage bark came from Lick, who stopped suddenly, her legs spattered with filth, her bared teeth white and gleaming.

"No, they're too big! Come on, Lick! Run, and the mud will slow the longpaws too!" Fear tightened Lucky's throat as he barked.

Mickey reached the bank, dragging himself up with his fore-claws, then turning to drag the floundering Bruno by the scruff of his thick neck. Snap clambered out too, shaking great clods of dirt from her coat, but Lick still stood there in the middle of the

SURVIVORS: THE BROKEN PATH

mud-field, barking savagely at the advancing longpaws.

"Lick, move!" Lucky snarled. Relieved, he saw Fiery reach the young dog, and the big dog nipped sharply at her haunches to drive her on. Reluctantly she turned and stumbled, her fangs still bared. But Lucky could hear muffled shouts of pursuit; the longpaws were close behind them now, jumping down into the mud and wading after them with their sticks.

Those aren't the same sticks, Lucky realized with a stab of terror. He recognized the ones they wielded now—long poles with looped cord at the end. His memory flashed back to a day that seemed ages ago, though he knew it'd only been a few turns of the Moon-Dog. *The day the longpaws captured me and caged me in the Trap House!* These were the same sticks that had caught him then, looping around his neck and tightening, choking, holding him fast.

Once those loops were around a dog's neck, it was impossible to get out of them. "Run, Lick!" he howled.

But she still hesitated at the bottom of the bank, snarling as Fiery scrambled up. "They're afraid of us!" she yelped in fury. "Those longpaws need sticks—they're scared, and we can drive them away!"

"No!" Lucky leaped down the bank, seized her scruff, and dragged her up after him. "We have to move!"

188

Fiery joined in, shouldering Lick up the bank as Lucky tugged at her. She stumbled and fell as he released her, panting.

"We have to change course," Fiery growled, with a glance back at the longpaws. "We're heading straight back to the Food House, to the Pack. We can't lead the longpaws there!"

"You're right. You go ahead!" barked Lucky as Lick scrambled to her feet, panting.

Fiery spun and pounded toward the thicker forest once more. Bruno, Mickey, and Snap followed, paws crunching on dry leaves again as Lucky shoved Lick to make her run faster. He could just make out Fiery's haunches as the big dog plunged through the trees. *We can get away!*

He and Lick broke out of the trees and into a shallow clearing just as Fiery reached its center. A flash of movement from above made Lucky flinch and swerve, but Fiery was still running hard as something fell from the high branches.

Lucky skidded to a halt, horrified, as the thing fell directly onto Fiery. The big dog tumbled head over paws, his legs still pumping. He was caught in a huge net of rope. Rolling over and over, tangled tightly, Fiery slammed to a stop against a tree root, his paws flailing through the thick, tangled web.

Lucky raced forward. "Fiery!"

He could only see one of Fiery's eyes, which rolled, showing the white, as the huge dog yelped in terror, slobber flying from his mouth.

"Lucky! Lucky, help me!"

CHAPTER TWELVE

Struggling to wriggle free, Fiery rolled again, his claws raking the ground. His teeth snapped uselessly at the rope that seemed to pull ever tighter around his muzzle; it had dragged the skin back so that his fierce teeth were completely exposed. The more he struggled, Lucky realized desperately, the tighter the rope-cage drew.

"Stop moving, Fiery!" he barked. "It's going to choke you!"

As the other dogs gathered around Fiery, whining in distress and trying to lick at their trapped Packmate through the ropes, he went still except for the heaving of his foam-streaked flanks. His paws twitched, as if he was desperate to run, but thankfully he was managing to control himself.

"What do I do?" he whimpered through his twisted muzzle.

"I don't know." Lucky licked his jaws and scraped at the ground, frustrated and tormented. "I don't know! I've never seen a trap like this. I don't know what the longpaws have done!"

Lucky heard the barks of the approaching longpaws—they were far too close now. Desperately he pricked his ears, hoping against hope that they would take a wrong path, but no; he could hear them crashing through the undergrowth toward the clearing. Lick shouldered past him.

"We have to get him out!" she whined.

"Stop, Lick!" Lucky darted forward to block her with his body. "There could be more traps. We don't know how this works."

"But we can't just wait—the longpaws are getting closer!"

Lucky stared past her, listening to the crunch of leaves and undergrowth, the racket of clumsy longpaws. Snap, Bruno, and Mickey were all watching him, their eyes terrified, and he knew they were expecting him to come up with some clever City Dog trick. *But I can't. I don't know what to do!*

"Packmates!" Fiery gave a strangled bark, and every dog turned toward him. "You have to get away. You can't save me; there isn't time. You have to get back and warn the others."

"No!" Lucky whined in distress. "We can't leave you behind, Fiery."

"Listen to me." With difficulty, Fiery licked his jaws. "If the longpaws wanted to kill me, I'd be dead by now. It's obvious that they only want to catch dogs. I don't know why, but my life's not in danger—not yet. You can't rescue me later if you get caught, too. Get out of here—go warn Alpha. . . ." Fiery's eyes burned into Lucky's. ". . . and Moon and my pups. Please."

Indecision gnawed at Lucky's gut. *It goes against everything I believe to abandon a Packmate.*

But he knew Fiery was right. There was nothing he could do for the big dog.

"All right," he said at last. "All right, Fiery, we'll go. But we will be back for you!"

"Good. Just go now!"

Lick started toward Fiery again, but Lucky grabbed her by the scruff and dragged her back. "He's right, Lick. We have to go!"

Reluctantly Snap, Mickey, and Bruno turned. Mickey gave a last reassuring whine in Fiery's direction, and they plunged back into the trees.

Lucky paused to peer through the tangle of branches. The longpaws burst into the clearing, stopping when they caught sight of the trapped Fiery. He was squirming again, fighting the ropes and snarling. *He's keeping the longpaws distracted,* thought Lucky.

The longpaws' barks had changed; they were making that huffing, rumbling sound he remembered from his days in the city. It meant they were amused; he knew that. It was their way of laughing. Once, it had meant friendly longpaws; it had meant he was safe and could expect only kindness.

Now, it just made his belly churn with anger. *We will be back for you, Fiery. I promise.*

They ran a long way through the forest; Snap led them in a wide circle before daring to head back in the rough direction of the longpaw settlement and the Food House. When she finally came to a halt, panting hard and still looking back fearfully into the forest, the others gathered around her, shaking their fur and regaining their breath. Lick spun and bared her teeth at Lucky.

"Why did we leave him? How could you do that, Lucky?"

Lucky panted, flanks heaving from the long, hard run. "There was nothing we could do."

"I don't understand!"

"How could it have helped if we'd *all* been caught?" he asked her. "If we escape, we can do something to help Fiery later. But if we got trapped, there would be no dog left to warn the Pack of the longpaw danger. The others would try to hunt, or they'd come looking for us, and soon all of our Pack friends would be prisoners!"

"Lucky's right," growled Snap. "We had no choice."

"It's true, Lick," added Bruno.

Lick was breathing hard, but at least she seemed to be calming down. She threw an angry glance back the way they'd come. "I wish I could teach those longpaws a lesson," she snarled. "I told you: They're afraid of us. One good scare, and they would keep their distance."

"It's not that simple." Lucky forced himself to ignore the aggression in her tone. He nuzzled her head gently, and gave her a nudge in the direction of the longpaw settlement.

"Come on," he murmured. "We need to get back to the Food House right now."

"No!" Daisy yelped in horror. "Fiery captured?"

The shadows were growing longer in the Food House, and to Lucky the dimness made everything seem even more unreal. He felt numb with shock.

"You left my Father-Dog with longpaws?" barked Beetle in disbelief.

Snap threw Moon a pleading look. "We had to."

Moon was very quiet, seeming dazed and miserable, but she at least was controlling herself. The rest of the Pack was in panicked chaos. Sunshine turned in a frantic circle as Martha licked her ears, trying to calm her. Dart murmured to herself, clawing the ground. Sweet paced to and fro, growling with anger. Alpha lay with his head on the ground, silent, his flanks heaving and his expression thunderous. Spring simply barked over and over again with frustrated rage, while Whine glared at Lucky.

"Betrayal is all you get from a Street Dog," sneered the former Omega.

"What did you say?" Lick's ears shot up.

Uh-oh! Lucky barged in front of her as she lunged, just in time to stop her grabbing Whine and shaking him to death.

"I don't understand!" barked Spring. "Snap, why would long-paws hunt dogs? Do they eat us now?"

"Of course not!" yelped Mickey. "Don't be stupid!"

"Who knows what they'd do?" snarled Alpha. "The Big Growl changed dogs. Why wouldn't it change longpaws?"

"They wouldn't," howled Daisy miserably. "They just wouldn't do that!"

"Then why?" asked Snap. "I don't understand it either, and I saw them. They thought it was funny."

"This only confirms what I thought before." Alpha got to his paws and gave Sweet a curt nod of his head. "We need to move on. Now. Every dog, get ready."

Moon lifted her head at that, frowning. She got to her paws and shook herself violently. "Alpha? You mean after we've rescued Fiery, right?"

"I mean now," growled Alpha. "The whole Pack is in danger. We have to get away from this place."

Lucky stared at him in disbelief. Surely Alpha didn't intend to abandon his third-in-command?

"No." Moon bounded forward until she was almost nose-to-nose with her leader. "I know you don't mean that. Leave Fiery behind, at the mercy of those longpaws? No, Alpha." She shook her head, her muzzle curling to show a gleam of teeth. "That is not going to happen."

All around them the other dogs went still, watching Moon and the half wolf as they faced each other down.

"Fiery took his chance when he went hunting in the forest," snapped Alpha. "He knew the risks. We can't afford—"

"You're afraid!" barked Moon, her dark eyes flashing with rage. "You never wanted to face him in the challenge. Now you don't have to, if you abandon him."

"Watch your muzzle, Moon," snarled Alpha. "I am your leader. This has nothing to do with your mate's stupid challenge."

Moon looked as if she might fly at Alpha's throat. *No!* thought

Lucky. He sprang forward to her side and licked her jaw gently, then turned to face Alpha.

"Moon's right," he said grimly. "Fiery insisted that we save ourselves—and I made him a promise that we'd be back to rescue him. I won't let him down. Lick didn't even want to—"

"Lick?" barked Alpha. "I should have known that evil little pup had something to do with this. Did she lead poor Fiery into this trap?"

Lucky's blood ran cold with anger and his fur bristled. "How can you possibly think this was Lick's fault? She doesn't even know about longpaws—she'd never seen one before today. How could she have led any dog into a trap?"

Alpha gave a low throaty growl. "She's bringing us bad luck. Everywhere we go—"

"You're just making things up now!" Lucky barked furiously. "You know that's nonsense, straight from the top of your skull. There's no bad luck, there's no 'evil' dog . . ."

His breath caught in his throat and he swallowed as he glared at Alpha.

"Go on, Lucky," growled the half wolf. "Do grace us with your 'wisdom.'"

Lucky clenched his teeth. "Maybe there is such a thing as an evil dog, but it isn't Lick. Terror talked about a Fear-Dog spirit. Well, I'm connected to the Forest-Dog, and the River-Dog watches over Martha. If anyone in this Pack has a link to the Fear-Dog . . ."

"What are you implying?" snarled Alpha. "How dare you, Street Dog?"

Lucky opened his jaws again, but he couldn't say more. *I've gone too far. I shouldn't have said it, but . . .* He kept his eyes on Alpha's glowing yellow ones. The growl in Alpha's throat was growing louder, like distant thunder before a Sky-Dog war.

"Stop. Both of you!" Sweet stepped between them, casting a hard glare at Lucky and then turning it on Alpha. "This does the Pack no good. It doesn't help any dog to have two of our strongest dogs at each other's throats all the time. You should both be ashamed!" Her teeth glinted. "We need to make a decision for the good of the Pack—together!"

Alpha stood up, hackles raised. "The decision has been made," he growled. "I lead this Pack and I consult no dog! Who do you think you are?"

"Your Beta!" she snarled.

"And I am your Alpha! We are moving on from this place; the whole settlement is a trap. Wild Dogs do not belong here!"

Moon leaped to her paws, her calm finally shattered. "I will not leave the father of my pups. If no dog will help me, I will go for him myself!"

For a moment, the air seemed to tremble with tension as the whole Pack stared from Moon to Alpha. No dog even seemed to breathe.

Then Spring's nose twitched, and she drew a breath. Lucky's head snapped around, and he too caught the scent. Every dog noticed it now, and their noses lifted.

"What is it?" whimpered Sunshine.

"Dog-scent," Mickey murmured. "Who . . ."

"I know that scent," growled Sweet, nostrils flaring.

"Every dog into battle line, now!" Alpha snarled. "We are under attack!"

CHAPTER THIRTEEN

There was no time to order themselves, Lucky realized as the Pack tumbled into a ragged defensive line. In the cramped room of the Food House the dogs could not even form proper ranks, and he could only push Daisy and Sunshine roughly behind him to make sure they were protected as much as possible. Whine shrank back out of danger, Lucky noticed, without his help. *That's typical of him!* Moon positioned herself snarling in front of Beetle and Thorn, but the two pups wriggled forward past her legs to take their places in the line. Moon's face softened just for a moment as she glanced down at them with pride.

Standing in the center of the line, facing the broken clear-stone entrance, Alpha drew back his lips to show his teeth. "You see? We can't even defend ourselves in this longpaw-place. If we get out of this alive, we are moving on—no arguments."

"Discuss it later," snapped Sweet, bristling as a shadow fell across the half-open doorway.

A nose appeared first, sniffing at the air. The door creaked a little wider, and Lucky cocked his head in surprise. Through the gap peered familiar puzzled eyes in a brown-and-white head.

"What . . . don't attack! It's me. Twitch!"

The strain snapped so quickly, Lucky could almost feel the muscles of every dog relaxing. Spring gave a growling sigh of relief, and Moon shut her eyes.

"Twitch?" Snap gave a low, suspicious rumble, and Lucky realized she was remembering their last encounter, and the terrible fight with Terror's Pack.

Limping forward, Twitch lowered his ears and head. He crouched, trembling. "Please. I had nothing to do with the attack in the forest."

"Who planned it?" growled Alpha. "Was it this 'Terror'?"

"Not really." Twitch shivered. "Terror doesn't really plan things. He just—"

"Then why are you here?" barked Alpha. "Not to beg for your Pack-place back, I hope. I have no use for crippled dogs." He glanced contemptuously at Twitch's three remaining legs. "Especially traitorous cripples."

Twitch winced, an expression of hurt flitting across his face, but his voice remained meek and respectful. "I don't ask for that, Alpha. I know you wouldn't take me back. I only came because we saw Fiery being captured. We were on our way to our camp after hunting, and we saw the longpaws take him."

"So you've come to gloat?" growled Alpha. "That would be stupid."

"No! I—you see, I know where they took him." Twitch glanced anxiously over his shoulder. "I know where Fiery is."

Hope leaped in Lucky's rib cage. Beside him, Moon gasped and sprang forward. "Tell me. Tell me, Twitch! Where is he?"

Alpha paced forward, pinning his ears back menacingly. "And why should we believe anything this crippled dog says? Why should you trust him? I know I don't."

Moon looked from Alpha to Twitch, her eyes desperate. She licked her chops doubtfully as Twitch gave a low, pleading whimper.

"Twitch, what's going on?" Lucky said at last. "The longpaws hunted dogs in the city. That's how they caught me and Sweet to put us in the Trap House. But I know why they did it there—because they don't like dogs roaming around their streets and parks."

"You said the longpaws shared their food happily," snorted Alpha.

SURVIVORS: THE BROKEN PATH

"Yes, some of them did. But others didn't like that, and they didn't like us dogs running free. They thought we made a mess, spoiled their pretty places. But why would they bother to catch dogs running wild out here? It doesn't make sense."

"No, it doesn't," Martha agreed softly. "And they can't be looking for Leashed Dogs. Not when they left all of us behind."

Twitch's tail thumped the ground once, unhappily. "I don't know what they're thinking. But I know which way they were going, and I can guess where he is. He's in the Dog-Garden."

That was enough to set the whole Pack barking and whining. "The Dog-Garden?" barked Bruno. "No!"

"That's where the Fierce Dogs come from," whimpered Sunshine.

Lucky's fur prickled. He had hoped they'd seen the last of the strange and sinister Dog-Garden, where the Fierce Dogs had lived their strict, rule-bound lives. Lucky and Mickey had rescued the Fierce Dog pups from there—and that had already caused so much trouble between the Packs.

"Are the longpaws working with the Fierce Dogs?" barked Dart. "If that's true, we don't stand a chance!"

"Can you imagine?" howled Spring. "Longpaws and Fierce Dogs!"

"Is that it?" demanded Alpha. "Is that what's happening?"

"I don't know," mumbled Twitch. "I just know what I've seen. When I was on my own—before I found Terror's Pack, I mean, when I was still injured—I saw the longpaws in the forest a few times."

"And didn't they hunt you?" asked Martha.

Twitch shook his head. "There aren't many things that are easier without a Pack, but it was much simpler for a lone dog to stay out of their way, and I didn't make much noise on my own. Most of them stayed around the Dog-Garden. They're up to something there. Something they must think is important. I don't know if the Fierce Dogs are still there, though. I never saw any."

Lucky scratched at his ear with a hindpaw, then thumped his tail thoughtfully. "Last time I was there," he murmured, "when I rescued the pups, the adult-dog scents were very faint and old. I don't think the Fierce Dogs make their home there now."

"But if the longpaws want to make a Pack with them . . ." said Snap doubtfully. "They might have gone back."

"And they will," growled Alpha. "Fierce Dogs want to be with longpaws. That's why we call them Longpaw Fangs, remember?"

"They do seem to worship the longpaws," murmured Mickey. "And not the way we did. It seemed very . . . odd."

With a shudder, Lucky remembered Fang's ears, mutilated in imitation of the way the longpaws treated the Fierce Dogs. But he could hardly mention that now. "Remember the last time Blade's Pack attacked us? They were too far from the Dog-Garden—they'd never have come all that way from their territory to retrieve the pups. It doesn't make sense."

Daisy shivered. "Who knows what makes sense to a Fierce Dog?" she yelped.

"And what would a City Dog know, anyway?" sneered Whine.

Lucky bared his teeth at him, then gave Daisy a reassuring lick. "I don't think the Fierce Dogs are at the Dog-Garden," he told her. With a glance at Moon, he added, "So I don't think we need to worry about them hurting Fiery."

Moon stepped forward determinedly. "But we still need to rescue him."

"Yes," agreed Lucky. "Who knows what the longpaws are up to?"

"No," snarled Alpha. "The most important thing is the safety of the Pack." He glared around at them all. "How do we know the crippled dog isn't lying? He's weak—he always was. He could be luring us straight into a trap of Terror's. I have no doubt the mad dog wants revenge."

Because that's the way your mind would work, thought Lucky, but he kept his muzzle shut.

"I promise I'm not lying," whined Twitch. "I'm telling you the truth. It's the only reason I came here."

"Then you wasted your time," snapped Alpha. "We are moving on. Now."

Whine was the first to creep forward to Alpha's side. "Well, I'm leaving. Alpha is the leader, isn't he?"

Dart nodded, then padded over to Alpha. Snap and Spring looked at each other, hesitant. They took a few paces, paused again, then followed as Alpha led the way confidently out of the Food House. With an apologetic glance back at Lucky, Bruno joined them, and so did Mickey. Daisy and Sunshine crept out too, in the shelter of Martha's big, protective body.

"Wait!" barked Moon, her pups at her side. "What's happening? Are we really leaving a dog behind?"

The others looked away, but Sweet growled, "It's Alpha's decision." Lucky thought she didn't look at all happy about it.

"And if Alpha was caught in a longpaw trap?" insisted Moon, her eyes narrowing. "Wouldn't he want to know his Pack was coming for him?"

"I wouldn't get caught in the first place," sneered Alpha.

Lucky's hackles sprang erect, and he felt a growl rise in his throat. Sweet shot a warning glance at him.

"Lucky!" she barked. "Don't start."

Disbelieving, he bared his teeth. If she was trying to calm him down, she was having the opposite effect. Anger swelled inside him like a threatening storm.

"Why not?" he barked. "Why should I listen to you, Beta?"

Alpha snarled and took a pace toward Lucky, but Sweet interrupted. "That's enough, Lucky."

For long moments he stood still, furious but undecided. *Why should I listen to Sweet?* he thought. *She supports him even when she knows he's wrong! Never mind Fiery,* he thought. *Sweet should have challenged Alpha herself, long ago!*

Lucky swiped his tongue across his jaws, desperate to say everything he was thinking. But what would be the point? It would solve nothing right now. At this moment, the important thing was to free Fiery. To stop Alpha from abandoning him to his fate.

He shouldered past Sweet, almost knocking her off her paws as he ran out into the street, where the other dogs waited for Alpha's orders. Facing them, he straightened his back and lifted his head. *I have to look like an Alpha dog myself.*

"Saving Fiery is the only choice," he barked. "Alpha knows that as well as any dog in this Pack."

Alpha stalked to face him, snarling. "Don't think I don't know what you're up to, Street Dog. You want to lure my Pack into the same trap!"

Lucky stared at the half wolf in disbelief. How could any dog think that of him? He raised his head to the others. "You all know that isn't true!"

"As Pack-leader, I would be at the front of any rescue group." Alpha's eyes were hard as yellow stone. "That means I'd be the first dog to set paw in the longpaws' trap. And that would make the Pack yours to take—wouldn't it, Lucky?"

"That's ridiculous!"

"Is it? I'm not falling for your City Dog lies, even if the others have." Alpha scraped his claws along the hardstone track. "I am doing what a leader must do—protecting my Pack."

"Then why are you leaving one of them to die?"

Alpha raised his head to howl: "I have had enough of this bickering, City Dog! Go on a death-mission if you want to—but you'll go on your own. If you want to leap into a trap, you do it alone. You will not take my Pack with you!"

"Should we ask them?" snarled Lucky.

Alpha turned so fast, his tail lashed Lucky's face. Lucky took a sharp breath, as anger made his heart pound in his chest. *Don't let him provoke you into a fight—you can't know whether any dog would back you up right now.*

One by one, Alpha looked into the eyes of his silent Pack, every dog now gathered in the corpse-strewn road. The smell of death seemed thicker and stronger than ever.

"Any dog with a death wish, feel free to leave this Pack and follow Lucky." His muzzle curled back to show his fangs. "Every loyal dog: Come with me."

CHAPTER FOURTEEN

Lucky barged forward to Alpha's side. "It doesn't have to be like that," he growled. "There's no need to split up the Pack for good. That's foolishness!"

Alpha seemed ready to leap at his throat, but Sweet interrupted, watching Lucky closely. "What do you suggest, then?"

Lucky nodded to Twitch, who was sitting at the Food House door trying to look inconspicuous, his body hunched low and his ears pressed close to his head. "Twitch can lead a few dogs back to the Dog-Garden, show us where Fiery's being held. Alpha can lead the rest of the Pack farther along the path of the River-Dog, and start looking for a new camp."

"That might split the Pack up for good whether you mean to or not," pointed out Sweet, tapping her tail on the ground.

"Not if Alpha's group leaves a well-marked scent-trail. Then we can catch up later—me, and any dog who wants to join me."

Alpha opened his jaws, but Sweet interrupted before he could speak. "Good idea. We will leave a trail."

Lucky blinked. Sweet was Alpha's loyal Beta—yet Lucky's fur almost stood on end with the tension in the air between them. Alpha said nothing, but Lucky knew how significant Sweet's declaration was. She had made a decision against Alpha's wishes, and every dog knew it—but how could Alpha possibly contradict her now without looking like a fool?

What was more, Lucky realized, Sweet knew Lucky would return. She trusted him to find the Pack again, and that faith gave him a warm feeling in his stomach.

Clearly it didn't do the same for Alpha. The dog-wolf's throat rumbled with contempt. "All right, Beta. Let's pretend any dogs will survive Lucky's foolish mission."

Sweet dipped her head gently, but did not rise to the taunt. *I have to make sure her trust in me is justified,* Lucky thought. *I'll bring back any dog who comes with me. If any dog joins me in the first place . . .*

He wasn't entirely sure they would. The dogs were murmuring among themselves; tails tapped the ground indecisively. Whine sat close to Alpha, smirking; *Well,* thought Lucky, *I wouldn't have expected his support anyway. But what about the others?*

Moon immediately trotted over to his side. Beetle and Thorn raised argumentative barks, but Moon turned and murmured to them. "No, you're staying. That's final, pups."

"But we want to help rescue Father-Dog!" yelped Thorn.

"No. I told you, I have to know you're safe. If I'm worrying about you two as well, I won't be able to concentrate on helping Fiery. Do you see?"

Beetle dipped his head unhappily. "I suppose so."

Moon licked each pup on the head. "I'll find him; don't worry."

Lucky nodded to Moon as she joined him. She was the one dog he knew he could count on to join him—now, what about the others? He flattened his ears, trying not to hear their quiet discussions. If he wanted to return to this Pack, he couldn't nurse resentment against any of these dogs.

It's a free choice, he told himself, glancing from Bruno to Martha to Snap. I have to let them make it.

Sunshine's expression was mournful, but she had the courage to meet his eyes. *It's all right, Sunshine,* he tried to tell her, just with his blinking gaze. The little dog must know she would be more of a hindrance than a help, anyway. It didn't mean she wasn't loyal.

Bella, on the other paw? He didn't know how he'd react if his litter-sister let him down. . . .

But as his eyes met hers, he realized he needn't have worried.

Calmly she padded to his side. Lucky found his wagging tail bumping into hers.

Sweet sat on her haunches a little apart from the other dogs, gazing at nothing. Feeling as if a rabbit-bone was stuck in his throat, Lucky rose and went to her side.

She didn't turn her head, and he knew immediately. "You're going with Alpha, aren't you?"

Sweet gave a regretful whine. "I'm his Beta, Lucky. I don't have a choice."

Inwardly he flinched. *She's choosing Alpha over me. Again.* "Every dog always has a choice." He couldn't keep the resentment from his voice.

"You don't understand, Lucky."

Lucky got to his paws, his muscles tense and trembling. "For once, we agree, Sweet. I don't understand at all."

Martha sat beside Bella, her expression calm and determined. *Good old Martha,* thought Lucky. *Martha, Moon, Bella, and me—I suppose this is a good-sized rescue party.* Too many dogs would be too confusing. He paced over and nudged himself gently between them. *This is my team.*

Lick bounded up, sending small stones flying. "So when do we start?"

Lucky's belly felt as heavy as a stone as he gazed into the young dog's eager eyes. "I don't know, Lick."

She sat down, looking puzzled. "What do you mean? Let's go as soon as possible!"

"No! I mean . . ." Lucky took a deep breath. "Lick, I don't think you should come. The Dog-Garden is where you were born."

"So what?" she barked. "What's the problem?"

Lucky shut his eyes. He hated having to say it, but Lick had to know. And there was no way he could take her; he was sure of that now. "Lick, I don't think you're ready for a job like this."

"What do you mean?" she barked in disbelief.

"You aren't in control of your instincts yet. It'll come, but you're too young. I've seen you lose your temper. On more than one occasion," he added as she tried to interrupt. "You get angry too easily, and you let it rule you. And . . ."

"And what?" Her eyes flashed.

"You've been meeting secretly with Fang," he reminded her quietly. "Deep down, you're still attached to your Fierce Dog family. That's understandable! I know it'll take time, but . . ." He heaved a sigh. "I don't think it's wise to take you back to the Dog-Garden. Not yet."

Lick's hackles sprang up and her fur bristled. "I'm loyal to this

Pack and I'll prove it to you! Take me. I will be useful!"

Now he almost understood how Moon felt, having to say no to her impetuous pups. Lucky shook his head. "You must stay with the Pack this time, Lick. It's too risky. I'm sorry."

The young Fierce Dog held his eyes for long moments, breathing hard with anger. At last, without another word, she turned and stalked away.

The Sun-Dog was high in the sky, blazing brightly on the dusty streets when the rescue dogs said their sad farewells to the rest of the Pack. Twitch waited patiently a little way off as Moon licked Thorn's nose and nuzzled Beetle. Lucky gave Sweet a glance, but she was staring resolutely away from him.

Alpha, though, met his gaze. There was no expression on the half wolf's face, but Lucky knew their conflict wasn't over. Turning on his haunches, he barked to his small group of dogs and set off after Twitch.

"Good-bye, Lucky," barked Sunshine sadly.

"We'll see you soon." Mickey's farewell howl echoed from the Food House wall.

At the edge of the trees, Moon paused and looked back, and

the others turned with her. Distantly they could hear Alpha's barked commands as the Pack moved out of the longpaw settlement. Snap, Spring, and Daisy yapped their good-byes; now Lucky could hear Beetle and Thorn as well, their young voices clear among the others.

"Stay safe, my pups," howled Moon.

I hope we all do, thought Lucky. *And I hope we see each other again very soon.*

For a day in Red Leaf, the Sun-Dog held a lot of warmth, and Lucky was glad to enter the cool shade of the forest, for all its dangers. Twitch ran ahead, moving faster and more nimbly than Lucky had expected.

"You don't seem to miss your injured leg," Lucky told him with surprise.

"I know. It was holding me back, always worrying about it." Twitch pricked his ears as he darted on between the pine trunks. "Now it's gone, and I can get on with living on three legs. Dogs have adapted to worse things since the Big Growl."

That was true. Still, Lucky was impressed with Twitch's positive attitude to his loss. *Alpha dismisses dogs too easily,* he thought. Twitch could have been an asset to the Pack.

An acrid scent tingled in his nostrils, interrupting his thoughts. Lucky stopped and went still, sniffing. But the Sun-Dog was so strong, and the sky so blue . . .

"What is it?" Bella halted at his side.

Lucky furrowed the skin above his eyes. Sure enough, the sky between the high overhead branches had darkened, and there was a chilly breath of wind between the trees.

"Bad rain!" he growled. "It's coming."

Martha was beside them now. "And we're out here with no protection. The trees won't help much!"

"It's at times like these I see why Lucky liked the city," muttered Twitch, turning to pad back to the others. "All those places to shelter."

"There's no time to get back to the Food House," said Lucky. "Let's find what shelter we can."

Just as he said it, thunder cracked above them. Lightning was playing among the Sky Dogs, and that meant rain at any moment. Uneasy, the dogs ran forward, then spun and ran back.

"Where will we go?" barked Martha.

Lucky looked around the shadowed trees, their branches already shifting in the rising wind. Through the pines he could make out the slope of a ferny bank; beyond that stood a broad oak, twisted with age. "Come on, this way!"

The dogs bounded toward the bank and over the top. The roots of the ancient tree were thick, jutting from the earth, and its branches were thickly tangled.

"This is our best chance," barked Lucky, leading them in among the roots, close to the gnarled trunk. The dogs jostled and huddled close together, glancing up anxiously into the dark leaves above them.

It's as good as we can hope for, thought Lucky, *so long as the rain doesn't fall too heavily. We'll just have to pray to the Sky-Dogs.*

Thunder crashed again, and Lucky pricked his ears as huge raindrops began to clatter on the foliage above them. The high pines roared in the storm, wind and rain howling and hissing in the branches.

As raindrops splattered to the earth, Moon flinched back, bumping into Lucky's flank. Lucky's heartbeat thudded, and he heard Bella gave a whine of fright. A few more drops hissed on a thick root and trickled toward him.

It's coming through! Lucky realized desperately.

The smell of the rain was stronger and closer, scorching

his nostrils. Lucky coughed in disgust, and heard Bella whimper. More fat drops splashed around them, sizzling on the soil, shriveling grass blades like flame. Twitch, at his side, trembled uncontrollably.

"It's all right," barked Lucky above the noise of the storm. "Don't worry. The rain has to pass soon!"

"It's not that," yelped Bella, wincing as a raindrop spattered between her forepaws. "What if the rain burns Earth-Dog? What if she loses her temper and growls again?"

"I'm sure that won't happen," whined Lucky. *I'm lying,* he thought, shivering. *I'm not sure at all.*

Rainwater was finding its way down the tree trunk, trickling in tiny runnels and pooling on the ground. Moon shrank from it, whimpering, but there was no patch of ground the rain wouldn't reach, Lucky knew. He covered his eyes with his paws. *Please, Earth-Dog. Please don't growl now. We've done nothing wrong; don't punish us.*

Twitch struggled to his paws, backing away from pooling water as it trickled faster down the gnarled trunk. "We have to move!"

He's right. We need better shelter. Lucky sprang up, shaking off a few spatters of rain before they could sink through his fur. The forest was dim under the black clouds, but he could see a gleam

SURVIVORS: THE BROKEN PATH

of pale gray, just a few rabbit-chases farther into the trees. "Follow me!"

Hesitantly the other dogs rose, shaking themselves, unsure; but Lucky sprang from the shelter and ran. Moments later, he heard their frantic, running paws and their harsh panting as they came after him.

Lucky shut his eyes as he raced, forced to find his way blind for fear the rain would get under his lids. *Am I even going the right way now?* Panic clenched his chest, squeezing his heart, and his paw-steps faltered.

Then he felt hard rock scraping under his claws, and he opened his eyes. "Here!"

The stony outcrop was small, but its slabs jutted out some way over the bare earth. Lucky skidded onto his flank and slid beneath it, feeling Bella crash into him a moment later. He squirmed farther into the hollow; it went deeper into the slope than he'd first thought. The other dogs were piling after him now, a flurry of paws and fur and thrashing hearts. Crammed together, they all wriggled around and stared out at the driving rain as thunder rolled across the clouds.

"Just in time," murmured Moon, her body trembling against Lucky's.

Lucky twisted his head, dislodging Twitch's one remaining forepaw from his eye. The earth beneath him was damp and cool, and reeking with a multitude of scents. Beneath the rotted leaf-smell there was the odor of long-dead mice and snail slime; he could even make out the territory marker of some old badger. Lucky shivered at that, feeling a twinge in his old, healed wounds.

I don't want to stay in here too long.

Neither did the others. He could hear their uneasy whines, feel the trembling in their muscles, and already the dampness seemed to reach his bones.

"If this rain doesn't stop soon," murmured Martha, "I'll be able to swim out of here."

"Maybe this whole mission was a bad idea," growled Twitch. "Look, I'm sorry. If you want to go back and join Alpha, go ahead. You'll catch up fast if you run. And at least you tried."

Lucky clenched his jaws, and held his breath. *I shouldn't speak. They have to decide for themselves.*

"I'm not leaving Fiery!" declared Moon. "The rest of you go back if you want to."

"No way!" yapped Bella, sounding annoyed. "We started this together, and we'll finish it that way."

"Quite right," grunted Martha.

Lucky's muscles went limp with relief. *There's still hope—I couldn't have chosen better companions on this mission.* With comrades like these, there was a good chance they could rescue Fiery after all.

And maybe we'll discover what those yellow longpaws are up to.

CHAPTER FIFTEEN

The Sky-Dogs' mood was fickle today, Lucky thought as he peered nervously out of the cave. One moment there was a torrent of lashing rain and whirling black ash, blurring the landscape and hissing where it burned the earth. The next it had slackened to a few spatters, and Sun-Dog's rays poked weakly through the treetops. The pale light gleamed off sodden bark and wet leaves, sparkling in puddles. Lucky licked his chops. However thirsty he was, he wouldn't touch those rainwater pools.

At least Earth-Dog didn't grow angry and shake off the bad rain, he thought with relief, turning to the others. "Come on, all of you—there's been no Growl. We have to get to Fiery as fast as we can!"

Twitch untangled himself from the group of dogs, dragged himself on his one forepaw to the cave entrance, then stretched. "Let's get going, then."

The three-legged dog limped ahead of them as they picked their way down the bank and into the forest. The ground was drying fast where the light of the Sun-Dog touched it, and as they traveled on, it grew easier to avoid the pools of rainwater.

Martha raised her head and sniffed, then shunted Lucky with her shoulder. There was an excited gleam in her eye. "We're getting closer to the river."

"That's good, I think. Doesn't it run near to the Dog-Garden?"

Martha's nostrils flared, and a tremor ran along her flank. "It's the bad part of the river. The part that was poisoned by the Big Growl."

"Well, at least we know what to expect." Lucky yapped to the others. "Listen, don't drink from the river when we reach it. It's the bad stretch. But at least we know we're on the right path to the Dog-Garden."

Moon growled in agreement. "Good. We've taken too long as it is. Who knows what's happening to Fiery?"

Long, yellow grass parted as the dogs pushed through it, and there before them lay the silver line of the river, glittering temptingly in the Sun-Dog's light. *It looks so safe,* thought Lucky bleakly, *yet we can't touch it.* He knew the others' throats must be as parched as his; his tongue felt swollen in his mouth.

Twitch halted abruptly, forcing Lucky to stop behind him. "Lucky, wait! There—on the other side."

"What is it?" asked Moon, as she, Bella, and Martha came to a halt behind Lucky and Twitch. All their hackles were up, every dog alert for danger.

Lowering his body, Lucky crept on his belly through the grass until he had a clear view of the far bank. Dogs! He recognized them at once, just as Twitch must have.

They were small and scrawny with hunger, and they cowered on the ground as Terror raged and howled, pacing back and forth in front of them. *Twitch's Pack. We cannot let them see us.*

Terror's high, cracked voice drifted clearly across the river. "You do not show respect for the Fear-Dog! None of you! Quiver before him; beg for mercy! Fear his wrath!"

"So he's still up to that old nonsense," muttered Lucky. "Fear-Dogs indeed!"

Twitch gave him a frightened sideways look. "You don't believe in the Fear-Dog?"

"Of course not," scoffed Lucky. "Terror spreads these lies to intimidate his own Pack. It's an insult to the true Spirit Dogs."

Twitch shivered. "But what if the Fear-Dog is real? There could be Spirit Dogs we've never heard of."

"He has a point, Lucky," whispered Martha as she stared across at the ranting Terror. "How can we know all the Spirit Dogs that exist? Back in the city, when Bella and I lived with longpaws, we didn't even know about the Sky-Dogs!"

"That's true," murmured Bella. "You told us all about them, Lucky. Perhaps there are Spirit Dogs we don't know."

Lucky felt doubt creep over him again.

Drawing a deep breath, he sighed. "You're right. I can't know all the Spirit Dogs that guide us; no dog can. But I don't think there can be any such thing as Fear-Dog."

"But how?" pleaded Bella.

"Can't we all tell when a dog is communicating with the Spirit Dogs?" whined Lucky. "Think of the Great Howl, and how you feel. Have you ever felt a Fear-Dog then? Any of you? When Martha is linked to the River-Dog we sense it—we know it's right. We know the spirit is there; we know it in our bones and the roots of our fur. But look at Terror now." He jerked his head at the raging, pacing dog on the far bank. "The only place Fear-Dog lives is inside that mad dog's head!"

"But Terror says—" began Twitch.

"That's just it. You don't sense the Fear-Dog, do you? Terror has to tell you about the Fear-Dog because he's the 'only dog who sees him.' Your Pack—you all relied on his stories. You've never seen or felt the Fear-Dog, but Terror convinces you. He's an unstable bully. He collapses in a fit and calls it a 'message' from the spirits! It's all nonsense. Why do the dogs in his Pack listen to a word he says?"

"It's easy for you to say that," argued Twitch nervously, "but what if—"

"Twitch," said Bella slowly, "you know, I think Lucky's right. I saw a dog like Terror once."

Twitch's ears flicked, but Lucky laughed. "Another like him? Impossible!"

"I did," insisted Bella. "The way you described him—his body jerking, his eyes rolling? Well, there was a dog who behaved like that at the vet's."

"The what's?" asked Moon.

"The vet's—it's a place our longpaws took us to in the city, whenever we were ill. There was a longpaw in green fur who healed us in his shrine."

"Huh. I've heard it all now." Moon twitched her nose in disbelief.

Taking no notice of her, Bella went on: "Well, sometimes he stuck a sharp thing in your scruff for no reason, but you always felt better afterward. That one time, I'd eaten something bad, and I was with my longpaw in the little room where you wait to find out if the vet-longpaw will agree to heal you. And another dog was brought in, a little thing with white fur. She acted just like Terror—twitching and gasping and flailing around on the floor of a cage, her eyes rolling like a dog with water-madness. I think her long-paws had put her in a cage so she wouldn't bite them. Maybe she was talking to the Fear-Dog, but I don't think so. She just had this terrible fit, and the vet-longpaw agreed to take her into his shrine."

All the dogs were silent, taking in Bella's terrible story.

"She never came out again." Bella gave a sad whine. "So you see, I don't think she was talking to Spirit Dogs. I think she was just very, very sick. The longpaws knew things like that, and the vet-longpaw was wise and kind. I think Terror has the same sick-ness as that little white dog."

Lucky licked his jaws. The Leashed Dogs could still surprise him with their strange knowledge, and in a way Bella's story reas-sured him. There might be an explanation for Terror's madness after all.

But before he could answer his litter-sister, a snarling ruckus broke out among the Pack on the other side of the river. Lucky and his friends started, alarmed.

"How dare you!" howled Terror, lunging at a small black dog. He landed on him with his forepaws, crushing him beneath his weight. "Who are you to question the mighty Fear-Dog?"

The rest of his Pack was whimpering hysterically, but the dog he had attacked lay cringing beneath him, paws twitching in panic.

"Terror," whined another dog, trembling as he stepped forward, "Great Terror, please. I don't think Splash meant to—"

With a screaming howl, Terror spun and grabbed the shivering dog with his jaws, shaking him violently before pinning him to the ground. Splash was trying to creep away, pressed so tightly to the ground it was as if he was trying to melt into it.

Twitch's voice was hoarse as he muttered to Lucky, "You see? This is how Terror keeps his Pack in line. Who will argue with a dog like that? You'd be amazed how obedient you feel when you never know what your Alpha will do next."

"His Pack isn't crazy at all," whined Moon. "They're terrified."

"Exactly," growled Twitch. "They're not bad dogs. They're stuck with Terror out of fear. Like me."

"You've taken a huge risk by helping us," murmured Moon.

SURVIVORS: THE BROKEN PATH

"I've only just realized how huge. Thank you."

"Should we get involved?" Martha shuddered nervously. "Help those poor dogs?"

Bella shook her head. "I think we need to keep as far away as possible. It's especially important that he doesn't see Twitch with us."

Twitch shot her a grateful look, wagging his tail.

"I'm much more concerned with finding Fiery than watching that mad dog," said Moon. "We should get out of here."

"Then we'll take a long way around to the Dog-Garden," agreed Lucky. "I don't want us to be in earshot or scent-range of Terror. There's no telling what he might do."

"Don't worry," muttered Twitch. "Trust me, Terror sees and smells nothing else when he's in one of his rages."

On silent paws, Lucky's group backed into the long grass and crawled away among the trees. This close to the river their paws sank in the sodden earth; scents were hard to place among the dank odors of wet bark and rotting plants. *At least that'll make it hard for Terror to scent us,* thought Lucky as he yanked his paws free of a patch of clinging mud.

Sounds were easier to catch, though. The dogs came to a squelching halt as they heard the rustling of paws in fallen leaves.

"What now?" Bella gave a growling whine. "Why is this forest a meeting place for every dangerous dog in the land? It's full of them!"

Moon pricked her ears and paced a slow circle. "Where do you think that dog is?"

Lucky tilted his head. "Behind us. If we keep moving forward, we might simply outpace it, and we won't seem like a threat. Pretend we haven't even noticed. But let's form a flank-to-flank line."

They formed a line as Lucky suggested, and walked on with only an occasional backward glance. Moon was at Lucky's right flank, and Bella at his left as they padded cautiously through the trees. Catching his friends' darting eyes, Lucky could see that they too still heard the crunching paws of a dog behind them.

"I don't like this," he muttered after many rabbit-chases. "Whoever that is, this dog isn't giving up. I think Moon and Bella should move farther to the sides and slow down. I'll keep going. If that enemy dog follows me, you'll both end up behind it. Then we can turn and hem it in, find out why it's after us."

Moon and Bella nodded, and he watched them from the corners of his eyes as they veered off and faded into the trees like shadows. Bella, he was proud to notice, was almost as silent and crafty as the Wild Dog Moon, her paws soft on the forest floor.

Twitch and Martha drew closer to him, taking Bella and Moon's places at his sides. Lucky hated walking on like this, all the time aware of the enemy dog creeping behind him; his skin twitched with his bristling fur, but he forced himself not to look back. The sound of the softly treading paws was growing steadily closer, the dog-scent stronger. A little nearer and he might even identify the smell as one of Terror's Pack, or a Fierce Dog, or a complete stranger.

Surely Bella and Moon had maneuvered themselves behind it now? Lucky slowed, hesitating, and a gentle breeze brought the dog's scent straight to his nostrils.

"Now!" he barked, and spun on his haunches.

Twitch and Martha twisted around with him, flying at their pursuer. The strange dog stopped, startled; the Sun-Dog dazzled Lucky's eyes, but he could see the light gleam on a glossy hide and packed muscle.

Fierce Dog! There was no time to change their minds and run; they'd face her down, whatever she was up to. Snarling, Lucky hurtled toward the surprised dog. He half turned, as if to flee, but Bella and Moon were right there, closing in fast, their teeth bared in snarls of warning.

The dog hesitated for just a moment, but that was enough.

Lucky reached her first, flinging himself onto her and rolling her backward into the undergrowth. Moon was there an instant later, helping him pin the Fierce Dog to the ground, where she writhed and struggled, muscles rippling with the effort. Martha, Bella, and Twitch surrounded them for backup, snarling as they blocked every escape route.

It had happened so fast, Lucky had barely breathed in. When he did, slobber drooling from his jaws, the dog's scent caught him full in the nostrils. Shocked, he leaped back. The dog threw off Moon and struggled to her feet.

"Lick!" barked Lucky in disbelief.

She stood there, legs straight and head slightly lowered, her tail flicking just a little. Her glossy sides heaved and she glanced around, shamefaced.

"What in the name of the Earth-Dog are you doing?" yelped Lucky. Moon, Twitch, Martha, and Bella backed off a little, sitting on their haunches and staring at the young Fierce Dog.

"I wanted to help," whined Lick. "And you wouldn't let me come."

"I told you why!" barked Lucky.

"I didn't want to stay with Alpha and the others," she said, her voice lowering to an unhappy rumble. "And no dog tried to stop me. Actually, I don't think any dog noticed me leave."

"But Alpha will be furious when he finds you gone!" Bella pricked her ears forward.

"No, he won't," Lick growled. "He'll be glad to see the back of me."

Lucky licked his jaws, anger and uncertainty warring inside his chest. He couldn't help but feel a pang of sympathy for Lick. To Alpha—and some of the others—Lick might as well not exist. And Lucky was forced to admit to himself: He hadn't recognized her. *She's not a pup anymore. When I attacked, I thought she was a fully grown Fierce Dog.*

A fully grown dog without a proper name . . .

Lucky shook himself, irritated as much by his own softness as by Lick's behavior. "None of that matters. This was reckless! You could have put us all in danger."

"You don't understand!" She flopped onto her belly and gazed up at him, pleading. "I have to help; I can't just wait and watch or I'd go crazy. It's like eating or sleeping. My whole body tells me to do it!"

Lucky shook his ears, trying to clear his brain. The others were all looking at him now, waiting for him to make a judgment. *I'm their leader on this mission. I have to decide.*

He sat down on his haunches, his expression grim. "You can't go back now, Lick." He showed his teeth. "Even though I want to make you."

Lick pricked her ears hopefully.

"It's too far, and I can't risk sending you alone. By the Sky-Dogs, Lick, I'd like to let Alpha give you a good beating!"

She whimpered apologetically and pressed herself lower, resting her jaw on the ground.

"But if I send you back, you'll get lost—or worse, you might run into Terror. You'll have to come with us."

Lick sprang joyfully to her feet. "Thank you, Lucky. I'll help; I promise!"

"You'll do exactly as you're told," he growled. "Don't think I'm happy about this!"

Moon curled her lip. "You're right, Lucky. We don't have a choice. She'll have to come."

Bella, Martha, and Twitch all glared at the young Fierce Dog. *At least she has the grace to look ashamed,* thought Lucky. *But that doesn't make things right.*

"It's agreed, then. We go on, and you come with us. But Lick, you put a paw out of line and you'll answer to me. Now let's find Fiery."

CHAPTER SIXTEEN

Sharp-snow pelted from a black sky. Lucky dodged and rolled, ducking his head to avoid the sting of its hard little pellets. They bounced off the grass and settled again, falling until they lay as thick as soft-snow. Beneath Lucky's paws, Earth-Dog grumbled and shifted in pain and anger.

Please don't be angry with me, Earth-Dog, begged Lucky. *It's the sharp-snow that's hurting you.*

But the ground trembled beneath his paws again. Either Earth-Dog didn't hear him, or she didn't care.

As the land gave a sudden heave, Lucky ran, fleeing the Growl and the sting of the sharp-snow. He plunged into a forest, hoping the trees would shield him, but as he looked up the sky brightened from black to a dazzling silvery white. Lightning was barking again, louder than Lucky had ever heard him, turning night to day. The mass of sharp-snow shattered into tiny pieces, and now the pellets hurtled between the leaves and the branches, and he couldn't avoid them.

It's just a dream. Just a dream!

But it didn't feel like one. Dread clung to his fur like wet mud. He should be afraid. He should be running, fleeing, racing to escape . . . something. But there was only this heavy, fateful horror. There was no Fear-Dog here; there was no Fear-Dog at all. But that wasn't the reason he wasn't afraid.

He didn't feel afraid because he knew there was no escaping the Storm.

The knowledge hit him like a pawstrike from Lightning. It was far more horrifying than the sharp-snow. The real Lightning barked again, slashing his claw into a tree that cracked down the center and toppled with a crash. Earth-Dog replied with a rumble of fury.

Please don't growl again, Earth-Dog. The world couldn't bear another Big Growl. It couldn't survive a war between the Spirit Dogs. . . .

If they chose sides in the Storm of Dogs, it would be the end of everything.

Lucky jerked awake, shaking the dream from his fur like pellets of sharp-snow. Dread still churned in his gut, deadening all other feeling until he suddenly felt a pattering against his hide. Panic choked him. *Sharp-snow? Is my dream real?*

No, he realized; it was only rain. And it was normal rain, too; the drops didn't burn his flesh or singe his fur. Relief swept through him and he gave a trembling wag of his tail. A tongue swept the raindrops off him, and he recognized Lick's scent. She was licking him gently awake.

"Are you all right, Lucky?" Her voice was full of concern.

"I'm fine, Lick." Lucky was breathing hard. Swallowing, he nuzzled her coat. "It was a bad dream, that's all."

Lick cocked her head. "Are you sure? You looked so scared, Lucky. Your dreams must be terrible. And your legs were jerking like you were running in your sleep. What were you running away from?"

Lucky gave a yelp of amusement. "The longer you live, the more you worry, and the worse your dreams are." He gave her ear a lick. "Have you had any more dreams? The ones about Fang?"

"No," whined Lick softly. "It's as if telling him I'd chosen our Pack made him stop coming. But I did have a horrible dream just now. That's what woke me."

"You did?" Lucky gave her ear a lick. "What did you dream about?"

"I'm not sure. It's fading a bit now, but it was frightening at the time. There was this sharp, icy water that fell from the sky and hurt my skin. And I think Lightning was fighting Earth-Dog. It was weird."

Lucky felt a prickle of unease run through his skin. He shook off the strange sensation, and said, "Let's start moving. We have to get to Fiery."

"Good," barked Lick. "This rain is horrible, even if it isn't poisoned!"

Of course Lick's fur was much thinner than his, Lucky realized as he licked warmth into her glossy hide. *She must feel the cold a lot more than I do, yet she hasn't really complained.*

The two of them nudged the others awake, and all five dogs stretched and yawned and scratched.

"What's our next move?" asked Twitch, glancing brightly from one to the other. "This rain doesn't look as if it's stopping any time soon. It'll be hard traveling in this mud."

Bella gave a thoughtful yap. "Can we travel far at all without finding food?"

"No," said Lucky, "and that's a good point, but let's not waste time. We can keep our eyes open for prey as we walk."

"I agree," barked Moon. "We've taken too long to get to the

Dog-Garden as it is." Without another word she turned and set off in the direction Twitch had been leading them.

It was just as well Moon had taken the lead; Twitch had been right about the ground. He was having particular trouble, stumbling on three legs through the soft, muddy earth.

"Are you all right?" Lick asked him anxiously. "Do you need help?"

"I'm fine," he barked gruffly. "Just keep moving. I'll manage."

"He'll be fine, Lick," said Lucky. "He's learned to cope better than a lot of us. But I want you to walk in front of me."

"Keeping an eye on me?" asked Lick. Her brow furrowed and her muzzle wrinkled.

"Yes," he told her shortly. He didn't have the time or the energy to get into an argument with the young Fierce Dog. The rain wasn't slackening as the dogs walked; it poured down in a relentless torrent, streaming into their eyes and nostrils and wetting them to the skin. Lucky could hear Lick grunting with the effort of every step.

As they reached the top of a grassy slope, the young dog lost her paw-hold altogether and slipped, then slid helplessly on her flank down the other side. She couldn't avoid Bella, in front of her, and both dogs tumbled to the foot of the slope.

Springing to her paws, Lick barked angrily at the earth. "Why are you doing this? Why?"

Lucky slithered down awkwardly until he was beside the two dogs, helping Bella to her paws and nuzzling Lick to soothe her. "Lick, it's all right. It was an accident."

She wouldn't be calmed. "Earth-Dog is making it as hard as possible for us to get to the Dog-Garden. She doesn't want us to get to Fiery!"

With an anxious glance at Moon, Lucky hushed Lick. "No, it's just that we need to be careful. It isn't Earth-Dog's fault."

"Really?" barked Lick, clawing the ground to rake angry gashes. "How would you know? She could help us, but she won't!"

"Lick, that isn't how it works—"

"It could be! Earth-Dog might have sent the Big Growl because she's angry with all dogs, and wants to destroy us!"

Lucky licked his jaws, tasting rainwater. He rubbed his streaming eyes with a paw. He didn't want to answer Lick, because he was suddenly afraid to. *I never thought of it that way. Earth-Dog wouldn't turn against us all so violently. She protects dogs . . .*

Doesn't she?

* * *

When they finally glimpsed the Dog-Garden's wire fences through the trees, Lucky was too tired to be relieved. Lick's paws dragged on the ground ahead of him as she blundered forward, dazed and exhausted, and he had to nip gently at her haunches to bring her to a halt. Moon took a scared breath as she shook rain from her face.

"The Dog-Garden," she whispered. "Fiery . . ."

Forbidding fences still surrounded the place, seeming high enough, thought Lucky, to touch the clouds in the night sky. Within the garden, the strange, low houses lay in shadow, their walls sodden with rain. Faint light gleamed on barred clear-stone.

Beside Lucky, Bella shivered. "It still feels like a terrible place," she murmured. "Let's be very careful."

"I remember," Lick whispered, trembling, the whites of her eyes showing.

Lucky nuzzled her flank gently. *Of course she remembers. It's her birthplace, the place her Mother-Dog died. It's the place where she spent her earliest days starving with her litter-brothers while a dead pup lay close by.*

Lucky wondered if he'd made a terrible mistake in not telling Lick to return to the Pack. What forest dangers could have been worse than this for her? She might not be able to cope.

It was too late. All he could do now, he reasoned, was keep a close eye on her.

Bella was already leading the dogs around the fence, staying low to the ground and moving very cautiously as she nosed for the gap the dogs knew was beneath the fence. She spent a long time scraping at the overgrown grass with her claws, tilting her head, and sniffing. At last her puzzled expression cleared and she gave a low growl of frustration.

"Here, I've found it. But the longpaws must have filled it in. There's dirt stuffed into it, and stones."

"Oh no." Lucky's heart sank as he and Moon and Twitch scratched at the patched wire.

"What now?" whined Moon in despair. She rose up on her hind legs to place her forepaws against the fence. "We have to get in!"

"Wait a minute." Twitch dug awkwardly at the soil with his forepaw. "They haven't done this very well. I think we can break it."

All six dogs dug at the earth and clawed at the wire. The metal was shinier where the longpaws had fastened new patches, and the weak tendrils of wire were easy to see. Using their teeth and claws, Lucky and Moon managed to loosen it, while Martha scraped at the filled-in hole. The original opening had been made much bigger by the escaping Fierce Dogs, but even so it was hard work clearing the new earth. Half of every pawful rattled back into the hole as soon as it was dug out. All the dogs were panting with exertion by the time they had made enough of a gap.

"I'll go first," said Lucky firmly. "I brought you all here, so if there's danger I should face it first."

Taking a deep breath, he squeezed his head into the tunnel and hauled himself forward with his forepaws. Stones scraped his ears painfully, but with a bit more scrabbling and pulling, he felt his shoulders slip through.

Lucky spat out soil and tiny stones, shaking his head free. For a horrible moment, as he tried to drag his haunches after him, he realized his backbone wouldn't bend the right way.

I'm stuck! Panic choked his throat and he coughed. Fear gave him a surge of strength, and with one shove of his hind legs he shot forward out of the hole, and tumbled onto clipped grass. His back was scratched and sore, but he was free!

Free inside the Dog-Garden, anyway . . .

Still, he couldn't stop his tail wagging with relief. With a soft bark he called the others, and Moon, Bella, Twitch, and Lick took turns crawling after him.

"I hated that," muttered Lick, shaking dirt from her shiny coat. The others were spitting out tiny stones and scratching their ears. Martha came last; as Lucky had hoped, the rest of them had made the hole big enough for her to squirm through.

Moon's dark eyes shone. "We're almost there," she whispered. "Not long now, and we'll have Fiery back!"

"Who's been repairing that fence?" asked Martha darkly. She stretched and shook her head. "Look at this place!"

Lucky's mouth dried with fear as they all gazed around at the Dog-Garden. Last time he had seen it, on the night he and Mickey had rescued the Fierce Dog pups, the grass had been wild and overgrown. Now it was trimmed as neatly as close-cropped fur, and bright lights shone on it in patches, turning it silver. Once cracked and sagging, the low dog-houses had been patched with some kind of white mud, and the holes in their roofs had been covered with ribbed metal. The scattered and dirty dog bowls were back in neat rows, polished shiny and clean.

"There must be a lot of longpaws," whispered Bella. "Far more than we thought. We'll have to be careful."

Yes, thought Lucky, *and I've led my friends into even more danger than I realized. It won't be as easy as rescuing the Fierce Dog pups.*

The memory of that night sent a stab of anger through his

guts. *I rescued three. And now one of them is dead, and one of them has joined Blade. Some rescue!*

The worst of the changes was obvious when they crept around the corner of one of the low houses. The Dog-Garden had been taken over not just by longpaws, but by loudcages.

The monsters crouched, sleeping on a patch of hardstone. Lucky halted with the others and stared in horror. These were different from the loudcages he'd known in the city. They were much bigger, very long, with many round, black paws, and blank eyes.

The scents around the loudcages and the dog-houses were confusing; there were so many, it was hard to tell if they were old or recent, close or far away. Treading quietly from the clipped grass to the rough hardstone, the dogs crept around the loudcages, sniffing at the acrid smells of their round paws. Moon lifted her muzzle to the body of the longest one, daring to flare her nostrils at its flank.

There was no sound, at least; nothing but the chirrup of insects in the grass and the distant whisper of the forest's highest branches. *If we keep quiet, we can find—*

Moon's whimper rose to a strangled wail. "Fiery!"

"Moon!" growled Lucky, alarmed, as he ran over to her. She

was crouched beside the loudcage, staring up at it in disbelief, nose trembling. "Moon, what is it?"

"Fiery!" She lunged toward the loudcage, flinching back just before her nose could touch it and wake it. "Lucky, he's in there! Fiery is in its belly!"

"Quiet! You'll bring the longpaws. Moon, please—"

But clearly Moon could bear it no longer. Her voice rose in a howl of distress.

"He's been eaten alive! Lucky, help me. I've got to get him out!"

CHAPTER SEVENTEEN

Moon scratched frantically at the beast's belly, where a hatch was set into the metal of its body. Her claws made a screeching, horrible racket but she couldn't seem to stop. The hatch hung slightly loose, but some kind of hook kept it from swinging wide. Pawing and tugging desperately, Moon whined to her mate.

"I wish Mickey was here," whimpered Bella, licking Moon's scruff. "He's good with longpaw doors."

Martha nudged Moon gently aside. "I think I might be able to do it," she said. "Let me try."

Pulling the door as wide as possible with her teeth, Martha worked one of her huge paws in behind the hook. "Now, if it's like . . . and I can just . . . there!"

Lucky and Moon instantly stretched up to pull at the widening gap, almost falling over each other as they struggled to tug on it. It was wide enough now for a squirrel, but not for any of the dogs.

"That's not the way. Let me try," growled Lick. "I want to get out of this rain, anyway!" Wriggling beneath Martha, she shoved her nose and one paw into the creaking space, then seized the edge of the metal with her jaws. "All you have to do is pull hard."

"If it was that easy, we'd—" Lucky fell silent, awed as Lick's packed muscles worked, and the door wrenched open with a screech.

"Wow," breathed Twitch.

"Well done, Lick!" exclaimed Martha.

Lucky could only stare after the young Fierce Dog as her haunches vanished inside the beast's belly. *She's so young—but so strong.* And Lick hadn't even hesitated—she just knew she could do it.

But there was no time to worry about Lick's strength. Moon had already sprung after Lick into the wounded loudcage, and Bella and Martha jumped up into the hole to follow her. In moments Twitch and Lucky were the only dogs left outside.

"I'll keep watch," Twitch whined. "Go and get Fiery. Quickly!"

There was light inside the loudcage, though it was dim and Lucky had to blink until his eyes adjusted. Slowly he turned, amazed at the size of the beast. Its belly was like a huge cavern.

Cages lined its gut walls, stacked up on one another and reaching from one end to another.

"It's a Trap House," Lucky whispered to Bella. "A living Trap House."

It wasn't like the Trap House where he'd met Sweet, where the Big Growl had caught them. Most of the captives in the cages weren't dogs at all. In fact, he realized, as Moon bounded up to one of the cages and whined and pawed through the wire, Fiery seemed to be the only dog here. He was lying on the floor of his cage, his flanks heaving—he barely had the strength to raise his head and whine gratefully at the sight of his mate.

In the other cages, birds flapped at the wire in a panic, instinctively trying to fly. A sharpclaw hissed and spat at the dogs, its orange fur greasy and matted. Other cages held a thin and exhausted-looking coyote, and next to it, a deer that couldn't even stand up in its small prison. Its eyes held the distant stare of an animal too frightened to struggle for its freedom. There were foxes, too, but they were no threat now; the scrawny gray creatures looked sick, their fur scabbed and patchy and their eyes dull. Smelling rabbits, Lucky peered into the depths of a cage to see two of them huddled, quivering in the shadows. *I'm not even tempted to eat them,* he realized with a lurch of horror.

"What is this place?" Martha's voice trembled.

"I don't know." Lucky shook his head slowly.

A cracked, mocking voice came from the coyote's cage. "Visitors. How nice. Stay long, do they?"

Bella shuddered. "What have the longpaws done?"

The coyote gave a hoarse, bitter laugh, but he didn't answer. Hackles bristling, Lucky sniffed at the air, trying to pin down the strange odors that swirled around him. Moon was still whining at the cage that held Fiery, her body pressed close against the wire.

Sickness, thought Lucky. All of these animals had been sick recently. Lucky could smell something fresh but foul, like the yellow blood that only leaked from poisoned wounds and old sores.

And the reek of their breath . . .

"It smells as if they've all been drinking the bad river-water," he said.

"Is this a place where sick animals come to be healed?" murmured Lick nervously. "Like the place the Leashed Dogs talk about?"

"I don't think so," growled Lucky. "These animals do not look like they are being cared for."

"We aren't," came a low snarl from Fiery's cage. The huge

dog was pressing his head as close to Moon's as he could through the wire. "You're right, Lucky; the longpaws are not interested in helping us. They want to hurt us."

"How could that be?" breathed Bella, horrified. "Longpaws aren't always kind, but they'd never deliberately hurt a trapped dog!"

"These ones do." Fiery licked as well as he could at Moon's nose; his tongue looked dry and swollen. "They've been giving us the bad water, so we'll drink it and get sick." He nodded toward a bowl that'd been pushed into the corner of his cage. It was half-full of water. Lucky peered closer and saw that there were scummy bubbles around the edges of the bowl and a shimmering film over the surface of the water.

"Big dog right," whined one of the foxes, before subsiding into exhausted silence again.

Lucky pushed through the others to stand next to Moon. "Fiery, are you sure they're doing it on purpose?"

"Of course they are," whined Moon angrily. "You can see how sick he is!"

Fiery's eyes were red and watery. He looked thin, and his glossy, shaggy fur was dull and patchy.

"I didn't want to drink the water," he wheezed. "I was just so thirsty."

He seemed so weak he could barely raise his head to look at them, and there was a crust of something unnaturally yellow and foul-smelling around his nose and muzzle.

Lucky shuddered. "But why? Why make all these creatures sick on purpose?"

"They come with sharp sticks," yipped the coyote. "They come poking and prodding. Checks our teeths, pulls out our hairs."

"I think . . . they're testing us," Fiery groaned. "To see what drinking the water does to us."

"Maybe they're trying to see if it's safe for longpaws to come back without those shiny, yellow furs!" Bella suggested.

Lucky glanced around at the pathetic creatures. *It doesn't look safe. Not if they don't know how to find water that's not poisoned.*

Moon shivered and whined, pawing the wire. "These long-paws are evil. Where are they?"

Fiery raised his head. "They have long loudcages of their own, on the other side of the Dog-Garden. I smelled them when they first brought me here—they smell bad, and so do the longpaws who live in them."

Lucky raised his muzzle to sniff the air, trying to block out the odors of sick animals and chemicals. "I can even smell it from here," he said quietly. "It's their fire-juice."

Lucky's hopes rose, and he gave Moon a comforting lick. "It means the longpaws will sleep soundly. And they'll sleep for a long time, too. That's what always happens when they drink lots of fire-juice. They get noisy and harsh, and then they sleep for a long time." He shivered, catching a faint pup-memory of that longpaw who used to kick him and shout—the one who reeked of fire-juice.

Bella pricked her ears and glanced up. "It's raining."

Sure enough, Lucky could hear the metallic *ping* and the growing clatter of hard raindrops on the body of the loudcage. In only moments, it was so loud he had to raise his bark.

"Let's get moving. We need to get Fiery out of here!"

"Wait." Fiery looked at him steadily, but Lucky could see the exhaustion and illness in his eyes. "Not just me."

"What do you mean?" Moon licked her mate's nose desperately through the wire. "We have to free you, Fiery!"

Fiery nodded at the next cage. "This is no ordinary Trap House—it's far worse. No creature deserves to be here. You must free us all."

Lucky hesitated, then gave a nod. Despite the sense of unease that crawled in his skin, he knew Fiery was right. No living animal could be left behind in the belly of this terrible loudcage.

He licked his chops, glancing down the rows of cages. Every trapped creature was staring at him, except the ones that were too sick to do more than hang their heads. *They're frightened, and wild, and desperate. Some of these animals might attack us as soon as they're free.*

Still, he didn't have a choice. He dipped his head to Fiery. "You're right. We'll let every animal go—but you first. You're why we came."

"Yes," whispered Moon. "No arguments. You first."

"Leave this to me." Impatiently Lick squeezed between Lucky and Moon, swiping a powerful paw at the latch on Fiery's cage. Hooking it with her claws, she hauled and tugged, her haunches straining as she leaned back. For an awful moment Lucky thought her claws might snap off before the door gave way, but then the young dog twisted her head and sank her teeth into the wire.

Lucky felt a jolt of realization. *Lick has her full, adult teeth. She's reached the age of Naming!*

There was a snarl deep in Lick's throat as the wire mesh bent and buckled. Fiery shoved his body against the cage from the other side, and abruptly the door popped open. It shuddered back with a clang as Lick dodged aside.

"Fiery!" Moon sprang forward, licking his face with gentle, eager strokes of her tongue. Fiery nuzzled her, growling softly.

What is that . . . ? Lucky's tingle of relief was swamped by horror at Fiery's smell. Out of the cage and moving, the big dog's scent was overwhelming—and it was bad. Lucky tried to stop himself from shuddering as he watched the two mates greet each other.

Though weak, the big dog's head was high and proud as he paced forward. "Thank you. But now we must free the others." Then he sagged as his voice slurred. "I won't leave any creature here. Friend or enemy. Prey, even. And the longpaws—they may be drinking fire-juice, Lucky, but they'll come soon. They visit in the night."

Lucky gave a gruff bark of agreement. "Let's not waste time, then."

"Do what I do," Lick told them, a gleam of determination in her dark eyes as she attacked another cage with claws and teeth.

They didn't hesitate. Now that they had seen the young Fierce Dog do it, the dogs tore and bit at the wire screens with new confidence, and one by one the doors crumpled and buckled and sagged open. Martha ripped with her enormous paws, and Bella and Lucky joined forces to gnaw at the wire, ignoring its sharp coldness against their teeth. With Moon at his side, Fiery set to the task with more enthusiasm than any dog.

One after another, animals crawled and tumbled from their prisons. The rabbits cowered in fear, but they crawled out on their bellies, then shot between the dogs' legs. The deer did not even have the energy to flinch, but when it had stared at its open door for long, stunned moments, it staggered out, half fell, then fled limping into the night.

Lucky found himself gnawing determinedly at the wire that held the orange sharpclaw. His side teeth ached from the effort, but his heart pounded with determination. *And all for a sharpclaw! Who'd have thought I'd struggle so hard to help a dog's enemy?*

The sharpclaw had stopped spitting now, and glared warily but silently at him as he ripped the door loose. As it sprang open, the sharpclaw stood straight, arched its back, and lifted its tail, fuzzed out to a huge size.

A low yowl came from its throat, and Lucky went still. That was its warning threat, he knew—but this was no time for a battle with a vicious sharpclaw.

The creature froze, its yowl dying. It lifted its head just a little, and blinked its yellow eyes. Something rumbled in its throat that wasn't a snarl; but before Lucky could react, the sharpclaw darted between his legs and shot out of the loudcage door.

Lucky felt a lurch of shocked amusement as he stared after his natural enemy.

I've just been thanked by a sharpclaw!

CHAPTER EIGHTEEN

Almost all the cages were empty now, their doors swinging loose and creaking eerily as the sounds of scampering paws and desperate hooves faded into the night. Every released animal with meat-tearing teeth—except for the sharpclaw—had turned to help the dogs, and Lucky was surprised and pleased at how fast they managed to open every wire prison. The sour smells of illness and injury were already dissolving into the night air through the gaping hole in the loudcage.

The coyote paused in the doorway of its broken cage, its large ears twitching with suspicion, then took a hesitant step to freedom. Lucky tilted his head to keep an eye on it as it passed him, then poked its head out of the wound in the loudcage's belly. Its muscles tensed, and Lucky stiffened. Beyond it, he saw the orange flash of the freed sharpclaw as it scrambled up a tree on the edge of the forest.

Lucky gave a rumbling growl, deep in his throat. *I know what you're thinking. But not when we've just freed that sharpclaw from the longpaw prison!*

The coyote gave him a thoughtful backward glance. At last it dipped its head slightly, then sauntered out of the loudcage and darted through the rain toward the fence. It squirmed into the hole under the wire, its tail vanishing.

Most of the prisoners were free now, and Lucky longed for fresh air to chase away the stench of the loudcage's belly. He stood in the doorway, inhaling the scent of the downpour through flared nostrils.

That smells so good. . . . Lucky sighed, then pricked his ears as he caught sight of a flash of fur. Through the pouring rain he could make out the coyote, just emerging on the far side of the fence. A shape bounded from the bushes and began to lick its ears frantically. Pausing, it glanced up, and straight at Lucky, its eyes steady. Then it tumbled joyfully together with the freed coyote, and the two animals whined and nuzzled each other.

Another coyote, Lucky realized. *She's his mate! She must have waited for him, all this time. . . .*

Coyotes weren't exactly Lucky's favorite cousins, any more than foxes—especially after that pack of them had tried to eat

Lick and her litter-brothers. Still, he couldn't help feeling happy that he'd saved this one to return to its mate.

Fiery was right. Freeing the others was the right thing to do.

Behind him, there was a low snarl from far back in the loud-cage's belly. Alarmed, Lucky spun around, his hackles stiffening. Another dog! So Fiery wasn't the only one after all. . . .

He dashed back inside, and saw Martha standing stiffly in front of a larger cage, one that was hidden far back in the shadows, behind a solid screen. *So that's why we didn't see him.*

A Fierce Dog stood quivering at the door of his cage, which had been torn away by Martha. His lips were pulled back over his savage teeth, and his trimmed ears were stiff and erect, but his black eyes avoided those of the rescuers, and his head hung low.

All of the rescue dogs were staring at him now, in silence but for the rattle of raindrops on metal. Lick gave a small shiver.

With a low growl, the Fierce Dog turned to swipe his tongue across the bare patches of skin on his flank, then faced them again. His eyes blazed.

"So I've been rescued by . . . who?" At last he raised his eyes, and his contemptuous gaze roved over Lucky and his friends. His muzzle curled. "Or should I say, what?"

Lucky snarled in anger. "Are you insulting us? When we've just set you free?"

"No. I just never thought I'd be reduced to this." The Fierce Dog shook himself violently and grunted. "But I suppose I should thank you."

"Oh, you're welcome," muttered Bella.

The Fierce Dog jerked his head up abruptly. "The longpaws will pay for this! They are not like my masters. My masters were good, and strong, and clever. But my masters are gone, and I am a Free Dog now. No creature keeps Axe in a cage!"

"No!" Lucky started forward, alarmed. "You can't make those longpaws pay for anything. We need to get away from here!"

"My friend Lucky speaks sense," growled Fiery. "We're getting out of this awful place—not hanging around to take vengeance and get caught again."

"Have you mutts gone mad? No longpaw gets away with treating a Fierce Dog like this!" There was a wild light in Axe's eyes. "They've had us cowering here—don't you care? Because I do, and I'll show them what real fear is!"

"We know what fear is," said Moon quietly, her flank pressed against Fiery's. "Lucky's right: We need to escape. Trying to fight for no reason—risking capture again—that would be madness!"

Lick darted in front of Axe and stood, legs straight, ears trembling only a little. "Please listen to Lucky. He's not a Fierce Dog, but he's clever. He knows how to survive."

Axe glanced down as if noticing the young dog for the first time. He gave a sharp bark of disdain. "You're one of Morningstar's pups, aren't you? Yet you're a traitor to your own kind! We Fierce Dogs do not take orders from lesser dogs!"

Lick's throat rumbled. "Lucky's not giving you an order—he's making a sensible suggestion." She tilted her head up and glared at Axe. "And don't insult him. I won't stand for it!"

Lucky felt fear rise in his chest. He stood up and wagged his tail amiably.

"Don't worry, Lick. Listen, Axe, we can discuss our next move once we're clear of the Dog-Garden. Let's focus on escaping!"

Neither Fierce Dog seemed to hear him. Lick and Axe faced each other, their forepaws planted square on the ground as they lowered their shoulders and bared their fangs.

"We didn't have to help you at all," snarled Lick. "We could have let you rot in that cage, but Lucky came here and set you free."

For just a moment, Axe's glare faltered, and he glanced sideways at Lucky. Then he snapped his head up again, drool dripping from his jaws in his rage.

"You're right," he growled savagely. "This dog Lucky is not to blame. I should turn my anger on the ones who deserve it. The longpaws who locked me in here!"

Before any dog could react, Axe had gathered his haunches and sprung out of the loudcage, knocking Lick aside with a glancing blow. She scrambled up swiftly and turned to Lucky, eyes wide.

"After him, quick!" barked Lucky. "He'll attack the longpaws and get us all captured!"

The dogs tore out of the loudcage Trap House into the torrential storm, paws slipping on wet grass, crashing into one another as they rushed to catch up with Axe. But the huge Fierce Dog was already at the fattest of the far loudcages, standing on his hind legs to slam his forepaws into its flank and letting loose a volley of challenging barks:

"Get out here and face me! Come out, you cowards!"

Moon yelped in fear. "We should leave him, the fool!"

"No!" To Lucky's shock, Lick was racing well ahead of them to Axe's side, barking her support. "He's right. Teach these longpaws a lesson, and we'll make the forest safe for all dogs!"

She hadn't quite reached Axe when the hatch of the fat loudcage burst open, spilling out a yellow-furred longpaw. This one had a proper face, Lucky realized in horror, not a blank, black mask, so Lucky could see his eyes widen. The longpaw staggered, reeling back as Axe rushed at him through the rain.

"I'll have my revenge," barked Axe wildly, "for all that you've done to me! To my Pack's home!"

The longpaw spun on his heel, and for a moment Lucky thought he would dash back to the safety of the loudcage's belly. Instead he grabbed something from just inside, and turned again, unsteadily, to face Axe. The longpaw was brandishing something that chilled Lucky's blood, and made every hair on his body stand on end.

Loudstick!

And the longpaw was pointing it straight at Axe's chest.

CHAPTER NINETEEN

"Every dog out of here," barked Lucky, skidding to a halt. "Now!"

Paws scrabbling on the wet grass, the dogs raced for the hole in the fence. Now the wind was driving the rain into their eyes, and Lucky could barely make out the black shadow of the muddy, churned gap where every animal had escaped. He felt a rush of relief as his forepaws slithered into it, jarring his whole body. It stank of sharpclaw and coyote and fox, but he had never been so glad to smell those scents.

"Quick! Go through; I'll follow." He yanked his paws out of the hole, making way for Fiery and Moon first, then Bella and Twitch.

Lick trembled at his side, making no effort to dive into the hole. "What about Axe?"

"Axe has brought this on himself," snarled Lucky, "and maybe on us too. We have to leave him!"

Martha was struggling through the gap now, her hindpaws raking the ground in her desperation. Lucky shoved her haunches with his shoulder, butted her with his head.

"We can't leave a dog behind!" yelped Lick. "You said—"

"Axe had his chance. We gave that to him!" Lucky shook rain out of his eyes as Martha finally squeezed her bulk under the fence. "We don't owe him our lives too."

Still Lick hesitated, staring back through the driving rain, her whole body trembling. More longpaws were staggering from the fat loudcage now, clutching loudsticks and giving rough barks of alarm. One gave a rasping laugh and yelled something.

"It's too late, Lick!" barked Lucky. "We have to go!"

A longpaw raised its loudstick to its shoulder and it jerked with a flat crack. Axe leaped, then tumbled over onto the grass and lay there, jerking. *There's something strange about those loudsticks,* Lucky realized. *The sound is different. It's not that awful bark that hurts a dog's ears. It was more like a hissing paw-slap.*

"Axe!" yelped Lick. "We have to help him!"

"No, we don't," growled Lucky grimly. One of the longpaws was running to the loudcage's head and clambering in. "He's woken it up!" he barked in horror, as the loudcage's eyes opened and blazed light across the Dog-Garden. It roared, and Lick stumbled back, panicking at last.

"What is that monster? What is it?"

"Something you don't want to fight." Roughly Lucky seized a mouthful of her neck fur and yanked her toward the hole. Rolling onto her paws as he released her, Lick wriggled hastily through to the other side of the fence, Lucky at her rump.

The others waited in an impatient cluster. "Come on," yelped Moon.

"Where to?" barked Martha, glancing around. "The loudcage is awake!"

Fiery said nothing. He stood with his head hanging low, his breathing harsh and shallow. Alarmed, Lucky saw that some of his wounds had reopened and were leaking yellow blood onto his hide, but the heavy rain was washing it away even as it plastered his remaining fur to his body.

"We have to get to the densest part of the forest, on the other side of that hill," barked Bella, indicating the slope with her muzzle. "The loudcages can't go among trees. They're fast, but they're not very agile."

"And too fat to fit between tree trunks," agreed Martha.

"Let's go," barked Twitch, lurching into a fast three-legged run. The others followed him, desperate to reach the trees and put as much ground as possible between them and the terrible Dog-Garden.

Lucky overtook Twitch as they pounded up the long, shallow slope. It seemed to go on forever. *Is the Forest-Dog against us too?* wondered Lucky in despair. *I wonder what Alpha and the rest are doing right now? I hope they've found safety. . . .*

As his muscles worked painfully in his pounding legs, and his blood drummed in his ears, he could still hear the furious barks of the longpaws and the roar and screech of their loudcages. He was almost sure they were growing more distant. The slope must have slowed the great creatures, because by the time the dogs reached the crest of it, even the glaring eyes of the loudcages had faded in the darkness. The dogs paused, panting hard.

The downward side of the hill was far steeper, and Twitch gave a yelp as Lucky crouched to spring down it. "I can't! What if I break another leg? I'll only have my hind legs!"

Lucky turned on his haunches. "Come on, Twitch, we can lose them for good—if we can get to the trees down there. I won't let you fall!"

"But my legs," whined Twitch uncertainly. "My good foreleg . . ."

Lucky loped back to him, ears pricked, as Bella and Martha raced past and plunged down the slope toward the dark line of the forest. Lick was close behind; at last even the limping Fiery passed them, supported by Moon's shoulder.

"Twitch, you have to come," Lucky told him urgently. "Whatever happens, it won't be as bad as being caught by those longpaws. I'll stay beside you, but we have to get to the trees."

Twitch gave a scared glance over his shoulder. Lucky's reminder about the longpaws had clearly worked. "Yes. All right."

Cautiously the two dogs clambered down the rocky slope, slipping in mud and sending small stones rolling. Ahead Lick yelped as dislodged pebbles hit her.

"Nearly there," growled Lucky, panting.

They were only a little over halfway down, and Lucky could see the others waiting expectantly at the bottom, when Twitch's forepaw slid from beneath him. Losing his balance altogether, the chase-dog went tumbling head-over-paws, crashing sideways down the slope.

Lucky gave a sharp howl. "Twitch! Are you all right?"

A bark floated up to him through the driving rain. "I'm all right. I'm at the bottom!"

Relieved, Lucky bounded down the rest of the slope.

"Now—into the trees. I can hear the loudcages again."

Sure enough, the angry rumble was growing louder once again, and flashes of the loudcages' eyes lit up the trees some distance away. *They're so fast!* They had come a long way around, thought Lucky, beyond the flank of the hill—but they were still on their trail.

"Go!" he barked as a loudcage roared over a shallow rise and its blazing eyes blinded him.

The dogs turned and sprang for the trees, weaving and dodging through the first thin trunks. Lucky's heart thrashed against his rib cage as his legs pounded the earth, and for a horrible moment he thought the loudcage was going to roll over him, crushing him right into the paws of the Earth-Dog. Then he felt the grass and earth give way to dry leaves and fallen twigs. Low branches slapped his muzzle.

We made it!

No dog slowed pace until they were far into the trees. By that time the loudcages and the longpaws who rode them were far behind, cursing and barking at one another at the edge of the trees. One by one the dogs slithered to a halt in a ragged group, panting hard, flanks heaving. Fiery swayed where he stood, and Moon pressed her flank anxiously against his.

SURVIVORS: THE BROKEN PATH

"That plan was brilliant, Bella!" barked Lucky, licking his litter-sister's ear. "It worked. We lost them."

"We should keep going, though," said Martha, with a nervous glance back toward the distant longpaw barks.

Twitch set off again, plunging nimbly between the low branches on three legs. The pace was easier this time, but still Lucky saw Moon casting anxious looks at Fiery, and he heard her mutter reassurances in the big dog's ear. At last she gave a despairing bark, and Lucky turned.

Fiery was limping to a halt. "I need to rest," he whined. "I'm sorry."

"No, it's fine," Lucky told him cheerfully. "We're safe for now. Let's find cover. Twitch?"

"There's a thick copse of trees, just a little way ahead. No rocks, but the branches are not bad as shelter." Twitch cocked his head doubtfully at Fiery, then led them on a last few rabbit-chases. Together they limped under the cover of the tightly grouped pines, and slumped in exhaustion to the ground, panting.

Despite the thickness of the branches above them, the rain still dripped through to soak their fur, and none of the dogs could shake themselves dry. Instead they huddled close together for shared warmth. Beside Lucky, Bella's muscles shuddered with tiredness.

"Are you sure we're safe?" she whined, resting her head on Martha's back and pricking her ears at her litter-brother.

"I can't hear anything," offered Twitch, raising his head.

"But I'm not sure we'd hear them over this rain and wind, would we?" Bella cocked her head nervously.

"Maybe not," Lucky told her comfortingly, "but we'd smell them. You know how strong the scent of their juice is. I'm sure they couldn't sneak up on us in here."

"Best to be certain," said Moon, her eyes on the trees as she licked Fiery's scruff.

"I can't smell anything." Lucky raised his head and flared his nostrils. "Truly, Moon, there's noth—"

He froze. A scent did tickle his nose; he could taste it on his tongue. Not loudcages, but . . .

"Lucky," whispered Lick. "What is it?"

"Other dogs," he growled.

Rising to his paws, he shared an anxious look with Bella. Lick's muscles tensed as she stood up too.

"It's him," she growled, hackles bristling. "That mad dog."

Twitch gave a high whine. "Terror!"

Lucky shifted his position, turning slowly as he stared into the trees. Between the darkness and the driving rain, he could make out barely anything. But there were shadows there; he knew it. As he watched, they moved, creeping closer: the dark forms of dogs, stalking them through the pine trunks.

An acrid stench cut through the odors of mud and rain, making Lucky shake his head and paw his nose. *Foul water,* he thought. *I saw Terror drinking it. That must be what made him mad.*

Or just madder.

"In the name of the Fear-Dog!" A howl echoed through the night, rebounding from trees until it seemed to be coming from every direction. "I will not see His Name insulted, nor my territory challenged!"

Lucky's fur bristled, and he snarled loudly. "What 'territory'? Do you claim the whole forest, Terror? And the longpaw settlement too? The Spirit Dogs won't allow such greed. You can't have it all!"

"I'll have whatever territory I choose," Terror raged. "And I will mark it with the blood of any dog foolish enough to cross me and defy the Fear-Dog!"

"You're insane!" snapped Lucky, still turning cautiously as he tried desperately to locate Terror among the shadows.

"I will kill the challengers!" the mad dog howled. "By the will of the Fear-Dog! And I will start with the traitor Twitch, and his friends."

Every shadow seemed to move at once. Dogs hurtled from the forest, piling onto them from all directions, howling and barking. Lucky stumbled over Martha as he sprang forward, and for terrible moments there was chaos as the Pack dogs panicked and spun.

"Fight them," barked Lucky. "They're all around us!"

Panting, his small band of friends regrouped swiftly, forming a rough defensive circle as they fought off the wildly attacking dogs of Terror's Pack. Lucky clawed and bit at a dog who lunged for his flank, driving him back, but another, the small, black Splash, was instantly at his other shoulder, sinking teeth into his flesh. Lucky flung him off, then seized a dog who was tearing at Bella's throat. She yelped with pain as he ripped him away from her, but there was no time to make sure she was all right. Another dog was at his flank, and he lunged—

No! It's Lick! Lucky swerved just in time. The darkness and the rain was making it too easy to fly at a dog who was an ally.

Terror's Pack, on the other paw, had no such worries. They simply ripped and tore and clawed at anything that moved, whether a dog was from their own Pack or from Lucky's.

Lucky felt teeth dig into his hind leg, and he tried to roll away, but the enemy dog's grip was too firm and he dragged him helplessly through the mud and twigs. Lucky felt his haunch crash into another dog's legs, almost tripping her up. It was Lick, but she leaped straight back up and into the attack, tussling and snarling with an enemy. There was a truly terrifying ferocity to her in a real fight, Lucky realized, yet he could see shivers running along her flanks. She was cold and scared, and her fear was making her even angrier. She could so easily lose control.

Flinging off his own attacker at last, Lucky raced across to Lick, snapping his teeth into her opponent's shoulder. "Get away, Lick!" he barked. "We can find you later."

"No! I won't run away."

"Lick, you have to—"

"Help!"

Lucky's head snapped around at the familiar howl. Moon was backed against a tree.

"Moon, I'm coming!" Lucky lashed a paw at a dog who leaped for his throat, sending him tumbling away, stunned. He sprang toward Moon, then crashed into another yelping dog who barged into his path. Growling with frustration, he tried to shake him off, but although he was small he held on to him like a sucking insect. "Moon!"

He was close enough to Moon and her attackers to see them snapping their drooling jaws. Circling behind her, Terror's yellow eyes glowed with hate and bloodlust, and Lucky could see that despite Moon's defiance, the three of them would rip her apart in seconds. He had just managed to pin down the fierce, small dog and rip at his ear when he heard Moon whine again, this time in terror.

"No, Fiery! Don't!"

Lucky spun around just as Fiery stumbled into Moon's attackers, snarling. The huge dog looked exhausted and bloodied, but he was lunging courageously for Terror's throat. Terror gave a screaming howl of fury.

"Kill him! Kill this stupid dog!"

CHAPTER TWENTY

Lucky ran through the battling dogs, knocking aside all challengers in his panic, but Terror and his two Packmates had already turned on Fiery. The big dog was knocked sideways, crashing heavily into a tree trunk, and as Moon howled in distress, Fiery disappeared under the teeth and claws of his snapping, snarling enemies.

Lucky slid to a halt in the lashing rain. He couldn't even see Fiery among the writhing mass of soaked fur that was Terror and his two Packmates. Their paws flashed down; their claws and fangs glinted. Worst of all, he could see blood streaming and mingling with the rain, forming pools. Lucky could smell it: bad blood and sickness leaking from too many wounds.

"Fiery, no!" Moon flew at the heap of fighting dogs, but one of them turned and lunged for her. Terror's second Packmate joined him, and together they dragged her away and pinned her down as Terror tore with his jaws at Fiery's limp form.

Now, though, Lucky could see where to aim his blows and bites. He bunched his muscles to spring at Terror, but a dark shape flashed past him, beating him to it. Lick flung herself bodily onto Terror, fastening her jaws in his scruff and wrestling him off Fiery.

Both dogs fell to the ground together, Lick's teeth clamped in Terror's neck. She dug her claws into the ground and dragged him away, then slammed herself on top of the crazed dog to hold him down, ignoring his snapping, slashing jaws. Terror's hind legs kicked hopelessly at the mud, sending showers of it spattering onto both their hides, but Lick was kicking too, raking her hindclaws along his side. Her whole weight was on his head, shoving him down into the mud.

Lucky opened his jaws to bark at her to stop, but the words stuck in his raw throat. *Let her kill him. Let her take revenge for Fiery!*

Fiery! Lucky raced toward his friend. Moon's attackers fled as she gave one of them a last savage bite on the muzzle. Scrambling up, she reached Fiery just before Lucky did, flopping down at his side and licking desperately at the bloody wounds.

"Fiery, I'm here! I'm here." She whined and shifted her muzzle to lick his jaw. As Lucky slid to a halt in a shower of mud, Moon spun with a defensive snarl, but then recognition flashed in her eyes, and she turned back to her mate.

Lucky stared at Fiery in horror. His sides still rose and fell with his breaths, but the movement was small and shallow, and the big dog's tongue lolled into the churned mud. Moon licked his side again, spitting and coughing between each stroke of her tongue. She turned helplessly to Lucky.

"His blood—it's bad! What's happened to him, Lucky?"

"I don't know. The longpaws—"

"Yes, but what can we do?" In despair she rested her jaw on Fiery's side.

"I'm not sure, Moon," whined Lucky. "I don't know."

An angry, squealing growl made him turn. Lick! She was on her side now, and Terror had struggled out from under her; he was shoving her down, biting with his slavering jaws at her neck. Lick was fast, though, and agile; she twisted her head away from his teeth and her lithe body squirmed loose. Then she rolled onto her belly.

"No, Lick!" Lucky dashed toward her. "Don't give him your back!"

It was too late. Terror sprang onto her spine, pinning her and snapping his jaws onto the side of her neck. Lick gave a screaming yowl of agony.

With a howl, Lucky reached and flung himself onto Terror,

seizing the nearest bit of flesh in his teeth. It was the mad dog's ragged ear. *Good!* He savaged it viciously, and Terror gave a scream and fell sideways off Lick. Lucky tumbled with him, his teeth locked in the soft flesh of the ear, dragging Terror farther from Lick.

Terror wriggled and kicked, then tore his ear free; Lucky felt a spurt of blood strike his muzzle. Slipping and slithering, Terror clambered to his paws, growling his hate.

He didn't even feel it, Lucky realized, and his gut turned over. *He's too crazy, too sick! Or does the Fear-Dog stop him from feeling pain? Is there something to his crazy stories?*

Lucky shuddered, but there was no more time to wonder. With a high-pitched scream, Terror charged.

Lucky braced himself, lowering his head and snarling, but Terror never reached him. Lick leaped forward again, meeting Terror head-on, and they staggered and rolled in a fury of claws and teeth.

She's too brave! Pride burst in Lucky's heart at the same time as a terrible fear for her. *Great fighter or not, if she's not careful, he'll kill her!* "Lick, no!"

The scene turned silver, and Lick and Terror were outlined in a pure, blinding dazzle. Lightning. The Spirit Dog leaped across the sky, his brilliance piercing the branches just as the two dogs crashed together once more, their jaws colliding.

For an instant, Lucky could see nothing. But as Lightning's flash died and Lucky's vision returned, he saw that Lick's jaw had locked with Terror's. Both dogs smashed into the earth, and with a great wrench Lick tore herself away.

Lucky's breath stopped. The young Fierce Dog shook her head violently, dropping a lump of flesh to the churned mud. Her flanks heaved, dark with rain and sweat and blood, and she glared down triumphantly at her enemy.

Lucky started forward, afraid Terror would rise to attack again, but he didn't. He lay twitching, blood pouring from his mouth into the sodden earth.

Then Lucky saw clearly. Terror's lower jaw had been ripped clean away from his face. The frenzied, yellow eyes rolled, and a horrible gurgling came from his throat.

The sounds of fighting died around them until there was only the rush of the rain, the harsh panting of exhausted dogs, and that awful, choked gurgle from the dying Terror.

A pitiful, petrified howl sliced through the night, and suddenly Terror's Pack was scrabbling, sliding, fleeing in panic.

"Terror!"

"Our leader! Our Alpha is dead!"

"Run for your lives!"

Mud showered the clearing as they skittered and slid and tried to flee, shouldering one another aside in their desperation. When the last enemy had plunged whining into the undergrowth, Lucky took a trembling step forward and stared at Terror. There was a dull roaring in his ears, and his own rasping breath. Then the other sounds returned, louder than ever.

Twitch gave a whimper of fear. "Is he dead?"

"No," growled Lucky, watching the blood soak into the earth beneath Terror's destroyed head. "But he is dying."

Martha shuddered and turned away, but Lick moved closer to her beaten enemy. Idly she stretched out a paw and prodded his flank. *She's not shivering anymore,* Lucky thought with a strange surge of dread. *She doesn't seem to even feel the cold now.*

Lick tilted her head hopefully toward Lucky. "Should I make sure the mad dog does not attack us again?"

Lucky's spine chilled. Her question was so straightforward, so honest. *She's trying to help,* Lucky told himself, staring into her bright, innocent eyes. *She wants to protect us all. . . .*

He shook himself hard. "No," he barked. "He won't survive that wound. Leave him to Earth-Dog. She'll take him now."

"Earth-Dog is welcome to him," snarled Lick, flicking the bloody stump of Terror's ear with a claw. "I hope she punishes him."

Before Lucky could say anything, a frantic howl split the air.

"Fiery's dying. He's dying. Help me!"

CHAPTER TWENTY-ONE

Every dog seemed to snap out of a horrified trance, and they rushed to Moon, who lay grieving by Fiery's side. The big dog struggled up onto his forepaws, his eyes glazed, but the effort was too much and he slumped back to the ground, spattering himself and Moon with mud. The rain was easing at last, and the breeze shook showers of it from the branches above; it was easier now to smell the stench of Fiery's blood. Lucky's heart weighed in his chest like a stone; the Forest-Dog seemed to whisper to him that there was no hope for Fiery now. If they were near the longpaw-place that Bella called "the vet's," maybe they would have a chance. . . .

But not out here, in the middle of the woods, when the only longpaws nearby were the ones that had done this to Fiery.

Moon's low whine was full of agony as she pressed her face to her mate's. "Fiery," she whispered. "Please. You're so strong.

You've always been strong. You fought Terror . . . please fight this now."

"Terror was outside me." Fiery choked out blood, his voice hoarse and ragged. "This is inside me, Moon. I can't fight it."

"I know you can. My strong Fiery. Please try." Moon shut her eyes tight, pressing close to him.

With a huge effort Fiery raised his head and nuzzled her. "I can't win this fight, Moon. I'm going to die."

Moon released a grief-stricken howl. "Don't talk that way. Earth-Dog will think you want to die. She'll take you!"

"Yes, Moon," he said softly. "She will. I have no choice now. It's my time."

The rain was a steady, sad drip around the dogs as they stood, sodden and bloody, their tails tucked between their legs. A shred of moonlight trickled through the overhead branches, gleaming on puddles. Twitch lay down awkwardly on his belly, his eyes filled with misery. Still standing guard over the dying Terror, Lick stared at Fiery and Moon, trembling.

"Lucky," she whispered. "We have to help him."

Martha nudged her gently. "We can't, Lick. I'm sorry."

"Martha's right," murmured Lucky, taking a pace back. He raised his head to meet his friends' eyes. "We should give them some time together. Moon needs to say good-bye to Fiery. Then . . ." He sighed. "Then we have to go. We need to find the Pack again."

Twitch climbed stiffly to his paws and he, Martha, and Bella crept away from the terrible scene, but Lick stayed still. Her eyes were locked on Fiery, but she didn't move from her post above Terror.

"Lick." Lucky turned back to her. "You have to come."

"I'll guard Terror," she growled.

Lucky sighed. "He isn't going anywhere. Give Moon and Fiery space, Lick."

"But—"

"I said come." He let the hint of a growl enter his voice.

Clearly reluctant, Lick gave Terror a last contemptuous glare, then padded over to join the others, keeping a respectful distance from the two mates. Lucky, Martha, Bella, and Twitch sat on their haunches, looking at one another, or at the ground. As the faltering rain dripped and the Moon-Dog rose higher in the sky, Lucky felt Lick lean against him. At last she nestled down, warm at his flank, as sleepy and affectionate as a pup again. Was this the Fierce Dog warrior who just ripped off another dog's jaw?

He found it so hard to believe; if he hadn't seen it himself, he would have scorned any dog who told him what she had done. Raising his eyes over her sleek, soaked head, he met Bella's sad eyes.

"Oh, Lucky," whined his litter-sister softly. "This was a wasted journey. We lost Fiery after all."

Lucky swallowed, but he didn't lower his gaze. "I don't think we wasted our time, Bella. We couldn't have left Fiery to be poisoned by the yellow longpaws."

"But we didn't save him."

"I know. But we tried. And in a way, we did save him. Fiery's going to die free, at his mate's side."

"And we killed Terror," murmured Lick drowsily, half-asleep. Her tongue came out to lick her bloodied jaws.

A shiver rippled through Lucky's fur, but he nodded. "Terror's Pack might have a chance to thrive now. They had no proper Pack life with a leader like that."

"I wouldn't have sacrificed Fiery for them," murmured Bella sadly. "Or for those other animals we freed."

"Neither would I." Lucky gave her a comforting whine. "But it's what's happened. And now we know, too, how bad the yellow longpaws are. We know where their camp is, and we know to avoid them at all costs. We've seen what happens to any dog they capture." He lifted his muzzle to scent the breeze from the trees. "As for the other animals—well, I know foxes and coyotes and sharpclaws aren't exactly our allies"—he saw Bella flinch at that—"but I'd rather they were roaming the woods than being tortured and poisoned by those evil longpaws."

"I agree with you," murmured Bella, lying down with her head on the ground. "But that doesn't make up for Fiery dying."

"No. All we can do is take these lessons with us, and protect the Pack in the future. That has to be worth something, doesn't it?"

"Lucky's right." Lick stood up suddenly, and Lucky wondered if she'd really been asleep. "Fiery's death is terrible, but the Pack can learn from it. The Pack will be stronger for this."

She's dealing with this so well for such a young dog, Lucky thought, licking her muzzle. But of course, her earliest memory was the death of her own Mother-Dog, and she lay with that other dead pup for a long time. Lick was born in the shadow of Earth-Dog, after her Growl had faded away. *Perhaps she isn't as frightened of death as she ought to be. . . .*

Was that a good or a bad thing? Lucky wasn't sure.

A terrible, whining howl broke into his thoughts, and every

dog turned to Moon, sitting up on her haunches by the unmoving body of her mate.

"Fiery," Moon bayed in grief. "He's dead. My mate is dead."

Hesitantly Lucky padded forward to her side, pressing his warmth close to her shuddering flank. He licked her shoulder gently. "Oh, Moon," he said softly. "This should not have happened. But Earth-Dog will protect him now."

"We have to give him to her." Moon's growl was choked. "I won't leave him here."

"Of course not." Lucky nuzzled her neck. "We'll help you."

The earth was soft, a mire of mud and pine needles; at least that made it easy to dig out a hole with their forepaws, though water kept pooling in the bottom of it. Martha and Bella came to help, raking out the clumped earth until it was heaped up at the side of a deep trench. Twitch hobbled to the edge, looking on mournfully.

"I'm sorry I can't help, Moon," he whined. "My foreleg . . ."

"That's all right." She paused, lifting her earth-spattered face to give him a lick. "I know you liked Fiery, and that you'd help if you were able."

As gently as they could, the dogs tugged Fiery's corpse to the edge of the hole, and rolled him into it. For long moments they all gazed at his unmoving body before reluctantly scraping back the sodden earth with their hindpaws.

"Earth-Dog," whimpered Moon. "Take my Fiery. Look after him. Give him to the world."

Lucky laid his head on her back and closed his eyes in grief. "She will," he said.

He hoped that sounded convincing. Because, for the first time in his life, he wasn't sure if it was true. *How could the Spirit Dogs treat us like this? If they really exist, if they're really watching over us, how could they let such terrible things happen?* He gave a small, helpless whimper.

"What about Terror?" Bella stepped back from Fiery's grave.

And Lick? Lucky realized he had almost forgotten her in the hard, sad work of burying Fiery. He furrowed his brow as he turned to find her. *She didn't help. Why not?*

Lick was standing over the limp body of her enemy once more.

"The mad dog is dead," she yapped. "At last. Should we dig a hole for him?"

Lucky blinked, looking from Lick to Terror. The dead Alpha was a shapeless mass on the ground, sodden with mud and blood, barely recognizable as a dog at all. It was as if the rain had already tried to wash him away.

He was dying, thought Lucky. *We knew that.*

He raised his gaze to Lick. Her face was calm, her eyes gentle and clear. Curious under his intent stare, she tilted her head to the side and pricked her ears.

Terror couldn't survive that wound. That was obvious.

Lick wagged her tail slowly, hesitantly. Seeming bewildered, she gave Lucky a soft, questioning whine.

It's probably better for Terror that he has died.

Yet something about the corpse made Lucky uneasy. He turned to look at it once more. Had it moved? Was there anything different about the way it sprawled there? Was there a new expression in its staring eyes?

Lick couldn't have. There was no need.

Right?

The Sun-Dog glowed bright gold through the branches as the exhausted little party set off again. The dogs were dazed and forlorn, paws dragging in the sodden ground. Moon went ahead, not looking back, head raised high but her ears drooping and her tail low. Twitch limped a little way behind her. Behind Lucky, Martha and Bella brought up the rear, keeping each other company in unhappy silence.

A little way behind Twitch, Lick walked alone, the tip of her tail twitching slightly, her ears pricked for danger. Lucky found he didn't want to catch up to her just yet. She seemed lost in thought. *Are they dark thoughts? Lick, I don't know what to make of you now. . . .*

Falling back a little, Lucky walked beside his litter-sister. Bella glanced at him.

"Do you really think you can control her, Lucky?"

Surprised, he lifted an ear, but he didn't look at Bella. He stared at Lick, still padding calmly along.

"I don't know," he murmured at last. "Maybe I don't have to. She's obviously going to be a great warrior. Dogs do what they have to do to survive, don't they?"

"Do you think that's all it is?" Bella pricked her ears at him, her face solemn.

Lucky sighed. "We can all be savage when we fight, can't we? Instinct brings out the beast in us."

"But this was different," Bella prodded.

"Yes. This was . . ." Lucky shook his head sadly. "She has a killer instinct. It's not surprising that she used it to battle Terror, is it?"

But I still can't shake the feeling something happened back there, when the battle was already over. That something was done while my back was turned. . . .

And if it was? I didn't hear any savage barking or tearing. Is a killer still a killer if death comes as a mercy?

A little way ahead, Moon halted and gazed up at the sky, sighing distantly. "The Sun-Dog has nearly finished his journey. He stays such a short time in Red Leaf season; perhaps he hates that the frost is coming. It always seems like he tries to set the trees on fire, but they never burn away."

Lucky licked her ear gently. "We should make a camp for no-sun," he said. "Every dog is tired."

"Will it rain again?"

Lucky's heart turned over at the sorrow in Moon's voice. "I don't think so. The sky is clear. Let's sleep under these trees, and move again at first light."

"We should howl for Fiery," Moon murmured. "We'll do it when the Pack is together again." She turned her sleep-circle, exhausted, and settled into a leafy nest, closing her eyes. "We'll howl to the Spirit Dogs for him, and send him on his way."

CHAPTER TWENTY-TWO

The forest was especially silent during the darkness of no-sun, with barely a rustle of insects or a whisper of breeze to disturb the dogs' sleep. Yet Lucky found himself restless, waking often, shifting his position, and fidgeting. Every twig and tiny stone seemed to dig into his hide. He kept seeing strange and horrible things— visions from his dreams of the Storm of Dogs mixed with the vicious fight with Terror's Pack. He was afraid that if he slept soundly, another of those terrible dreams would visit him. Even the stillness of the trees unnerved him.

A new sound broke into his shallow doze, and he lifted his head. *Pawsteps. And they're nearby.*

He got up as quietly as he could, not wanting to disturb Moon's exhausted sleep. Was it Terror's Pack, sneaking back for revenge?

No, the paws aren't coming toward us. He blinked into the darkness, making out a moving shadow. *It's Lick! And she's creeping away.*

Perhaps she just needed to stretch her muscles or make waste, but Lucky felt an intense urge not to let the young Fierce Dog out of his sight. Softly he padded after her, catching up at the bottom of a shallow slope. Lick turned, blinking, but she didn't look surprised or guilty.

"What are you doing, Lick?" he murmured.

She glanced away, into the trees. "Nothing, Lucky. I just wanted to be alone. I feel . . . guilty." She sighed.

His fur bristled with renewed suspicion. "What about?"

"I'm not sure. I don't like the mood of the others. It's strange, that's all. It's nothing definite, but I can tell. They think I'm bad, don't they? Evil and vicious, like Terror."

Lucky licked his dry jaws, his gut twisting. "To be honest, Lick, I was surprised at the way you fought Terror. That doesn't mean it was wrong," he added hastily, "just that you didn't hold back, not even a bit."

"Should I have? Am I evil?" Her dark eyes met his, anxious.

"No! I know in my gut you aren't." He sat down on his haunches and gazed at her. "There's anger in you, but that's not surprising. And you're fiercely loyal, and passionate. You want to protect your friends. That's not evil!"

"But I think . . . maybe . . . I could be." She shuddered and shut her eyes. "Like Blade."

"Lick." He nuzzled her gently. "That's why I want you to stay close to me—to all of us. Stay with the Pack. Without the Pack, you might find your rage getting the better of you, taking control of you. Do you see?"

Lick shuffled down onto her belly, gazing up at him with pleading eyes. "I won't grow up to be like Blade," she whispered fiercely. "I don't want to! I want to be a good warrior and a good Packmate—not a savage killer. I want to be a good dog!"

Lucky rested his muzzle affectionately on her head, closing his eyes and ignoring the gnawing uncertainty. It was a nagging voice in his head, asking him over and over again how such a natural-born killer could be good.

What would Alpha have said, he wondered with a shudder, if he had seen Lick fight Terror?

What would Sweet have said?

The nagging voice faded, and he felt a flare of rebellious anger in his rib cage. He didn't know what they would have said. But he knew very well what they should have said.

They should have thanked her for it. They should have been

grateful. *Lick is the only reason the dogs who left the Wild Pack are returning.*

"Listen to me, Lick. We didn't save Fiery—but we'd all have died if it weren't for you. And I'll make sure every dog knows it."

Her head came up and her sad eyes brightened with gratitude. "Really?"

"Come with me, Lick," he said softly, nudging her to her paws and shepherding her back to the sleeping dogs.

"Thanks, Lucky." Lick yawned and trod a circle.

Together they lay down, curled together, and he felt her muscles relax and her breathing deepen. In a short time he knew she was fast asleep.

Lucky wished he were, too. For all the comfort he'd tried to give Lick, a voice of warning still barked in his head. All he could see when he closed his eyes was Lick, standing stiff-legged over the corpse of Terror. Terror, who'd been dying so slowly, bleeding into the earth, and who had been so suddenly, so entirely dead.

What happened, Lick? What did you do?

As slivers of pale dawn light penetrated the trees, the dogs stretched and rose. Lucky's head was fuzzy with lack of sleep, but he knew there was no point worrying. There was only one way to take his mind off his tiredness, and wake himself properly.

"Bella," he whined, nudging her with his muzzle. "Let's hunt some breakfast."

Eagerly she got to her paws and trotted alongside him. There were no rabbits in the dense woodland, and the birds stayed frustratingly in the treetops, whistling and chirping taunts at the dogs, but with patience and persistence the two managed to stalk and kill some fat squirrels that were too Red Leaf sleepy to escape.

"Three, and a weasel." Bella sniffed at their haul. "Shall we try for more?"

"This should keep us all going for a while," said Lucky, pawing at the limp weasel. "It's not much, but we should get moving, I think."

Back at the camp, the dogs shared the prey without regard for Pack status. Moon, though, sniffed at a squirrel haunch, but turned her head away.

"I'm really not hungry," she murmured. "The rest of you share this."

"Moon, no." Worried, Lucky licked her nose. "There's a long journey ahead of us. You must eat."

Reluctantly she nibbled at the chunk of flesh, but did little more than paw it like a sharpclaw with a mouse. After only two proper mouthfuls, she shoved the haunch away again. She turned her head, coughing harshly.

"I can't. That'll have to do, Lucky."

"All right." He nuzzled her neck. "I understand."

But I'll keep an eye on you, Moon. You must stay with us—I won't lose another dog.

Still tired, and hobbling with their aches and pains, the small Pack set off again, letting Martha take the lead this time. Before long the huge, black dog had sniffed out the River-Dog, and Lucky felt a little energy return to his bruised body as he gazed at the glinting, silver water.

"We just have to follow the stream," he said, wagging his tail limply. "We'll be back in the longpaw settlement soon, and then we'll have the Pack's scent to lead us."

Soft grass and earth gave way under their paws to the rough hardstone of longpaw tracks, and the shadows of houses stretched across their path. Padding through the streets, they scented the ground, seeking out the trail of the Pack. Was it Lucky's imagination, or was the stench of death fainter than it had been?

Perhaps it's because Red Leaf is growing colder. Or perhaps the longpaws are finally being taken by Earth-Dog. With a stab of sadness, he thought again of Fiery in his lonely grave.

"We won't know which way the Pack went," whined Lick dolefully.

"Of course we will," barked Lucky. "Sweet—*Beta*—promised to leave a scent-trail, and I trust her. Don't worry. Use your nose." He brightened. "There! Smell someone familiar?"

Lick sniffed the ground hesitantly, and her head popped up. "Sunshine! And Beta!"

"I knew they wouldn't let us down." Lucky felt happy for what felt like the first time in days. "If the scent stays strong, we'll find them again. I promise!"

His muscles ached and his paw pads stung by the time they had followed the trail out of the longpaw streets and down into another narrow valley. How must the others be feeling? He wondered. Lucky made his legs work on, one pawstep at a time. He felt that if he ever stopped walking, he wouldn't be able to start again. He'd simply curl up and sleep forever. . . .

Something tingled in his nostrils, and he halted, one paw lifted. "What's that?"

Bella raised her head. "I'm not sure."

"It's like nothing I've smelled before." Twitch wrinkled his nose, curious.

It was strange, thought Lucky: a tangy, salty scent that floated on the air. It wasn't coming from the grass or the river or the trees—it was as if they could scent something vast, and wild, far away. He curled his upper lip, trying to identify it, but it remained tantalizingly distant. There was nothing to do but walk on, every muscle hurting. Twitch was limping badly now, and Lucky felt a prickle of anxiety.

The Sun-Dog slipped farther down the clear sky, and Moon-Dog was stretching and rising into the dusk. She was not quite full, but she was huge and white, and Lucky's eyes kept returning to her as she rose high. They would not catch up with the Pack tonight, he knew. *The others are as exhausted as I am, and no-sun will be here soon.* Indeed, the Sun-Dog had already curled to sleep below the horizon, staining the sky gold and orange.

We have to stop. But I don't want them to lose heart at not finding the others. I must do something to raise their spirits.

Moon-Dog, help me. . . . Lucky tilted his head back to watch her, glowing silver above him.

And suddenly he knew. He wagged his tail as energy returned to his limbs.

"Stop, all of you," he barked. "We'll camp for the night."

Every dog paused and eyed him wearily.

He turned to Lick. "We're going to do something we should

have done already," he barked. "A special ceremony."

Lick took a breath, her eyes brightening with hope, and she licked her chops uncertainly. "You don't mean . . . ?"

"Yes." Lucky bounded onto a nearby slab of rock. The eyes of every dog were on him, livening with interest. "Packmates, look at Lick. She is not a pup anymore; she has truly come of age. She has traveled a long way with us, and survived a terrible journey. And"—he turned, meeting the eyes of every dog—"she saved our lives."

Moon gave a soft bark of agreement. "She did."

"She has proved herself a worthy Pack member." Lucky took a breath. "If Alpha was here, he would not deny Lick her name now."

Martha exchanged a doubtful glance with Bella. "Are you sure?"

Lucky curled his muzzle. "If he has anything to say about what we're doing, I'll defend my decision. With my teeth, if I have to."

As he waited, the silence stretched. Bella turned anxiously to Moon, who glanced at Twitch. Lick sat very still.

Don't they think she's ready? he thought.

Martha raised her eyes to the sky. "It's not a full moon."

Twitch cleared his throat. "We don't have a white rabbit."

Moon only looked thoughtful. *She's the most senior Pack Dog of all of them,* Lucky realized. *It will all rest with her.*

Moon's tail twitched, then thumped the ground decisively. She lifted her head. "Lucky, I think it's a wonderful idea. And who says ceremonies can't change? We are not there for them—ceremonies are there for us. The only important thing is that Lick is ready, and that she wants this." She turned to the young Fierce Dog. "Do you, Lick? Are you ready?"

Lick dipped her head to Moon, then raised it, her eyes shining. "I've never wanted anything more," she whispered.

"Then climb up here," barked Lucky, leaping down from the rock slab. It wasn't as big as the stone where Beetle and Thorn had been named, but it was pale in the moonlight, with veins of silver. "We can't offer you a rabbit fur, but we can bring you gifts. Come on—every dog find something to celebrate the dog who saved us from Terror. Let's honor Lick's new name!"

It was as if Lightning had struck the little Pack and filled them with his sizzling energy. Exhaustion was shaken off as the dogs darted happily into the trees in search of tokens for Lick.

Pale things were easy to find in the gleaming Moon-Dog light. Martha trotted back with a smooth, white pebble in her jaws, and clattered it down on the stone in front of Lick. Moon padded back and forth among the bushes, and at last seized a white flower in her teeth, snapping it off and bringing it to the rock. Its petals shone pale and perfect. Twitch hobbled out of the trees carrying a stick in his mouth; Lucky saw it was a birch twig, still sheathed in silver bark. Bella's offering was a delicate, gray leaf that gleamed in the Moon-Dog's beam.

They've done a bit too well, thought Lucky, amazed and rather aghast. *What can I bring to the rock?* Hopelessly his gaze scoured the ground.

There! It isn't white, but it's perfect.

At the edge of the trees was a gigantic gnarled oak, its exposed roots twisted through the bare ground beneath it. Lucky padded to the base of it and carefully picked up a tiny acorn, still in its cup. Gently he laid it on the rock at Lick's paws.

"For you, Lick," he told her solemnly. "You're still young, but I think you will grow to be something great, something strong. Especially with powerful roots among our Pack."

The young Fierce Dog still sat motionless on the rock slab, dazed. For long moments she was silent, her eyes closed and her face upturned to the Moon-Dog, but Lucky could see her heart beating against her chest. *What must she be feeling?* he wondered.

Memories swirled around his brain—the running feet of the longpaws, the yellow hair of their smallest Pack member, the acrid tang of the red-tipped stick, and the frightening death-smell inside their house. Their alarmed cries and barks rang inside his head: the noise that helped him find himself. Lucky. *I was Lucky. I still am. I'm with a Pack who like and respect me as an equal member. I'm helping another young dog discover her fate and the way the world works. I'm teaching her how to be part of a Pack: a noble, valuable, loved dog.*

The young dog's eyes snapped open. New raindrops began to fall, trickling down her muzzle, dampening her fur. She blinked around at the other dogs as Lucky waited, his heart tight with anticipation.

Distantly Lightning leaped across the sky, and thunder rumbled overhead. *Quickly, Lick! Before the Sky-Dogs fight and the Moon-Dog hides away . . .*

The young Fierce Dog drew herself up proudly and gave a bark of joy.

"Storm. I choose the name Storm."

At once the other dogs began to yelp in delight, bounding forward to congratulate their newly named Packmate. Even Moon barked her approval, happy for Lick despite her grief. Only

Lucky stayed where he was, rooted to the ground as firmly as the great oak.

A shudder ran through his bones. *Surely it's only a coincidence.*

But what if it wasn't? What if the Storm of Dogs was beginning, right now?

Oh, Storm. Will you be at the heart of the war?

SURVIVORS

BOOK 5:
THE ENDLESS LAKE

Lucky awoke with a shiver to a cloudless night. The dogs were by the riverbank, huddled together beneath a bush. The warmth of their bodies wasn't enough to keep out the freezing wind. It whipped over the water, burrowing under Lucky's golden fur.

He looked about him. Bella's head was resting on Martha's huge black flank, and Lick—no, she was *Storm* now—was nestled between the water-dog's paws. *Oh, Storm, why did you have to choose that name?* Lucky's stomach clenched. He couldn't shake the feeling that her choice was an omen of some kind. Could the young

Fierce Dog have a part to play in the gruesome battle that haunted Lucky's dreams?

The Storm of Dogs?

He still didn't know exactly what it was, or when it would happen . . . but it *was* real. He sensed the chaos, the frenzy of snapping teeth. His tail drooped against his flank. Storm looked so peaceful with her head resting on her brown forepaws, her ears flopping back. But Lucky couldn't forget the savagery with which she'd attacked Terror, the crazed leader of Twitch's Pack.

Twitch was sleeping on his side, revealing the stump where one of his forelegs had been. Moon slept with her back against Lucky, her paws covering her eyes. The Farm Dog's lip trembled, revealing one fang, and she whined softly. "Fiery, I'm here . . . .I'm here. . . ."

She must have been dreaming of her mate. Maybe in her dreams, the great hunter had survived.

If only they were back with the Wild Pack already. Fiery's illness and death had left Lucky feeling exposed. His mind returned to the Dog-Garden, where black-faced, yellow-furred longpaws had built a Trap House in a giant loudcage. The dogs had found Fiery locked inside, along with other animals. Foxes, rabbits, a coyote . . . even a ginger sharpclaw. And every creature was sick.

The dogs had managed to free them all, escaping with Fiery into the forest, only to come across Terror's Pack.

Lucky shuddered. Fiery had been such a powerful fighter, but his time in the Trap House had left him as feeble as a pup. He hadn't been able to defend himself. Lucky whined softly as he remembered the gaunt dog with watery eyes that the once-mighty Fiery had become.

He smelled bad too. . . . His blood was foul, like the poisoned river.

By the time they'd found him, it had been too late. Poor Fiery . . .

The dogs had formed a circle around Moon when they'd settled down for the night, as though they could protect her from her loss, as well as the bitter wind. Lucky rose carefully so as not to disturb her, and trod over Twitch's tail, stepping out from beneath the bush. Frost clung to the small green leaves and sparkled on each blade of grass. Even Lucky's fur was stiff beneath its icy touch.

He edged around the bush, looking out across overgrown fields that rose and fell in peaks and valleys. He turned back to the river, crunching over the frozen grass to the bank. The water hadn't turned to ice, but it was so cold it scalded his tongue, and he drank only a little.

Lucky smelled salt on the chill night air. It had grown more powerful as the dogs had wandered downstream, but he couldn't work out where it was coming from. Lowering his muzzle, he caught the scent they'd been following: Alpha, Sweet, and the rest of the Pack must have passed this way. They couldn't be far ahead—a day at most. It still stung that Sweet had gone with the dog-wolf, refusing to look for Fiery after the yellow longpaws had captured him. But Lucky was grateful that Sweet had left careful scent-marks along the way, just as she had promised.

Moon and the others would be happier among more dogs. And Lucky had been feeling isolated since the battle with Terror and his Pack—if a brave, powerful dog like Fiery could fall so easily . . . He lowered his head. That crazed Pack was still out there somewhere, as were the Fierce Dogs. He and his companions would be safer once they were reunited with the Wild Pack.

DON'T MISS

DAWN OF THE CLANS

WARRIORS

BOOK 1:
THE SUN TRAIL

For many moons, a tribe of cats has lived peacefully near the top of a mountain. But prey is scarce and seasons are harsh—and their leader fears they will not survive. When a mysterious vision reveals a land filled with food and water, a group of brave young cats sets off in search of a better home. But the challenges they face threaten to divide them, and the young cats must find a way to live side by side in peace.

DIVE INTO
RETURN TO THE WILD
SEEKERS
BOOK 1:
ISLAND OF SHADOWS

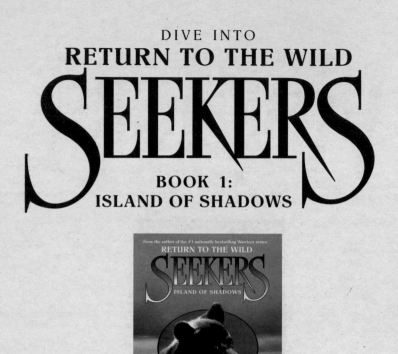

ERIN HUNTER

Toklo, Kallik, and Lusa survived the perilous mission that brought them together. Now, after their long, harrowing journey, the bears are eager to find the way home and share everything they've learned with the rest of their kinds. But the path that they travel is treacherous, and the strangers they meet could jeopardize everything the Seekers have fought for.

ERIN HUNTER

is inspired by a fascination with the ferocity of the natural world. As well as having great respect for nature in all its forms, Erin enjoys creating rich, mythical explanations for animal behavior. She is also the author of the bestselling Warriors and Seekers series.

Visit the Packs online and chat on Survivors message boards at www.survivorsdogs.com!

FOLLOW THE ADVENTURES!
WARRIORS: THE PROPHECIES BEGIN

In the first series, sinister perils threaten the four warrior Clans. Into the midst of this turmoil comes Rusty, an ordinary housecat, who may just be the bravest of them all.

HARPER
An Imprint of HarperCollins Publishers

www.warriorcats.com

WARRIORS: THE NEW PROPHECY

In the second series, follow the next generation of heroic cats as they set off on a quest to save the Clans from destruction.

HARPER
An Imprint of HarperCollinsPublishers

www.warriorcats.com

WARRIORS: POWER OF THREE

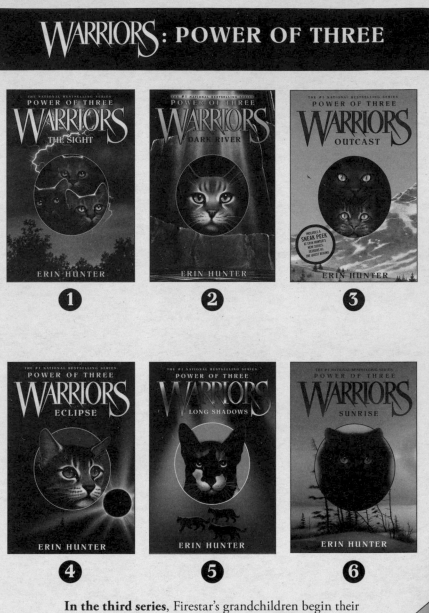

In the third series, Firestar's grandchildren begin their training as warrior cats. Prophecy foretells that they will hold more power than any cats before them.

NEW LOOK COMING SOON!

WARRIORS: OMEN OF THE STARS

In the fourth series, find out which ThunderClan apprentice will complete the prophecy.

ALSO BY ERIN HUNTER:
SURVIVORS

SURVIVORS: THE ORIGINAL SERIES

The time has come for dogs to rule the wild.

SURVIVORS: BONUS STORIES

Download the three separate ebook novellas or
read them in one paperback bind-up!

HARPER
An imprint of HarperCollinsPublishers

www.survivorsdogs.com

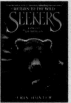